THE VIRGIN NEXT DOOR

A STUD RANCH STANDALONE NOVEL #3

STASIA BLACK

"The ugly duckling is a misunderstood universal myth. It's not about turning into a blonde Barbie doll or becoming what you dream of being; it's about self-revelation, becoming who you are."
- Baz Luhrmann

1

MACK

SOMETIMES PEOPLE NEEDED TO DIE. There was a certain kind of evil where there was nothing to do but to kill it.

Mackenzie 'Mack' Knight had learned this lesson early. He'd gotten a full ride academic scholarship to Harvard and hadn't come home for Thanksgiving because he'd been busy studying for finals. But he'd finished his Philosophy term paper early. He wanted to make it home to surprise his mother on her birthday.

That was when he found her on the floor. Two black eyes and a broken nose.

"He didn't mean it." She kept repeating it over and over. "He's a good man. I upset him. He didn't mean it."

When she wouldn't give him a name, Mack tore through all her shit. Found her phone. Found the fucker's name.

Mack tore out of the house. But not before grabbing his baseball bat.

Then he went and took care of evil.

The only thing he regretted when the police took him away in cuffs three hours later was that he hadn't finished the job.

2

LIAM

LIAM SLAMMED the hot blonde up against the back of the women's restroom door after shutting and locking it.

He kissed her deep and ground his erection into her stomach unabashedly. After all, she was the one who pulled him into the bathroom after a short ten minutes of heavy flirting. If she wasn't going to bother being subtle, well, why should he?

"You're the hottest girl I've laid me eyes on." *Tonight anyway.* He didn't add that last part. A little flattery was expected with these things.

His hand roamed up from her waist to cup her breast. He paused when he felt how unnaturally firm they were. Like two hard little melons. Damn, even girls out here in the middle of nowhere got boob jobs? Was nothing sacred anymore?

But hey, boobs were boobs. Liam plucked at her nipples through the thin little nothing spandex tube top she was wearing.

Then she pulled back from him. "I want to blow you. Is that okay?"

Liam's eyebrows went up. "Well, who am I to deny a beautiful woman when she wants what she wants?"

She giggled. "I love how fancy you talk."

It never failed. His Irish accent got him almost as much tail here in America as being a famous playboy billionaire had back in Dublin.

She dropped to her knees right there on the restroom floor and reached for his pants. Liam leaned back against the door and crossed his hands behind his head. He couldn't help smirking as her little hands fumbled with his belt and zipper.

He could help her, sure, but watching the show like this was more fun. Eventually she managed to get her greedy little hand in his slacks. She yanked out his cock.

Ow. "Gentle," he hissed, his hands dropping to her bleach blonde hair.

She looked up at him through her eyelashes and smiled. "Sorry. I just want to taste you so bad. I didn't mean to be rough. I've seen you at the bar before and I was always hoping we might..." She glanced down like she was bashful.

She had her hand on his knob, her lips an inch away from his crown and she was going to pretend to be shy now? Come the feck on.

Liam wanted to growl at her to shut up and get her mouth on his dick already. He stopped himself at the last second. An Irish accent would only get a lad so far.

And wasn't the whole reason he'd taken this extended vacation to America because he was tired of everyone bowing and scraping at his feet no matter how he treated them? He was trying to learn how to be a decent human being for a change.

He put on his most charming smile, the one he knew brought out his dimples. The bettys went mad for dimples. "Well looking hot as fuck in that little red minidress was sure a good way to get me attention."

She pulled his cock toward her mouth and gave a long, sloppy lick up the bottom side of his shaft. She repeated the action several times, licking him up and down. In a way that reminded him of a deer at a salt lick.

"Why don't you suck me?" He put a little pressure on her head. "Pretend I'm your favorite flavored popsicle, yeah?"

"Am I getting you hot?" she asked, holding the base of his shaft and smiling up at him. Some of her lipstick had smeared onto her chin while she'd been licking at him. Liam had to fight to keep his cockstand.

"Yeah," he said, less than enthusiastically. "So now why don't you suck me in your mouth? That'll get me even hotter."

She grinned like he'd just said Christmas was coming early and popped the crown of his cock in her mouth.

Fucking finally. Liam was just about to relax against the door and enjoy the ride when she suddenly gagged and yanked back from him.

"Sorry," she said. Jaysus, the lipstick situation was even worse now, a little bit of saliva dripping from her bottom lip. "I have a really sensitive gag reflex."

So why'd she fuckin' go down on him in the first place? This was getting less and less fun by the minute.

"Look, maybe this was a bad idea." Liam pulled his pelvis back from her mouth and would have stepped away except she still had an iron grip on his dick.

"No, wait!" Her eyes flashed panic and she jumped back to her feet. She leaned in for a kiss but Liam turned his head, not wanting to make contact with her manky lipstick smeared mouth.

She just rolled with it, though. She went up on tiptoe so she could whisper in his ear, hand still on his cock. "I just want to be with you. You can stick it anywhere. Up my ass if you want."

Well shite. A woman went and made an offer like that, what was a lad to do?

She finally let go of his knob and sauntered over to the sink. She wiped her mouth with her forearm, which helped clear off the smeared lipstick. She was sorta pretty. In the same generic way a hundred other girls were. Liam wasn't sure if it was worth it. Sure, he hadn't got his oats off in a while, but the rest of the guys were outside and he'd already been gone too long—

Then the woman—Brittany? Betty? he couldn't remember—bent over at the waist, her arse pointed toward Liam. She yanked up the nothing little scrap of spandex that was her miniskirt and *damn*.

Her tits might be fake, but that was one-hundred percent genuine, Grade A American arse. She leaned to look at him over her shoulder, then widened her stance even further so that he could just make out the contours of her shaved pussy.

"Any hole you want," she repeated her earlier offer.

Liam's cock jumped. He dropped a hand to jerk his shaft up and down as he took a step toward her. He pulled a condom out of his pocket. Lessons that every good Irish boy learned early—never leave the house without a rain-slicker or a handful of condoms. The hope being that even if it was raining cats and dogs outside, a lad would always have a warm, safe place to stick his prick.

"Oh I'm clean," the woman said when her eyes dropped to the condom in his hand.

"That's nice," Liam said, rolling the condom down his cock as he stared at her tight little arse. This just might be her best side. Yeah she was pretty but she was obviously one of those birds who knew it. Tons of make-up, the fake boobs.

Liam slapped her arse and it jiggled just like a proper arse should. She yelped and glared at him over her shoulder. The glare lasted just a moment, though. The next second she'd softened her features and she licked along her top lip in a way that was obviously meant to be seductive. "Do you want me to help you get it in?"

"No, I got it. Just lean over. Face forward." He put his hand on her spine to urge her a little lower. His balls were aching and he really wanted to just fuck this chick and get out of here. It'd been almost a month and her pussy was better than his hand.

But it'd really go a lot easier if she just stopped fuckin' talking. His cockstand was already drooping again and that was just a fecking shame. Her face might only be a six but this arse really was a nine.

His hands dropped down and he caressed the round globes,

closing his eyes and pressing his condom covered cock into the crevice of her arse. He massaged and molded her cheeks until they cupped his hard-on.

"Jaysus," he whispered. "You got one fine arse here."

He reached around to strum at her clit, still half lost in the feel of his cock grinding her arse. But his eyes popped abruptly open when he touched her flesh and realized she was barely wet at all. What the fuck?

"Oh, that feels so good," she said breathily, wiggling her arse against his hard on.

"Does it?"

She must not have heard the skepticism in his voice because she just let out another breathy moan.

All right, well, fair enough. He hadn't done much to work her up other than shoving her up against the wall when they first got in here and then having her gag on his knob. He was willing to put in the work. Any woman who slept with him was damn well going to get off.

It was another of the promises he'd made to himself when he crossed an ocean to leave his old life behind. How many bettys had he fucked throughout his youth without bothering to see to their pleasure? They were fighting to throw themselves on his cock and service him without asking for anything in return. Okay, that wasn't true—they asked for plenty. Exclusive club memberships. Diamond bracelets. Trips to the Riviera. Just not orgasms. Because *that* might make them look too demanding.

Liam shook his head and tried to come fully back to *this* moment. This woman. This arse.

His forefinger quickly zeroed in on her clit and her body jolted when he made contact. Oh yeah. He hadn't lost his touch. He circled the small bud, loving the feel of how it hardened but all the hot flesh around stayed soft and yielding. He reached around with his other hand and dipped a finger inside her.

She hissed out in pleasure and pressed back against him. And for the first time, it didn't feel like a calculated move. That was goddamned right. He'd make her so crazy she'd forget to put on some stupid fecking show.

He leaned over and kissed the back of her neck, still circling her clit with a gentle, explorative touch.

After his misspent youth and finishing Uni, he really put in the time to discovering the mechanics of female pleasure. He nipped with his teeth at the back of her neck even as he slipped a second finger inside her.

"*Oh. God*," she whimpered, shuddering around his fingers.

"That's right," he coaxed, his cock coming back to full mast at her response. "Give it to me. Give it all to me."

"But you—" she tried to protest. "Stick it in so we can—"

"Hush." Liam finally increased the pressure on her clitoris, returning over and over again to one particular spot that made her words cut off and her back arch.

"Yes. Keep— Oh my God, *yes.*"

Liam used his thumb to continue strumming her clit. Then he tugged her hair so she'd look over her shoulder at him. He loved watching women while they came. No matter what they rated on the hotness scale, they became beautiful during climax.

"Now," he ordered, losing the cheerful joviality he'd had all night. "Come. Fucking now."

Her eyebrows lifted and then her whole face scrunched in surprised longing that almost looked like pain as she orgasmed. Jaysus, he loved that. That line between pleasure and pain. And how fucking fleeting it all was.

Her mouth dropped open and her head tipped back as the shudders racked her body. Liam kept stroking her all the way through it, more fucking turned on than he had been all night. He was finally hard as a rock against her.

Her body had barely stopped quaking before he had his cock nudging at her now drenched pussy. He grabbed his shaft and rubbed the crown back and forth over her swollen lips.

"Yes. Oh God, yes. Please, Liam. Make love to me. Oh my God," her voice was hoarse. "I've never made love with a billionaire before.

You're even more amazing than I thought— *Oh!*" She grabbed the sink and swiveled her head to look at him as he yanked back from her. "What is it, baby?"

"What did you just say?" He stared at her, willing himself to have misheard her.

She giggled and pushed a stray hair out of her flushed face, again putting on that fake fucking show of innocence. It made him want to fucking gag. In fact, everything about this little bar bathroom tryst was suddenly making him sick to his stomach.

"Just that I've never— well, you know." She blinked her eyes up at him in a way he imagined her practicing in front of a mirror. "Been with someone like you."

"Someone like me?" It took most of his newly acquired self-discipline to keep his cool.

"*You know.*" She lowered her eyebrows and whispered, "A *billionaire.*"

Liam jerked away from her like she'd slapped him. "Who told you that?"

"Nobody told me, silly." She stood up, not bothering to smooth down her skirt. The red fabric bunched around her waist, her pussy still exposed. She tried to take a step toward him but he held out a hand to stop her. She cocked her head to the side like she was confused.

"So how'd you know?"

She shrugged, smiling and taking another step toward him. Liam didn't move and she ran a hand down the buttons on his shirt. She did that thing where she angled her face down and then looked up at him through her lashes.

Another practiced fucking move if he ever saw one. Jaysus, this woman was as bad as any of those leeches back in Dublin. How did he not spot it earlier? He was out of practice, that was for sure. His hand shot up and he gripped her wrist, prying her away from him. "How did you know who I am?"

Her smile faltered as she tried to pull her arm out of his grasp. He didn't let go.

"How?" he demanded.

"Look, it's no big deal," she tried to laugh it off, pulling her hand back when Liam finally let go of her. "I was just curious about the new people in town, so I googled you. Everybody does it."

She was lying. "What'd you google? You don't even know my name."

She looked at the floor before trying on another insincere smile. "Well, Google has that feature where you can look up people by their faces now. So last time you were in the bar, I snapped a picture."

"Jaysus." He walked several steps back from her. She was a goddamned stalker. And he'd almost— *Jaysus*. He cringed even at the thought. He'd had a few obsessive women try to stalk him back in Dublin. Then there was the woman he'd had an affair with who tried to claim he was the father of her baby. That had been a fecking nightmare. No wonder this slag hadn't wanted to wear a condom. She was probably hoping she'd get knocked up and that she could sink her hooks into his life and his bank account permanently.

He was about to turn and get the hell out of there but he stopped. "Who else have you told? About who I really am?"

Her eyes went wide. "Oh I would never tell a soul. I know you wanted to get away from all that scandal and I would hate for any of that to get out—"

"Are you trying to fuckin' blackmail me?" he bit out.

"No!" she exclaimed and for once she sounded genuine. "I wouldn't want any of these other bitches getting a hold of you. Besides," her voice softened. "I know what it's like to be rich when everyone around you is poor. Daddy owns half the land in this county and people have been jealous of me my whole life. But I knew you'd understand me completely. It was like," she shook her head, "like fate brought you to me."

"What a crock of shite." Liam glared at her. "I didn't come halfway around the world just to pick me up another damn stalker. This," he waved between them, "is never happenin'."

With that he pushed past her and headed for the door. He unlocked it and swung it open, zipping up his fly as he went.

Only to find a thin lad standing on the other side reaching for the handle, a surprised look on his face when he saw Liam. Coming out of the women's restroom.

Then again, he was a dude reaching for the ladies, so he was obviously confused in general.

"Hey man, wrong bathroom. This is the ladies."

The lad just stared at Liam. He was wearing a thick flannel shirt underneath overalls and a dirty trucker's hat. Liam had seen him at the bar a few times. One of the sad little ranchers who lived around here. When he just kept standing there without saying anything, Liam wondered if he was slow. Jaysus, sometimes this little backwoods town was depressing as fuck.

"Ladies bathroom," Liam said slower, pointing to the stick figure with a skirt on the door.

"I *am* a lady. Um, a woman, I mean."

Oh. Shite. Liam's eyes immediately dropped to her chest but the flannel was too bulky to make out if there were any breasts hiding underneath. "Sorry."

When he looked up at her face, he could see that though her features were angular, if he tilted his head just right... yeah, she *was* female. Especially considering the way her cheeks were turning pink.

"Do you mind?" She glared at him.

Liam held up his hands. "Sorry. Sorry." He moved out of the way. She shoved the bathroom door the rest of the way open and disappeared inside.

Liam ran his hands through his hair. Way to feckin' step in it. He headed for the bar. He needed another drink. Or ten.

3

CALLA

HAVING her crush think she was a man was just the last in a long line of shitty things that had happened to Calla that day.

But nope. The universe wasn't done screwing her over. Because as soon as she got in the bathroom she saw Bethany Cunningham doubled over laughing and pointing a finger at her.

Calla's eyes shot back to the door. So that was why Liam had been coming out of the women's restroom. He'd been in here with Bethany. She thought of how his hair had been mussed and he'd been buttoning his fly.

"He thought you were a guy!" Bethany laughed even harder.

Great. So Bethany had heard the whole thing. The one person in the world who could make that humiliating experience even worse.

Calla knew how stupid it was to have a crush on a guy she barely knew. Lord, even the word *crush* made her cringe, but she didn't know what else to call it. She'd talked to Liam a couple times when he and the other guys from Mel's ranch came out to Bubba's. Granted, he'd been *very* drunk both times.

But she was done for the first time he'd flashed that gorgeous smile of his. Dimples. It wasn't fair. That accent *plus* dimples? Come on, God, couldn't you be a little fairer when you're distributing things? Why was it always people like Bethany who got the looks and the money? And the guy.

"You've really lived up to your potential. Weren't you voted 'Least Likely to Ever Get Boobs' in high school?" Bethany cracked up like it was the best joke she'd ever heard, wiping at her eyes. At least Calla had managed to make her smudge her perfect make-up. Bethany had little black mascara tracks running down her cheeks.

It was on the tip of Calla's tongue to shoot back: *weren't you the bitch on the yearbook staff who gave me that name?*

She and Bethany had hated each other ever since they started facing off in barrel racing competitions throughout high school. Bethany couldn't stand the fact that a nobody like Calla could wipe the floor with her in the arena. Out of all the times they went head to head, Bethany only beat Calla *once*. And even then, the bitch had done it by cheating.

But did Calla confront her or kick her teeth in like she wanted to after finding her horse overfeeding on an extra hay sack drenched in applejuice? This on top of the year when she was a freshman, all courtesy of Bethany starting rumors about Calla and the English teacher being in a lesbian love affair.

No. Calla had been an adult about it. Always. She'd turned the other cheek and gone on to compete as well as she could with her hay-heavy horse. Bethany's smile had been vicious as she claimed her blue ribbon.

Calla wished she was the kind of person who could face down the town bully. But she hated confrontation. She had ever since she was a little kid and would hide under the bed when her parents had screaming matches. Then Mama left when Dad got sick. Not before that one last fight, though, where she shouted about how she was still young and there was no reason to let Dad's illness ruin two lives.

"What about Calla?" her dad asked. *"What about your daughter?"*

Silence. Then, "I couldn't bear watching her get sick too."

"There's only a fifty percent chance she has it. It's just as likely that she's perfectly fine."

"And you expect me to live like that? Hoping on a coin toss? No. It's better if I leave now."

"Better for who?" Calla had never heard her dad's voice so bitter.

Another long silence. "I know I'm a coward. I don't expect your forgiveness. But I'm just not strong enough for this. Goodbye Edward."

Then she left. The house got real quiet after that. Years and years of quiet, her dad only talking to her when there was something to be done around the ranch.

All of this meant Calla didn't say a word to Bethany as she turned to slam back out the door.

"Just admit it," Bethany straightened up. "Your dad raised you like the son he always wanted. You couldn't even get that right. You lost him his ranch. Now what are you going to do? No man is ever going to want you."

Calla froze at the door, an alien fury burning in her chest.

Too far.

Too much.

She'd woken up that morning only to say goodbye to the only home she'd ever known.

All the land that had been in her family for three generations was officially sold to none other than Bethany's father, Ned. He'd been trying to buy them out for years. Dad always swore he'd never sell his land to a Cunningham. Turned out that between the failing economy, a few years of serious mismanagement, and Dad's worsening illness, the choice was made for them.

Not that Dad saw it that way. Last time she went to visit him at the home, he'd refused to even see her. If he'd had his way, they would have fought till the day the bank came and foreclosed on the place. And then Ned Cunningham would get the property anyway—at the bank auction.

Screw it. Calla was tired of keeping quiet and not causing waves. She swung back around to the blonde little Barbie wannabe.

"Well if being a woman means being a vindictive bitch like you, guess I'm happy the way I am. Besides, I don't need a man to validate my existence."

Bethany's mouth dropped open before she scrambled for a comeback. "Good, because the only man who'd want to fuck you would be a gay dude."

"Well at least I know I deserve better than a drunken hookup in the bathroom of a bar."

Bethany looked like she was about to spit fire. "Liam and me are meant to be. Not that I expect some he-she freak like you to understand. No one will ever want you. You'll die old and alone."

Enough. Calla's entire body was shaking as she shoved the bathroom door open. She refused to let Bethany know how well her words hit target.

Calla held her head high as she walked through the bar to the counter. Hey look, God answered some prayers. Liam was nowhere in sight as she walked over to her still mostly full beer mug.

"Hey Bubba," she said when she got to her stool, "I'm gonna cash out my tab." She pulled out her phone and clicked on the Uber app. Hawthorne had a total of two Uber drivers, but Wayne only drove on weekends. Tonight there'd only be Carl and he liked to be in bed by eleven. It was ten-thirty, so she was pushing it.

She clicked through the app. Okay, Carl was ten minutes out.

"Heading home so soon?" Bubba ran his hand down his long Santa like beard in the habitual way he had that Calla was sure violated some health code.

She smirked. "Been warming this stool since dinnertime."

Bubba leaned his elbows on the bar. "Prettiest face gracing my counter tonight."

Calla rolled her eyes. Bubba sure could tell a whopper with a straight face. "My tab?"

"All right, all right, if you're in a hip and a hurry." He pushed off the bar.

He came back with her credit card and a receipt to sign. She signed it and gave a generous tip. She couldn't afford it, or the drink for that matter, but what the hell. Bubba had been great company while they watched the game he had on. She'd almost been distracted from her shit life for awhile and that was worth throwing away a little money she didn't have to spend, right?

"Don't forget to get your fortune," Bubba said, fishing a fortune cookie out of the large jar he had set up beside his cash register.

Calla lifted an eyebrow. "You do realize this joint isn't a Chinese restaurant, right?"

"What? My Susie loves reading her horoscope every morning. And I'm always looking for little ways to jazz things up around here." He grinned, his ruddy cheeks pink and his coffee-stained teeth shining.

"Hey, I'll take all the luck I can get," Calla took the fortune cookie from him.

"Have a good night, gorgeous."

Calla rolled her eyes again. She heard a loud laugh from the far end of the bar that sounded a lot like Liam's—a fact she hated that she knew, and decided to wait for Carl outside. It wasn't just Liam. All night everyone had been flashing her pitying looks. Town the size of Hawthorne, everyone knew everyone else's business. She was sure she and Daddy had been a hot gossip topic lately.

She shoved the fortune cookie in her pocket and headed for the door.

"Night, Cal," a couple people called out as she walked by. She just nodded, avoiding everyone's eyes.

She kept her back straight, chin up until she was out of the bar. Once she was out of sight of everyone, though, she collapsed back against the brick wall. She squeezed her eyes shut as the events of earlier that morning flashed for the hundredth time.

Today was the hardest since she'd moved Dad into the nursing home six months ago. The ranch was so in debt they'd barely come out of the deal with enough to secure his long-term care. Huntington's Disease was degenerative and he only got worse as the years passed. But being so cash-strapped also meant that in addition to her truck, she'd had to sell her horse.

She'd taken Prissy out for one last ride before Chris Mendoza, a local trainer she'd sold him to, came to pick her up.

"Okay, girl." Calla had scratched down Prissy's long nose. "One last ride."

It was a warm June afternoon but Calla felt cold through and through. She smiled though, not wanting Prissy to pick up on her mood.

Prissy snorted and nudged Calla with her nose. Calla wasn't fooling her. Prissy knew something was off.

"Can't get anything past you, can I, Priss?"

Calla ran her hands along Prissy's sleek shoulder and flank, not wanting to lose a single second of contact during the short time she had left with her beloved mare. Her best friend.

Calla lifted a foot in the stirrups and then hiked herself up. Prissy neighed, throwing her head and stepping forward. Calla shifted her weight and got her seat right in time.

"Whoa, whoa, girl. What is it?"

But as Calla looked down the long road that led to her dad's ranch, her stomach sank.

No. Not Dad's ranch anymore.

She'd signed the papers just yesterday finalizing the sale. Ned Cunningham hadn't made any bones about the fact that he expected Calla off the property within twenty-four hours and that anything she left behind was forfeit.

Calla swallowed as she watched the progress of the truck and trailer rig. At least the Cunninghams weren't getting Prissy. The thought of Bethany owning Prissy was more than Calla could take. So she'd made arrangements with Chris, who was always looking for good barrel racing horses. Since Prissy was getting older, Calla had taken a loss on her. But it was better than that witch Bethany getting her.

The approaching truck kicked up dust and dirt as it rumbled closer. Calla's jaw clenched and she clicked her teeth. Prissy came to attention underneath her. When Calla squeezed her thighs, Prissy responded.

The movements were almost unconscious at this point. She and Prissy had been together so long, the horse was more like an extension of Calla herself. So it was barely a thought in her head before Prissy took off at a canter that quickly became a full gallop around the side of the house to the practice paddock.

The gate was open and Calla leaned back in the saddle as they sped toward one of the barrels that was still set up in a cloverleaf pattern. She pulled on the left rein and Prissy turned on a dime to circle the first barrel.

Calla urged her on with her legs and then they were flying toward the second barrel. She felt her hat flip off at the speed but she pushed even harder. Wind beat at her face as she leaned back and pulled on the opposite rein to circle the second barrel. Prissy made an even tighter turn than the first and then dirt flew as they went hell for leather toward the third and then fourth barrel.

Both Calla and her mare were breathing hard when Calla finally pulled the reins to bring Prissy to a halt right beside the paddock fence.

Calla leaned over and breathed in Prissy's familiar horsey smell as she clapped her on the neck. "That's right, my strong girl. You did so good. You never let me down. Not once in my whole life."

Calla got Prissy when the mare was just two years old. Calla was eleven and more often than not in the past fourteen years, Prissy felt like the only true friend Calla had in the world. And now she had to say goodbye.

A loud clapping shook her out of her thoughts. Calla swung around to see Chris standing by the gate. She'd arranged to sell Prissy to him a few weeks ago. Just a few years older than her, Calla knew Chris in the same way she did most people in Hawthorne—he was a friendly acquaintance she'd known forever.

Growing up, she told herself the reason she didn't have any close friends was just because there'd always been too much work to be done around the ranch. There was no time for socializing when you had to run home after school to see to the calving, or check the irrigation lines, or to help bring in the hay.

Dad started showing symptoms for Huntington's when she was twelve and she'd had to take on more and more of the physical tasks around the ranch every year as he got worse.

It wasn't until she got to college that she finally realized the real reason she didn't get close to people. Every year she watched her dad's health decline, she knew the same could be in store for her. *Would* likely be in store for her. She was a dead ringer for her dad— she'd looked at pictures of him when he was her age and they could have been twins.

She couldn't get the test to find out if she had the mutated gene that brought on the disease until she was eighteen. And by then she'd made such a habit of keeping folks at a distance that it was a way of life.

As for the test? Now twenty-four, she still hadn't taken it. Because even though she fully expected to test positive for the gene, there was some foolish little part of her that thought, *you never know. Maybe you don't have it.* Stupid as it was, she hadn't wanted to give up that hope by testing and learning for certain.

"If I wasn't already sold on her, that run would have convinced me." Chris looked admiringly at Prissy. "How fast was that? Seventeen seconds? Less?"

Calla swallowed hard, her throat thick. "Don't know. Just wanted one last run."

Chris's expression changed from impressed to sympathetic. Pitying. It was the same look everyone had been flashing her around town since news of the deal with Cunningham had been announced in the local paper.

Calla swung off of Prissy, her back to Chris. She took a moment to compose herself and then turned around to face him again. "She should make for a great training horse."

"Don't I know it." His admiring gaze was on Prissy before he looked back to Calla. "You can come visit her anytime you want."

Calla controlled her features. It might about kill her to have to go visit her beloved horse and then turn her back over for someone else to stable. She could only handle so goddamned much. "Maybe I will," she lied.

She turned away to unbuckle the cinch straps that secured the saddle. She ran her hand down Prissy's flank and gave her one last pat before tying the cinch and sliding the saddle off.

"Let me get that," Chris said, stepping forward.

Calla wanted to yank back from him. But he was about to own the saddle along with Prissy, so that was stupid. She handed over the heavy tack and he took it without complaint.

"I'll help you load her up." Calla made a clicking noise and Prissy fell into step behind her as she led her toward Chris's trailer.

After she got Prissy trailered, Chris pulled his wallet out of his back pocket and handed her a check. Calla wanted to shove it back at him the second her fingers closed around it.

Prissy let out an anxious, high-pitched neigh and shifted in the trailer, ears flicking back and forth. She knew something was wrong.

Calla's mouth went dry as she stared down at the check in her hands. Five-thousand dollars. Was she really going to sell her best friend, even for so much money?

After putting away money for Dad's care, she did have a little bit to live on. Maybe if she really scrimped, she could—

But then she forced her eyes shut as she shoved the check into her pocket. She'd already been over this a thousand times. Even if she didn't need the money to live on, she couldn't afford the boarding fees and all the other costs that came along with owning a horse. There was no way to justify spending six to seven hundred dollars a month when it wasn't an absolute necessity. Not if she wanted Dad to stay in the best nursing home around. It was the same reason she'd sold her truck earlier in the week.

So she squared her shoulders. "Could you drop me in town? I need to deposit this."

And then go get a stiff drink. Or ten.

She'd gone to the bank, then walked down to Bubba's where she'd been warming a barstool all night.

Calla stood up straight and swiped at her eyes when she saw Carl pulling up in his Honda Odyssey. Lord, she couldn't believe she'd let herself stand here in the dark and wallow like a little baby. So she'd had a crap run of luck lately. So what? Plenty folks had it harder.

She was young. Healthy, at least for now. And she had a place to stay and a good job for the foreseeable future.

No more pity parties. She took one more deep breath and jogged over to the back seat of the van.

"Where to?" Carl asked after she pulled open the back door and got inside. He was a bald guy in his late fifties who used to play poker with her dad.

"The Kent ranch."

Carl nodded and pulled onto Main Street. "I heard you was gonna go work out there after losing your dad's place." Carl was also one of the prime movers of gossip in Hawthorne. She'd often thought he might be a driver for the gossip as much as for the extra income.

Calla's mouth went tight but she nodded as Carl went on.

"Kent's a good man. None of us was too sure about him when he bought up the old resort and moved here. What with his face all mangled like it is."

Calla looked out the window, hoping to dissuade conversation but Carl wasn't put off.

"But he and that wife of his are good folks. Just look at 'em helping you out." Carl nodded, glancing back toward Calla. "Good folks."

Calla kept her gaze trained out the window. "It's been a long day. I'm just going to close my eyes till we get there."

"I bet. Heard you even had to sell your horse to the Mendoza boy. Awful sad. I remember seeing your picture in the paper with her when you won those first-place ribbons back in high school. Your daddy was so proud he carried a cutout from the Gazette and showed anybody who would give him five minutes."

Okay, Carl was clearly getting up there in years if he thought that had been her dad bragging on her. Yeah she and Prissy had won ribbons—first place in the regional rodeo her senior year— but Carl must be mixing her up with someone else's daughter. If her dad ever had anything to say about her, it was complaining how she wasn't keeping up with chores, no matter how hard she worked her butt off. It was never enough for him.

She leaned back into the seat and shut her eyes. Carl eventually got the picture and stopped talking.

She must have actually fallen asleep because it felt like only moments later when the car was pulling to a stop.

Calla sat up, looking around. The big ranch house was dark. Little wonder since most ranchers woke up before dawn. She pulled out her phone and glanced down. It was ten-forty-five going on eleven.

She tipped Carl and then got out. She'd moved her stuff in and gotten the key yesterday. It was probably foolhardy and sentimental to have gone back to her own place last night. But she hadn't been able to say goodbye knowing she could have one more night there. It wasn't any easier to do it today, though, so she might as well have gotten it over with yesterday.

She shook her head at herself as she pulled her keys out of her pocket and unlocked the front door. Carl waited until she was inside before driving off.

There were a couple of nightlights that lit up the central staircase and she went up as quiet as she could. She didn't want anyone waking up on her account. Mel and Xavier had three little boys all under six years old.

To her relief she made it to her room at the end of the hall without her encountering anyone. She flipped on her light. And then groaned when she saw all her still-packed boxes. The bed looked inviting. First, a shower, though.

Calla paused on her way to the attached bathroom, noticing a note lying on the pillow. She leaned over and picked it up.

Left a plate of food for you in the fridge in case you're hungry. So glad you'll be staying here. There was a little heart and then *Mel*.

Calla smiled. She didn't know Mel very well, but from the few times Calla had interacted with her, she seemed pretty great. Food sounded good but still—shower. If ever she'd needed to wash a day off, it was this one.

She paused when she got in the bathroom, looking at her reflection. She pulled her hair out of the stubby little ponytail and ran her fingers through it. It was almost long enough to touch her shoulders.

She'd worn it short since she was a little kid. When Mom left, Dad started cutting her hair and gave her the same cut he did himself —he slapped a one-inch guard on the trimmers and mowed everything else off. In her late teens she'd started going over to Betty's to get it cut there, but she'd still kept it short. What did she know about having girly hair? Nothing, that's what.

She tugged on the ends and frowned at herself. She still didn't know a damn thing about it, which was why she kept it tied back under the cap she always wore.

But maybe she could wear it down sometimes. When she wasn't doing ranch work anyway. She frowned and turned away, turning the shower to hot and then stepping in.

The steam loosened her muscles but fifteen minutes later after shampooing and shaving, her mind wasn't any quieter.

Maybe if she...

Her hand dropped down her stomach. And then lower.

But her usual fantasies weren't quite—

Hey man, wrong bathroom. This is the ladies.

"Ugh!" She slammed the shower knob to the off position and stepped out, toweling herself brusquely.

She wrapped a towel around herself and then paused for her nightly ritual. She lifted up her left leg. And waited, concentrating hard to see if there was even the slightest tremor in the limb. Yeah, her dad's Huntington's hadn't developed until he was forty-three, but plenty people experienced early onset. She dropped her left leg and lifted her right, going through the process all over again. Then her left and right arm.

She breathed out and leaned back against the bathroom door. And recited the alphabet backwards three times.

"E, D, C, B, A," she whispered, lifting a hand to her forehead. Safe for one more day. She shook her head and pushed back out into the bedroom.

She grabbed her overalls off the ground and the fortune cookie fell out of the pocket. She went to throw it in the little trash by the toilet but then paused.

Rolling her eyes at herself, she ripped the little package and pulled out the cookie. Cracking it in half, she slid the little paper out and read the message.

Live every day like it's your last.

She couldn't help but laugh. Wow. Spot on, fortune cookie gods. Considering any day could be the beginning of the end for her.

As shitty as today had been, what the hell would she do if tomorrow she detected a tremor?

She rolled her eyes again. God, she was being an idiot, letting a goddamned fortune cookie get to her. It was just a stupid gimmick. Bubba had probably ordered the damn things from Fortune Cookies R Us.

Popping the stale cookie in her mouth, she munched on it while she gathered her dirty clothes and tossed them in her laundry bag. She pulled on an oversized University of Wyoming t-shirt.

Then her stomach rumbled. Hmm. She glanced at the clock on the nightstand. Probably not the best idea to eat at eleven-fifteen.

But Mel had gone through all the trouble of making her a plate. Who was she to deny the woman the opportunity to be hospitable?

Calla headed back downstairs. Mel had showed her around yesterday so she knew where the kitchen was.

She flipped on the light and went for the fridge. She was leaning over to look for the plate Mel had left her.

And only remembered she was just in a T-shirt that skimmed the top of her thighs when a low, masculine voice said, "Well hello, gorgeous."

4

MACK

THE FIRST THING Mack knew was that he wanted her.

Whoever the woman with the sweetly curved ass currently pawing through the refrigerator was, he wanted her. Which made no damn sense because one, he didn't know her from Adam and two, he didn't go for that shit anymore.

He'd made it his business a long time ago not to want anybody ever again. Some people in this world were shit. They were born shit, and they'd die shit. He was one of those people. It had taken him a long time to accept it. He'd even tried going to college and pretending to be something other than he was. Lasted a whole four months. 'Cause fuck it. Truth was truth.

He tried not to spread his shit around too much. Kept to himself.

So wanting someone, anyone, but especially the owner of that particular sweet ass was a problem.

Then again, maybe this was just a dream. Maybe he was still upstairs, face down on his bed.

His sleep had been restless all week. It got like that sometimes.

Too many ghosts came out at night. You didn't spend eight years in lock-up without getting jumpy when the lights went out.

He'd come down to the kitchen to do what he always did when he couldn't sleep. He plotted. He went through, step by step, his plan to take revenge when the time was right.

"Well hello, gorgeous," he said, still half-convinced he was talking to a dream.

The way she squealed and jumped about a foot in the air sure seemed fucking real, though.

Shit. Mack hadn't meant to scare her. He sat back in his chair at the little table near the bay window and held up his hands.

She gasped and spun around.

Mack expected her to recoil once she saw him. Covered in tattoos from his neck to his wrists, he knew he could be an intimidating bastard. That was generally the point—but never when it came to women.

Her body relaxed when she saw him though and she let out a shaky laugh. "I didn't see you."

"Sorry," Mack said, still eyeing her up and down and waiting for her to flinch away from his gaze.

Instead she let the refrigerator door fall shut and she walked toward him, hand extended. "Hi there, I'm Cal. I've seen you around but I guess we've never officially met."

Chicks usually reacted to him one of two ways. Either they took one look at his tattoos and reacted like he was about to steal their shit and murder them. Or they saw him and thought *sex*. Couldn't say he minded either reaction, generally.

But Calla didn't flash him a smile or flip her hair or any of the other shit women of the second persuasion usually did. She just looked friendly, hand still held out.

Mack stared for a moment, then took her hand and gave it a shake. What was her deal? "Mack."

"Good to meet ya, Mack." Then she tilted her head and stared at him more intently. "So, you regularly sit in dark rooms ready to scare the bejesus out of people?"

He cracked a smile at that. She was cute. He held up his empty glass. "A glass of milk helps me sleep sometimes."

"Milk?" The edge of her mouth quirked up.

He shrugged. "Ran out of tequila."

She shook her head, the slight smile still in place. "Well good luck with that."

Then she turned back to the fridge and resumed hunting for whatever it was she'd been after in the first place. He watched her as she pulled out a plate that had aluminum foil covering it with a little post-it.

For Calla ONLY. He'd seen it earlier when he got his milk and smirked because Mel and everybody else knew that anything in the fridge was fair game unless marked. Which meant most the time the fridge was running on empty except right after the weekly groceries. Having six grown men on the property would do that.

Calla didn't look at him again as she pulled off the foil and then went over to the microwave, popping in the plate of meatloaf, potatoes and beans. It took her a couple tries to figure out the settings, but soon it was whirring and lit up as it reheated her food. She kept her body toward the counter, back to him.

Was she just pretending to ignore him? If there was one thing Mack could say about himself, it was that he provoked reaction in people. It was a little disconcerting to have her be so oblivious to him.

Unless it was an act. Chicks did that sometimes. At least the ones that were trying to play it cool.

Curious, he stood up, grabbing his milk glass and taking it to the sink. His path led him right by her.

She glanced his way and gave him a polite nod but then went back to watching her food cook.

All right, either this woman was the best actress he'd ever met or she genuinely didn't give a damn if he was there or not.

He should have walked away right then. Man he was, plans he had, he should have given her the silent treatment he did everyone else and forgot her existence. Forgot how her apple-bottomed ass had looked when she bent over to look in the fridge. He shoulda forgot how her clear, pale skin and moon eyes had looked at him so huge and innocent as she held out her hand to him.

But Mack was shit. Always had been and always would be. And if there was one truth about shit, it was that shit liked to stick. To dirty up clean things. To befoul them.

A thought which again, shoulda had him running the other direction.

One problem kept popping up in the way of sane, rational thought, though.

He wanted her.

He'd been feeling restless lately. He'd come out to this little patch of nowhere to kill time until... well, until he did what needed doing.

He thought he'd come out here and pass a few years under the radar. Wait it out.

It shoulda been enough just to live. To be a free man living in the world. When he first came to the ranch a couple years ago, just getting away from all the shit back in Jersey had been enough. He could go hang out with the horses when he got sick of people. The manual labor of the ranch was usually enough to clear his mind. He liked working with his hands.

It had been peaceful. Sort of. Until night came anyway. Then his hands were still and there was nothing to do except *think*.

Like tonight. He'd jolted awake with his fists clenched and his heart racing. Bone's goddamned voice ringing in his head. When he looked at the clock, he saw he'd barely been asleep for half an hour.

Losing himself in a woman could be just what he needed. Right after he got out, he'd fucked any woman that gave him half a glance. You didn't go without pussy for that long and not want to drown yourself cock-deep for a few weeks.

He'd needed to prove to himself he was normal, maybe. So there, he'd proved he could screw a chick no problem. Meant he hadn't been fucked up by all the shit that went down inside, right? Not permanently anyway.

But easy pussy got tiresome real quick. Plus, what did any of it mean except confirming he could still stick his cock in a hole, shut off his brain, and fuck till he came?

Great, his dick wasn't broken.

That had never been the problem though, had it? It was his *head* that had gotten fucked ten ways from Sunday in that place.

He moved out here and hadn't gone chasing tail since. His right hand worked just fine. Plans he had, he didn't need any woman getting caught up in his shit. Even if he was tempted, the town was so small and insular, well, he knew better than to shit where he ate.

Hadn't been a problem.

At least until now.

The woman said she'd seen him around and he wondered where the fuck she meant because surely, he would have noticed her.

He washed out his cup, looking at her out of the corner of his eye. She had a square face and strong features for a woman. Sharp cheekbones and an angular jaw. Pale, pink lips. Her chin-length hair fell over one half of her face and she tucked it behind her ear before looking over at him.

"You're staring," she said bluntly.

Mack cracked a grin. She was interesting. Mack couldn't remember the last time anything had interested him. "I am." He continued staring.

She narrowed her eyes at him. "It's rude to stare." The microwave beeped and she reached to pull the plate out but Mack beat her to the punch.

"Let me get that for you. Don't want you to burn yourself on the plate. They're ceramic. They get hot."

He tagged a kitchen towel from the oven beside the sink and popped the microwave door. He had to lean into her side to do it. An intentional move. His chest brushed up against her side as he pulled the steaming plate from the microwave. He didn't miss her quick intake of breath. So she wasn't completely unaffected by him.

She kept her head down while he set the plate on the counter in front of her. He didn't move away, though. He stayed right where he was, intruding on her personal space. It was a dick move but if she told him to back off, he wouldn't push it.

The devil in him was too curious to see how she'd react.

She finally turned her face his way. Her eyes were a golden hazel and they flashed at him in a way that had his cock stirring to life.

"Am I in your way or something?" she asked. She started to slide to the left but Mack moved with her.

"No. You're not in my way."

She paused at his words, her head tilted toward him and her eyebrows furrowing like she was confused.

"I'm right where I mean to be," he clarified. When she didn't try to pull away again, he dropped his hands to the counter on either side of her, caging her in.

That got him another little breathy inhale as her eyes searched his. Fuck, but it made his balls tight when she did that.

"You are?" Her eyebrows went up slightly. Her surprise seemed genuine. Then her eyes dropped to his mouth.

"Fuck yes I am," he all but growled. Her eyes flicked between his and then again to his mouth, like she couldn't stop looking at it.

He was close enough he could smell the clean scent of soap on her skin. He would have known she'd just come from the shower even if her light brown hair hadn't still been slightly damp. But it wasn't any flowery shit. Just a crisp, clean smell. Her skin was tan and there was a scattering of freckles across her nose.

Her chest rose and fell with each breath. Mack couldn't help his eyes tracing down her swanlike neck. Even in the shapeless T-shirt, he could see the outline of her pert little breasts, especially where the hard peaks of her nipples poked out. Was she just chilled? Or aroused?

Mack couldn't remember the last time he'd felt such an instant, animal attraction. And it wasn't just his cock responding to her. Even exchanging as few words as they had, he could tell she wouldn't be just another easy lay. There was more to her. She seemed *real*.

Had it been long enough, finally? Could he go to bed with a woman without all that other bullshit interfering?

One of her hands shot up to lay flat on his chest, over his heart. Like she meant to push him away. But she didn't put any pressure behind it. She just kept it there and the longer she did, the more it felt like a scorching iron of connection between them.

Mack couldn't help shifting his pelvis forward and her eyes widened when she felt his hardness through his jeans against her stomach. But they didn't widen in alarm. Instead, a flare of heat blazed.

That was the last straw. He was only a man for Christ's sake. Mack lifted his right hand from the counter and he cupped her cheek. He wasn't delicate about it either. He gripped her graceful jaw and traced his thumb over her bottom lip, tugging it down slightly. If he thought her little breathy noises from earlier were sexy, it was nothing to the way she gasped and leaned in to his touch at this. Jesus, she was responsive.

He'd just decided he needed to spend the next few hours exploring exactly *how* responsive when suddenly there was a racket outside the back door. Calla's face swung that direction moments before the door was shoved open and that bloody fucking Irishman's voice filled the kitchen.

"Not my fault I forgot me fecking keys at the bar. You're the one who thought a drinking game was a good idea. If you thought I was going to lose to some pansy-arsed American, well I fecking showed ya!"

Liam staggered into the kitchen, followed up by the twins, Tweddle dee and Tweddle fucking dumb.

Before Mack knew it, Calla had jerked away from him and tugged at the bottom of her shirt as the voices quieted. His housemates might be drunk as skunks but they were all brought up short at the sight of the beautiful woman all but in Mack's arms. A woman he'd been a hairsbreadth away from claiming for the night before these fucknuts stumbled in.

"Who's that?" one of the twins asked at the same time Liam took a lunging step toward where he and Calla stood.

"Hey, it's you." Liam pointed a finger toward her face. "You really aren't a dude. Huh. When'd you get so pretty?"

Calla had pulled away from Mack, but he still felt it the instant her back went ramrod straight. Her mouth dropped open and she looked horrified.

Mack's fist was flying toward Liam's face before he could even think it all the way through. He didn't know exactly what the fuck the bastard was on about, but it was clear he'd upset Calla.

And Jesus but it was satisfying when his fist connected with Liam's jaw. He barely registered Calla's small shriek or the other guys shouting. All he knew was he'd wanted to punch the fucker from almost the moment he'd met him.

Rich bastard parading around, playing at being a cowboy when the rest of them were here to earn a living. It made Mack fucking sick. So when Liam's head was knocked sideways and he stumbled backward a few steps before falling on his ass, Mack felt only the glow of gratification.

At least until he saw Calla shrink away from him, her hand to her mouth.

He didn't have more than a moment to register it, though, because the next second Liam was back on his feet and lunging for him.

"Ya cocksucker!" he yelled, fist swinging.

Mack blocked the first blow but when Liam followed up with a mean jab to his ribs, Mack wasn't fast enough.

And fuck but the bastard could fight, even when he was drunk off his ass. Mack barely had time to recover from the fist to his stomach before Liam swung again. He jerked back but Liam still clipped his jaw.

Which just fucking enraged him. You didn't survive super max for almost a decade without knowing how to fight, and he couldn't believe this pansy-assed motherfucker had actually gotten in two hits on him. He could count how many times that had ever happened on one hand. With a roar, he charged Liam and took the bastard to the ground.

Mack was just about to get a choke hold on him when a pissed off voice demanded, "What the fuck is going on here?"

Shit. The boss was here. But even that wasn't enough to stop him from trying to get the upper hand on the little Irish shit. He *almost* had him pinned—

Suddenly a huge hand jerked Mack off Liam and tossed him onto his back. Mack scrambled to try to get at Liam until he finally registered a very pissed off Xavier Kent standing over him.

"You want to fucking explain what the fuck you're doing fighting in my kitchen. I could hear you all the way from the stairwell."

Mack blinked, the haze of rage starting to clear from his vision. He looked around. The twins had grabbed Liam's arms and were holding him back. Calla stood behind the kitchen island, arms crossed over her chest, her features showing clear mortification.

"Well?" Xavier demanded, the mottled skin on the burned upper left of his face going all but white in his anger even while the other side reddened.

"Sorry boss," Mack said, getting to his feet and looking at Xavier. "Won't happen again."

"Sure as fuck better not," Xavier growled. "You two—" He pointed a finger at Liam, who was still on the floor although no longer being held back by Jeremiah and Reece. Next, he pointed at Mack. "—are on KP duty for the next four weeks. And I better not ever have to deal with this shit again."

With that, the big man turned on his heel and was about to stalk from the room when he seemed to notice Calla.

"Cal." When Xavier acknowledged her, his voice was still gruff but not angry. "Glad to see you made it here okay."

She cringed, glancing between Mack and Liam. "Sorry for all this."

She hadn't been afraid of him when she'd first seen him but there was a wariness in her eyes now. Dammit. He was usually so good at hiding his monster. Out of all the times to lose it on Liam, it had to be tonight? In front of her? He'd just gotten so pissed when Liam had openly disrespected her. He clenched his jaw all over again just thinking about it.

Xavier shook his head, taking a second to glare over his shoulder at Mack and then Liam. "Not your fault these two are assholes who don't know how to behave in front of a lady."

Calla smirked. "No one's ever accused me of being a lady before."

Xavier shook his head, his hard face softening. "Well that just goes to show you," he paused, glaring back at Mack and Liam, "if this little display didn't already—what absolute fucking idiots the male population is. Get some sleep. Day starts early tomorrow." He patted Calla on the shoulder and then pushed out through the door. She followed on his heels. A moment later, two pairs of footsteps, one heavy and one light, could be heard as they went up the stairs.

"Hey, who's food is this?" Reece asked as he pulled his blond dreadlocks into a ponytail and stepped toward the counter. "I'm starving."

Mack moved and snatched the plate off the counter before Reece could touch it. "Not yours," Mack growled, turning and leaving the kitchen without another word.

He knocked lightly on Calla's door once he got upstairs. It had to be hers. Isobel used to stay there but it had been empty since she'd gone to live with Hunter.

"You forgot your food," he said through the door.

No response.

Shit. Like she was gonna open the door to an animal like him.

He took a step back. Why the fuck did he even care? He'd come to terms with what he was a long fucking time ago. He'd done what he had to in order to survive. Become what he was. He knew there was no going back.

The image of her sweet, open face and how innocently she'd extended her hand to shake his flashed through his head.

"I'll just leave it outside your door." He set the plate down and then stepped back

He ran his hands roughly through his hair, then whispered a sharp, "Fuck," before striding down the hall to his own room and shutting the door firmly behind him.

5

LIAM

"Jaysus," Liam grumbled to Jeremiah, "no one should be expected to wake up at the arse crack of dawn every morning." He pushed out the back door of the kitchen and they headed in the direction of the stables. "It's just not bloody right."

Jeremiah nodded, clutching his head.

Mack and Nicholas had gotten out the door ahead of them but Mack turned back, apparently having heard him. "Well maybe you shouldn't go out drinking and whoring when you know you have to get up at five a.m. the next morning."

Liam's eyebrows narrowed and Jeremiah winced, hand still massaging his temple. "Would everybody stop shouting?"

Liam ignored Mack and grinned at his friend. His own head was aching a bit but he didn't feel anywhere near as bad as Jeremiah looked. Then again, Liam hadn't spent half the night throwing up. He clapped Jeremiah on the back. "That'll teach you to go playing drinking games with an Irishman. Even the smallest of me kinswomen could drink you lot under the table any day of the week."

"I think I'm gonna be sick again." Jeremiah clutched his stomach and bent over, one hand on his knee.

Liam jumped back. "Don't come anywhere near me. I've barely even worn in me new boots." They were black Lucchese cowboy boots, the best of the best. Just because Liam had given up playing billionaire didn't mean he had to give up all his creature comforts.

"God help us if your pretty new boots get mussed," Mack shot over his shoulder.

Liam lifted a thumb to his still aching jaw. Brawling at six in the morning would be a bad idea, yeah?

Didn't stop his fists from clenching. Jaysus it had felt good getting that sucker punch in last night. It had been a long time coming.

Liam didn't know what Mack's fucking problem was. Liam was perfectly affable when he'd gotten to the ranch two years ago. But about three seconds after meeting him, Mack acted like Liam's very existence was some great offense. Bastard thought he was better than everyone around him even though it couldn't be further from the truth.

If Liam had met gutter trash like Mackenzie Knight in his old life, he would have gotten him thrown out of whatever club they were in and that would be that. He'd never have had to see the wanker again.

But part of this great experiment was seeing how the common people lived. Which meant living across the hall from the biggest douchebag he'd ever met. And constantly having to put up with his shite.

Nicholas hauled the stable door open, silent and good-tempered as ever. Liam liked the gentle giant. And the twins were great for a laugh. Xavier and Mel were top notch too. If not for Mack, he'd be totally happy with his new life.

All right, he could do without constantly having to muck horse shit, but apart from those two things, life on the ranch was surprisingly enjoyable. He'd only meant to spend a month or two here. But it had quickly grown on him... and well, he hadn't been eager to face all the shite back at home.

Turned out not having your every step hounded by paparazzi was more refreshing than he'd expected. Plus getting away from the city. And his family. His last scene with his father had ended up with his fist in his da's face.

He knew twenty-seven was too old to be running away from home. But fuck it, half the point of being a spoiled little shit was that you never had to grow up, yeah?

And his best memories had been spending time in the stables when he was a little kid. They used to spend summers in a cottage just outside Kilkenny. To hear his ma tell it, it was where his da had first courted her. She'd been on the set of a movie she was shooting and he'd been passing through on vacation. Love at first sight, that's what Ma said. So they'd come back every summer.

Except ever since Liam could remember, his da never stayed more than a week or two. He was always traveling, running back to Dublin or flying to L.A. or London or God knew where.

So Liam and his ma would spend all summer riding horses and painting and eating lazy meals in the big cottage house on the hill. The brawny stablemaster, Craig, taught him how to saddle and ride his first pony when he was just four years old. He thought it was all magical.

At least until his parents got divorced and Ma started drinking and snorting whatever shite she could find to shove up her nose. Back when Liam believed in things like goodness and love and happy endings. Before he learned better.

Jaysus, why was he thinking about all this right now? It was barely six in the feckin' morning. If he was going to go wallowing, he might as well wait till it was late enough to justify a good stiff glass of whiskey.

"Calla. Hey. How long have you been up?"

Liam looked up at Mack's question and paused. It was the woman from last night. Liam cringed. The one he'd first mistaken for a lad.

She was wearing overalls again but instead of a shapeless flannel shirt underneath, she had on a form-fitting long-sleeved thermal that emphasized her small but toned arms. Her hair was pulled back in a tiny ponytail, little wisps escaping all around her face.

Damn, she *was* pretty. It hadn't just been his dick's drunken response to seeing a half-naked woman last night. Here it was, arse-o'clock in the morning and she was still pretty as a peach. He felt like even more of an eejit for mistaking her for a man.

She only glanced up momentarily from the stall she was mucking out. "Oh. Hey guys."

Jeremiah had finally joined them and several long moments of silence passed, everyone just staring at Calla. Mack finally whistled. "Damn, you've got five stalls done already. Trying to impress the boss on your first day?"

Liam was about to call him out for being a rude bastard but Calla only smiled and shook her head. "Just used to farm life. Been waking up at four a.m. for as long as I can remember."

Her voice was a low, soothing alto. And the more Liam looked at her, the more he realized that, fuck, she wasn't just pretty. She was *really* pretty.

Maybe not in an obvious way, with that square jaw and strong nose. More like a young Meryl Streep. As different as could be from the plastic fake-boobed betty he'd almost banged last night. This girl had a healthy tan like she was used to being outdoors regularly. And she was obviously used to hard work.

"You slackers gonna help me out or just stand there staring? I loaded up the hay nets a bit ago and have just started turning the horses out."

Nicholas nodded. "Mack and I will take the horses in the East Barn." He started toward the far barn door but Mack didn't move to follow.

"Why don't you take Jeremiah today?" Mack said. "I'm happy to stay here and help Calla."

She'd gone back to shoveling but looked up at hearing her name. Pink entered her cheeks as she locked eyes with Mack.

"I'll just get a pitchfork so I can join you." Mack's voice went almost soft as he said it. A small smile crossed her face before she went back to her work.

What the feck was going on? Mack hated everybody. And he

didn't smile. Ever.

Liam felt his jaw going hard as Mack walked to the far side of the barn to grab a pitchfork and shovel.

Was Calla actually buying into his bullshit? Last night was a little fuzzy, but if Liam remembered right, the two of them had been cozied up by the counter when he and the twins stumbled in the back door. He knew some girls got off on the thrill of the whole bad-boy tattooed thing. One glance, though, and he would have guessed this woman wouldn't be pulled in by that shite.

Then he cringed. Well, he supposed on *very* first glance he'd already shoved his foot in it by mistaking her for a man. That would be hard to recover from.

But if there was one thing in life Liam O'Neill was good at, it was charming women. And the occasional man if the situation was just right, but that was neither here nor there.

What was important now was saving her from being screwed over by Mackenzie. Mack was an ex-con, for Christ's sake. He'd done eight years hard time.

For whatever reason Xavier didn't seem to have a problem with that but Liam sure as hell did. And if it fell to him to save the fair maiden from the bastard's wiles, well, sometimes sacrifices had to be made.

And suddenly Liam was determined to do just that. Liam put on his most charming grin and walked over to where Calla was still shoveling. "I wanted to apologize for me behavior last night. Bad lighting and too much whiskey." He gave a short, self-deprecating laugh.

She looked up at him, eyebrows furrowing like she didn't understand why he was intruding on her space. Damn, she was going to be a tough nut to crack, wasn't she? Liam couldn't remember the last time a woman had posed a genuine challenge.

And the fact that he'd be stealing her out from under Mackenzie, who obviously wanted her too?

Just icing on the cake.

"So, ya like horses?" Liam leaned a shoulder against the stall she was mucking out.

Again she just looked at him like, *what do you want?*

Damn, had he really lost his touch that much?

"Why don't you run along and start your own work, laddie?" Mack tossed one of the shovels his direction and Liam barely managed to catch the heavy-handled tool.

Motherfucker, if he—

"Aren't you two supposed to be on kitchen duty this morning?" Calla asked, wiping her forehead and propping an elbow on her pitchfork. She looked back and forth between the two of them. "What time is breakfast anyway?" She glanced out the stable door like she was trying to gauge the time by the sun.

Liam cringed. Shite. He'd forgotten about that.

"I did my half," Mack said with a shit-eating smirk in Liam's direction. "Waffle batter's ready and the fruit's cut up. What about you?"

Liam wanted to smack the smug smile off his face. "Guess I should go start me prep."

"Don't worry, pretty boy, we'll leave you plenty of stalls to muck out."

No one would miss one more dead ex-con in the world, would they? He wouldn't even have to do it himself. Just one call to his fixer back in Dublin and—

"Chop chop," Mackenzie said, clapping his hands right in Liam's face.

Liam stopped himself just short of lunging for the bastard, and only because Calla was right there. No, he'd show he could be the bigger man.

"Great to officially meet you, beautiful." Liam winked at Calla and noted, with no small amount of satisfaction, that the pink came back into her cheeks again.

"You, too," she said, then quickly averted her eyes. Was it his imagination or did she sound a little breathless? He grinned as he headed back toward the house, all his instincts telling him she was checking out his arse as he went.

Oh yeah, he still had it.

6

CALLA

CALLA WASN'T sure how it was possible to burn *eggs*. But as she poked at the eggs that were slightly charcoaled along the bottom, she had to admit that apparently it could indeed be done. The unappetizing evidence was right there on her plate.

"What the hell happened to these eggs?" Xavier asked, his booming voice echoing around the open lodge area. The big man stood by the heating tray on the sideboard containing the ruined eggs. Everyone else was gathered behind him, plates in hand. They'd insisted Calla go first since she was new. She'd been grateful. She was ravenous after the long morning of hard work. Or at least she had been until she'd seen what was in the trays.

"Xavier," his wife Mel hissed, nodding toward the little boy she had cradled in her arms. "Language."

"They're not listening." Xavier waved to the other side of the room where their two oldest boys played chase. The twin with blond dreadlocks, Reece she thought his name was, would run after the boys and catch one every so often to swing them around until they got dizzy and fell giggling to the floor.

"What the hell!" shouted the younger of the two boys as Reece caught him again.

Mel glared Xavier's way and he tossed his hands up. "Blame whoever cooked this." He gestured at the tray. "How am I not supposed to react to seeing that."

"Sorry, guys," Liam said, lifting a hand to the back of his neck. "I read on the internet and it said to cook protein slowly." He frowned down at the tray of eggs. "But I guess I had the heat too high."

"Just get the boys waffles," Mel said, hiking the baby on her hip and heading toward her sons. "Hey guys, calm it down. It's not even eight o'clock in the morning. You'll have all day to roughhouse. But Mommy hasn't had her coffee yet."

"About that..." Liam trailed off when Mel jerked her head in his direction. "Well, the coffee was sort of the reason I forgot about the eggs. I remembered to set the timer on it last night, but I sort of forgot to put the carafe underneath it. So when I got back in the kitchen, the coffee had just spilled everywhere. I was trying to multitask and get it cleaned up while also cooking the eggs. Then I realized we were out of coffee and there wasn't enough for another pot."

"You can't have coffee anyway, babe," Xavier went over to her and lifted the baby out of her arms. Mel's back slumped. "Dang it, you're right."

"Uh, is there something you forgot to tell us, Mel?" Jeremiah looked at Mel, eyes widening.

Xavier put his arm over Mel's shoulder, a wide smile plastered across his face.

"We were going to talk to all of you about it this morning," Mel said, a little flush taking over her cheeks. "But yeah, Xav and me are pregnant again."

"You two Catholic or something?" Liam asked, looking from the two boys still screeching and horsing around on the other side of the room to the baby in Mel's arms.

Jeremiah slapped him upside the back of the head.

"What?" Liam said. "Soon they aren't going to need any of us around because they'll have their own labor force."

Mack came forward and landed a kiss on Mel's cheek. "Congratulations, you two."

"Yeah, congrats," Jeremiah said, joining Mack's side and reaching out to give Mel a hug.

"Thanks." Xavier was grinning so wide it all but transformed his face. The burned half didn't seem nearly so menacing when he smiled like that.

"It does mean that I won't be able to compete in the Extreme Horse Makeover competition this summer, though."

"The ranch signed up for three spots," Xavier said, his gaze moving over all of them, even Calla who was the only one already seated. "Mack and Liam are taking two, but there's a spot for one more if anyone's interested in the third."

Calla's heart leapt in her chest. She'd wanted to do the horse makeover challenge ever since she'd first heard of it. One hundred wild mustangs the BLM had rounded up were divvied up among volunteers who then had one hundred days to break and tame the horses. There was a competition at the end of the hundred days to see who'd trained their horse the best. Along with cash prizes. Serious cash prizes. Last year the winner got a hundred thousand dollars.

Plus it was for a good cause—the horses were auctioned so people could bid on them to give them a home.

Calla watched as Jeremiah and Nicholas looked at each other. But mainly Calla's mind was stuck on the cash prizes. With a hundred thousand dollars, she could start over. Buy herself a patch of land. Not a big one, sure. But still something she could call her own. Maybe get a loan and set up a little boarding and training place like Chris Mendoza had. Plenty folks were being forced to downsize and needed places to board their animals. She could—

"I'm still too busy with my online classes," Jeremiah said. Calla's eyes jerked back to the table. Damn, she was putting the cart before the horse. There was every chance one of these guys would want to snatch up the spot.

Nicholas shook his head. "Not this year."

"What about you, Cal?" Xavier asked. "It's fine if you don't want to take on too much since you just got here—"

"I'd love to," Calla cut in before he even finished his sentence. Then she felt her cheeks heat. "I mean, if no one else wants the spot, that is."

Jeremiah just held up his hands. "Like I said, I'm too busy."

[Nicholas nodded. "I'm out too."]

"Looks like you're on deck then, Cal," Xavier said. "We head out to pick up the mustangs after breakfast, so eat up. Only one of the trailers is hooked up and we need to be there by three."

Calla stared down at her plate. The excitement tingling in her chest felt so foreign. It had been years since she'd competed and almost as long since she'd had a new horse to train. She'd wanted to set up one of her dad's barns as a boarding and training stable. But like all the other options Calla had raised as ways to bring in more income on the ranch, Dad had vetoed the idea.

After all, keeping the land as just a cattle ranch had been good enough for his parents and grandparents and he wasn't going to go and 'reinvent the wheel.' Lord how many times had he stubbornly kept to that line? No matter how hard Calla tried to convince him they had to join the twenty-first century and accept that cattle ranching couldn't go on as it always had. The land couldn't take it.

But trying to get her dad to embrace sustainable ranching was like trying to convince an atheist there was a God—he wasn't willing to even consider it and he'd only mock her when she tried. He wouldn't have some *green cowboy* ranching his lands. He refused to hear her out about how they could be as much as tripling their profits if he would just get his head out of his ass. They could have at least *tried* some of the land management and revitalization programs that had turned some rancher's fortunes around.

But then it was too late and they lost it all.

"Cal. Calla."

Calla jerked her head up to Mel calling her name. "You want a waffle?" She gestured toward Calla's untouched eggs. "If you don't grab one now, believe me, there won't be any left."

Calla nodded and started to stand up but Mel just waved her back. "I got it." She plopped two waffles on her plate and then came over and slid one off onto Calla's.

"Thanks."

"No problem," Mel smiled. "We girls gotta stick together." She sat down beside Calla.

Liam plopped his plate on the other side of her, hiking up one lanky leg to straddle the bench seat, body turned toward Calla.

"So, beautiful. Want to ride with me today on the way to get the horses?" He flashed a gorgeous smile. "I'd love to spend a few hours getting to know you better."

Calla's stomach flipped at having him so near. She didn't know what the one-eighty in his response to her was about, but she couldn't help being flattered by it.

Which was stupid. It was obviously Liam and Mackenzie had some kind of rivalry going on. Was Liam's sudden interest only due to Mack's attention to her last night and this morning? Or did he just hit on every female he came into contact with—and seeing her in only her sleep shirt last night had finally convinced him that she was, in fact, female?

Neither option was especially flattering, but the more Liam smiled and leaned in toward her, the less she cared about his motives.

She'd had a crush on this guy ever since she'd first seen him. He was the kind of boyish handsome that Hollywood celebrated. Maybe that was shallow, but her attraction wasn't only about his looks. He always seemed to be the life of the party whenever he and his friends went out. His laugh was loud and contagious. He was everything her quiet, dour life wasn't and she'd been surprised by how much she wanted even a little bit of that shine to turn her direction.

"I promise I won't even bother ya by singing along with the radio. Unless a One Direction song comes on." He bumped her shoulder. "Then all bets are off."

Calla choked on a laugh, grabbing her water tumbler and sipping before her bite of waffle spewed everywhere.

"You a Harry Styles fan?" she asked, one eyebrow lifting.

Liam put a hand to his chest and pretended to pump it like a heart. "He's just *so* dreamy. That hair. How can you not want to run your fingers through it?"

His eyes lit up when Calla laughed again.

"You're a closet Directioner, aren't ya? Don't lie." He held up his hands. "I don't judge. I'll even help you hang your posters later tonight." He leaned in. "You don't mind inviting me into your room, do you?"

"Jesus Christ, some of us are trying to eat here," Mack said, finally sitting down at the table across from them with a stack of three waffles piled high, syrup making a pool on his plate. "Your sad attempt at flirting is turning my stomach. Oh wait, nope, that was your eggs."

Calla covered her mouth with her hand and coughed to cover her laugh. Then she cleared her throat when she saw Liam glaring at Mack.

"Do you want a little waffle along with that syrup?" Calla asked Mack, gesturing toward his syrup-drenched plate. "And maybe some oars to help you wade through it?"

The tiniest edge of Mack's mouth quirked up. "What can I say? I like things sweet and wet." His eyes did a slow survey of her body as he cut off a huge bite of waffle and shoved it in his mouth.

Calla grabbed her water glass again as her stomach contracted at his words. She rubbed her legs together under the table. The way Mack was looking at her... dear God but that was sexy.

She was used to being around men—she'd worked with ranch hands all her life. This was a far more comfortable environment for her than say, a room full of gossiping women. But she usually disappeared into the background, just another one of the guys. Being the object of focus was an entirely new experience.

Liam had certainly noticed that she'd ditched her flannel when he'd first seen her this morning in the barn. Being objectified, it was supposed to be a bad thing. But for a girl who'd never been looked at that way, she couldn't say she minded too terribly.

Was this what girls like Bethany felt all the time? No wonder women spent so much energy on their appearance. Cal's hand went to her hair, pushing some that had fallen out of her ponytail behind her ear. Did it look okay?

She almost rolled her eyes as soon as she had the thought. Dear Jesus, a couple guys looked her way and suddenly she was acting like Lady frickin' Godiva. What, was she gonna go to the salon in town and get her hair put in rollers next?

She took another few bites of waffle, feeling quickly full. The fact that Mack's intense gray eyes never left her might have had something to do with her nervous stomach. Liam was also impossible to ignore, his thigh brushing hers in a way she wasn't sure was accidental. She was glad when talk around the table moved on to other topics and off of her. She was all in her head and missed some of the conversation until a small piece of toast came flying across the table and hit her instead of the intended target, which was apparently Liam.

"Oh. Sorry Calla!" Reece said. He was sitting in the seat Mel had been in moments before. Calla looked down the long table and saw Mel sitting with her boys as they dug into their breakfasts.

"But you can't really think that," Reece continued. "It's so cynical."

"What is?" Calla turned to Liam.

He held up his hands. "I was just saying that I think all of life is a series of transactions. We're all using each other. We'll give but only if we get something back."

Calla frowned. "How do you mean?"

"In everything. From the biggest scale to the smallest. There's the obvious." Liam gestured around the table. "We're giving time and energy here on the ranch in order to get money back. We pay taxes so the government will do shite for us. But even on the smallest scale. Say one woman complements another. It's not just to be *nice*." He put the last word in air quotes. "The one doing the complementing is trying to gain favor. Increase her social standing."

Reece shook his head, scoffing. "What if she's already the most popular girl there?"

Liam shrugged like it was no big deal. "Maybe it's lonely there at the top and she wants companionship. Or she has a fear of not being loved or admired. Maybe she's trying to create a comfortable atmosphere so she can manipulate the other woman more easily. People do shite for a hundred different reasons, but always because they've got something to gain."

"That's so cynical!" Reece said, getting worked up. Calla had to agree with Reece. There was a certain kind of logic to what Liam was saying, but it was an ugly logic.

"Okay," Reece's eyes lit up. "What about Mother Teresa?"

Liam waved a hand. "Easy. She either liked the endorphins she got from all that do-gooding or she expected a big tiara in heaven." He shrugged, "Sure she was delusional about the heaven gig, but hey, to each their own."

Reece was still shaking his head. "What about couples?"

"Pffff. You kidding?" Liam leaned in and lowered his voice. "Sex is the ultimate transaction. *Tit* for tat, if you know what I mean." He winked and Calla felt her cheeks warm even though he wasn't looking her way.

"I mean people in *love*," Reece insisted. "Love is patient, love is kind, it does not envy, it is not self-seeking—"

"Are you quoting the Bible at him?" his brother Jeremiah turned to him, incredulous. "Aren't you Buddhist?"

Reece shrugged. "I don't like labels when it comes to the mysteries of the universe."

Jeremiah rolled his eyes but then Liam jumped back in.

"Romantic love is the most selfish of all. Think about it." He stabbed a finger on the table top. "What's people's greatest fear besides death? And taxes." A few people laughed. Liam looked around the table. "Being alone," he answered himself.

Calla shifted on the bench, poking at her half-eaten waffle with her fork.

"Think about it—it's nuts. When people get married, they're

trying to contractualize their way out of one of our biggest fears. To make another person legally obligated to provide companionship to you? What a fecking joke." He shook his head. "Of course, these days, you can just split when you stop getting what you want out of the deal. Is she not the pretty young thing she once was? Call the divorce lawyer. Is he still in the same dead-end job he had when you got married and you want to trade up? Call the divorce lawyer."

Reece dropped his elbows on the table and interlaced his fingers, propping his chin on his hands. He stared straight at Liam. "I feel sad for you."

Liam laughed, grinning. "Don't. I'd rather live with me eyes wide open to reality."

But all Calla could think was: *Did he get diagnosed with an untreatable condition that will ruin your life if you stay? Call the divorce lawyer.* Maybe there was more to Liam's theory than she'd like to believe.

She wasn't hungry anymore. She stood to take her tray to the kitchen when Mack sidled up alongside her.

"You should ride with me today," Mack said, voice only low enough for her to hear. "I haven't been able to stop thinking about you since last night."

Her breath caught and she jerked her head sharply toward him. Was he making fun of her? She saw Liam still sitting at the table, frowning in their direction. Was this some sort of game between Mack and him?

She felt her blood heat. "Are you fucking with me?" She didn't flinch from Mack's gaze.

He glowered at her and she was almost sorry she asked. Still, she stood her ground. "What do you mean, fucking with you?"

God, was he going to make her explain? She pursed her lips and looked at her feet. "Is this just some... joke? Or prank between you and him?" She jerked her head over his shoulder in Liam's direction.

Mack's head whipped back and his jaw hardened. "Did he say it was? That son of a—"

Calla winced and shook her head. "No. God." She took a step back from him. "Forget about it."

She felt her face flaming and she turned to go. Mack put a hand on her arm to stop her, stepping close again. "Look, Calla. I'm interested in you. I think we could have some fun together."

Her mouth went dry as she looked at him, absolutely floored. "You don't even know me."

"Well, isn't that sorta the point? I wanna get to know you." His grey eyes flashed. "And I know life's too fucking short not to grab ahold of something good before it's gone. And I think you and me could have something special."

Have some fun. Special. Her heart pounded wildly as she tried to clarify. "You mean like... sex?" she whispered.

He burst out laughing. Several heads turned in their direction at the sound. Crap. She was making a scene. Calla Carter didn't make *scenes*. She was about to get the hell out of there before her mortification reached truly epic proportions, but again Mack's hand on her arm stopped her.

Her jaw worked as she looked at the floor. She could really do with it opening up right now to swallow her. "I don't like it when people laugh at me."

"Sorry gorgeous," he said, his hand dropping to her hand where his thumb moved in little circles on her wrist. Oh wow, that felt nice. Really, really nice.

"You just took me by surprise there. You're so fucking direct." He ran a hand through his hair and laughed again. "It's refreshing."

Then he leaned down so that he was speaking right in her ear. She shivered at the warmth of his breath. "And I guess yeah, if I'm being honest I do mean sex."

"Can I take your plate, Cal?" Liam's voice was short as he stepped up right beside them. He flashed a glare toward Mack before his eyes gentled.

"Oh." Calla blinked and handed over her plate of half-eaten waffles.

"Not much of an appetite," Liam said, his gaze on her like Mack wasn't leaned over, his face still inches from hers. "I can understand that. I didn't find those waffles very appetizing either." His eyes flicked to Mack for just an instant.

Mack scoffed. "Did you eat any of your eggs? No wonder. Pretty sure they would have put me off food all day long."

Liam's head snapped toward Mack.

Okay, as nice as it was to be squeezed in between their two big warm bodies, the tension between them was getting to be too much. She wasn't interested in being the dog bone in some tug of war.

"I think this is my cue to exit stage left. See you two later." She patted Liam on the chest and touched Mack's arm as she took her leave. Then she called, "Mel?" toward the end of the table where Mel was cleaning up after her boys.

"What's up?"

"Is there space in your truck to ride with you?"

Mel glanced at the two men beside Calla, a small frown crossing her face. "You bet."

"Great. I'll go help get the trailers rigged."

Calla left the room without a glance back to either Mack or Liam.

"You just let me know if any of the guys get out of hand, okay?" Mel said as she and Calla drove down the highway toward Denver. They were alone in the truck—Xavier and Liam were riding in another and Mack in the third. "I don't know what's up with Mack and Liam, but the last thing in the world I want you to feel is uncomfortable while you're staying with us."

"Oh, it's nothing. I'm fine."

Mel glanced over at her from the driver's seat. "I'm serious. I'll kick their asses."

Calla couldn't help grinning at the picture that put in her head. "I'd love to see that, actually." She laughed. "But no, I'm fine. Believe me, I grew up around cowboys. I can do any ass-kicking I need to all on my own."

Mel smiled but it didn't fully erase the line of concern in her fore-head. "I don't doubt that."

"So where are you from again?" Calla asked, changing the subject. "I think I heard Xavier mention once you were from New York."

Mel laughed and shook her head. "About a million years ago, it feels like. But yeah. That's where I grew up."

"In the city?"

Mel nodded. "Lived there all my life till I was twenty-six. Moving here was a bit of a..." she paused before another slow smile crossed her lips, "a bit of an adjustment, that was for sure."

"So how'd you find yourself in Hawthorne, Wyoming?" Calla asked, more than curious about the beautiful and obviously sophisti-cated woman beside her. Truth was, Calla had admired her from a far for a long time. Ever since news spread around town that Xavier Kent had got himself a wife, Calla had been as eager as anyone else to catch a glimpse of the woman.

Xavier had been the talk of the town since he took over the old resort. A giant of a man like that, especially disfigured as he was, taking over one of the town's biggest properties was bound to make waves. The fact that he'd gotten it out from underneath Ned Cunningham's fingers was just a bonus for Calla. But the town gossips really hit the roof when they learned he had a woman out there in addition to all those horses, that he'd married her and even renamed his horse rescue after her.

It all seemed so romantic. Something special in a town that was full of a whole lot of dull, hard living.

"That's a bit of a long story." The way her eyebrows lifted, Calla could just bet.

"I'll take the CliffsNotes version."

Mel flashed her a smile before moving her attention back to the road. "Let's just say..." her voice dropped off like she was thinking of the best way to simplify something complicated. "Xavier helped my family out when we were in a rough spot. In return, I came out to help him with the rescue."

"And then you fell in love?"

Mel laughed. "Yeah, well, it wasn't exactly a smooth transition. We didn't get along at first. There *might* have been a few days that I wanted to gouge his eyes out. But we got there in the end."

Calla felt her own eyebrow arch at this. "Now *that* sounds like a story."

Mel grinned. "No doubt. Some other time. What about you? You got someone special in your life?"

For the umpteenth time that day, Calla felt her cheeks warm. She shook her head. "Hasn't been much space in my life for that."

Mel's face softened. "I was so sorry to hear about your dad." She reached out and gave Calla's arm a gentle squeeze. "How is he? He has Parkinson's?"

Calla swallowed and looked out the passenger window. Rolling hills covered in scrub brush whizzed by. "Huntington's."

"I haven't heard of that."

"It's sort of like Parkinson's," Calla said, fidgeting with a fingernail. "He's constantly got the shakes and is starting to get pretty forgetful."

"I'm so sorry, hon. I might not see my dad very often, but we were close. I can't imagine." Her eyes were full of sympathy when she glanced at Calla again.

Calla swallowed and looked down at her hands. "Yeah, well. That's life. What are you gonna do?"

"Just keep going," Mel murmured, like she'd had some experience with the punches life could throw. "One day after another."

Calla nodded. "Pretty much."

They didn't say anything for a long while. Just drove in companionable silence and watched the landscape roll by.

"So, Mack and Liam?" Calla asked, her mind always circling back to the two guys no matter how much she tried not to think about them. "What's their deal?"

Mel let out a huff and rolled her eyes. "Lord knows. They've been like fire and ice since they first met each other. It's funny too, because as different as their backgrounds are, they actually remind me of each other."

"How?" Calla asked, more than interested. She pulled her foot up into her lap as she focused on Mel.

"Oh, I don't know." Mel waved a hand. "Nicholas and the twins are pretty mellow. Well," she amended, "Reece more than Jeremiah. But Liam and Mack," she shook her head. "They're both passionate guys. You might not think it when you first meet Mack, he's so shut down all the time."

Calla was surprised at that. "He hasn't been shut down around me." The total opposite, in fact. One of the things she liked about him was his bluntness. He wasn't afraid to speak his mind.

Mel looked at her, a smile curving her lips. "That's the other thing. They're both these alpha tough guys on the surface. But they've got gooey centers. I've seen it." Then she sobered, her hands shifting on the wheel. "I don't think things have been easy for either of them in their lives. Sometimes I think about the ranch as our own little island of misfit toys, you know?"

"Well then I guess I'll fit right in," Calla joked.

"Welcome to the club."

They were quiet again, just listening to the radio. *Welcome to the club.* Calla had felt like an outcast all her life, out of step with her classmates and peers. And that had been all right because she had her dad and the ranch.

But what had all that self-sacrifice, putting everyone else's needs over hers, ever gotten her?

A big fat wad of nothing, that's what. She was a twenty-four-year-old virgin. She'd never even been drunk. Couldn't risk having a hang-over when there was always so much work to be done the next day.

Screw. That. She was done with living like a nun. She was going to have sex. A lot of sex.

Live each day like it's your last.

Okay, universe. She was ready to listen. She was going to have sex, and get drunk, and she was going to learn what it meant to *party.*

If Liam and Mack were being genuine in their interest, well, goddammit, she was going to take one of them up on their offer.

It was time to let it all fly.

"There's a big party tonight after the mustang assignments are handed out, right?"

Mel looked her way. "Sure. Most ranchers live so isolated that whenever we get together, everybody lets their hair down."

Calla knew Mel had been speaking metaphorically, but her hand still went to her own hair. She didn't know what else to do with it other than the awkward ponytail. She looked at Mel, who's long hair hung in attractive curly waves.

"Do you think you could help me with... Maybe we could go shopping or something before the party? I'm not really good with, you know," she waved down her body and the overalls that had become her uniform for, well...forever, "being a girl."

"Sure," Mel said, looking her way with eyebrows raised in surprise. "But I think you do a fine job at being a girl. From what Xavier says, you singlehandedly held onto your dad's ranch for years, not to mention you're a talented horse trainer. If I ever have a daughter, I could only hope she'd be half so dedicated, hard-working, and loyal."

Calla looked down at her short grubby nails, embarrassed at Mel's words. "Yeah, well, we lost the ranch. So what does that say about me?"

Mel's face softened. "That you're the kind of person who never stops fighting and sticks it out until the end."

Calla gave a short laugh. She wasn't sure that fighting her whole life for a losing cause meant much in the scheme of things. They were getting off track anyway. "So you'll help me get ready tonight?"

Mel gave her a long look but then just nodded before grinning and putting her attention back on the road. "Those boys aren't gonna know what hit 'em."

7

MACK

"YOU'RE gonna lose a few fingers with that one," Mack said, leaning over the fence and watching Liam try to feed an apple to the mare he'd been assigned.

Liam barely had a second to shoot a glare his way before yanking away when the spirited mare took a snap at him.

"Whoa, girl!" Liam said, managing to dance out of the way just before the giant horse teeth chomped down on his hand.

Mack didn't hide his laugh. Well, this was going to be more fun than he'd thought.

He'd only signed on in the first place because the day in day out grind of the ranch hadn't been doing the trick anymore. He thought routine would be good. Like he could just lose himself in his work and not think about shit.

Problem was, the opposite had happened. The more rote daily life on the ranch got, the more space his mind had to linger back in the past. He'd only done an eight-year stretch but sometimes he thought it might as well have been a life sentence. Part of him would always be stuck in that six by eight cell.

The restlessness got worse and worse till he actually thought about moving on. It'd be years before he could do what needed getting done—the fucker who needed dead was still in lock up and would be for four more years.

He thought about going to work on one of those ocean rigs. He'd heard it was grueling work that left a man so spent at the end of the day you'd fall asleep standing up.

Then, before he could decide one way or the other, Xavier mentioned the mustang makeover competition. Said he hoped some of them would go for it.

Liam immediately held up his hand. And Mack thought, what the hell, maybe it was just the distraction he needed. And if he could show up that privileged little Irish prick while doing it, all the better.

They'd gotten into Denver a little after two o'clock and headed straight to the Bureau of Land Management facility.

It had been organized chaos with the trainers from all around the country lining up to see what mustang they'd been assigned. Once given a mustang, the trainer then either loaded them up and headed home if they lived close. If they didn't, then the horse stayed in the holding pens until the next morning.

Xavier didn't like them making the six-hour drive there and back home on the same day. It looked like most folks felt the same from all the horses still in the holding pens. The hundred days to train the mustangs started tomorrow.

Mack had been assigned a mid-sized gelding. The horse was jumpy as any wild horse would be, but Mack felt good about him— he was certainly calmer than some of the ones he'd walked past. Including the she-devil Liam had landed.

Liam glared at him after jumping over the fence of the pen. "Where's yours?"

"Torpedo's over there." He pointed to the small cluster of brown horses hovering near the hay trough. "With the white patch between his eyes. Sweetest little gelding you ever saw."

"Poor fecker doesn't realize he got stuck with a gammy mog from the wrong side of the tracks," Liam shot back. "Frankly I'm shocked anyone would put a living creature in the hands of an ex-con who knows more about carving shivs than taking care of horses."

Mack's blood went hot. "You think you're going to do any better? Growing up with that silver spoon up your ass?"

"Better a silver spoon than all the cock I'm sure you took while you were a prison bitch."

Mack's blood lit on fucking fire.

"You don't know what the fuck you're talking about." Mack got toe to toe with the Irish bastard. "And if you're so confident, why don't you put your money where your mouth is? A hundred bucks says my mustang goes for more green than yours at auction."

Liam's eyes flashed and he stepped into Mack's chest, knocking him backward several steps. "You're on, you ruddy bastard. But let's make it interesting. One grand says my mustang kicks your's arse come September."

"Does it make you feel like a big man being able to flash your cash around like that?" Mack leaned in. "Makes it a little obvious you're overcompensating. But hey, we can't all be born stallions. I wouldn't worry, though." He clapped Liam on the shoulder. "I'm sure your bank account is enough to blind most women to whatever you may be..." He glanced down toward Liam's belt. "Otherwise lacking."

Liam's jaw went rigid and Mack let the edge of his lip curl up.

"I don't mind being a thousand bucks richer. You've got a deal." He reached out for a shake and Liam gripped his hand with a bone-crushing force.

Mack kept grinning and squeezed back just as hard. Liam thought he could intimidate him? He'd eaten little shits like this for dinner back in lock-up. He was an enforcer for one of the nastiest bastards on the inside. You didn't get that far up the food-chain without being one ruthless motherfucker.

Couldn't deny who he was even if he didn't like to think about that period in his life—he hadn't been sure for a while he still had a soul after all the shit he'd done. Wasn't till he started working with the horses at Xavier's that he actually found a ray of hope he might still be more man than monster.

Then he shut that shit down.

He needed the monster for the plans he had.

But this rich Mick wouldn't know a thing about making the hard choices in life or what kind of man it took to come out the other side. Mack had known people like Liam before.

When Mack had gotten a full ride scholarship to Harvard, he'd dated a couple rich kids who'd never known a hard day's work in their life. Blaire was old money on her mom's side and her dad was a famous hot-shot lawyer. When she paid attention to Mack, he thought it proved he wasn't just white trash from Jersey. That he could move up in the world. Be more than the nothing he'd been born. He didn't see it for what it was even after Blaire pulled him into those fucked up games with her boyfriend.

Wasn't until shit hit the fan and he got arrested that he realized the only reason they'd ever looked his way was because they got a thrill out of fucking who they considered to be 'the help.'

The same way Liam looked at Calla.

Mack's jaw hardened. "While we're on the topic of shit you oughta know better than to step in," Mack continued, voice hard, "back off Calla. She doesn't need some worthless user like you fucking her over."

"Worthl—?" Liam's nostril's flared. "She certainly deserves better than *you*. You were born trash and you'll die trash. How long till you end back up in prison? They got a bed still nice and warm with your name on it?"

"You wanna say that ag—?"

"What's going on here?" Xavier's booming voice made Mack's head jerk to the right.

Shit, the boss was heading toward them and he didn't look happy. Mack stepped back from where he'd been in Liam's face.

"Kitchen duty for a month still not enough to teach you two to play nice?" Xavier stopped between them, glaring at one and then the other. "I'm not going to be embarrassed by two of my men acting like jackasses, am I?"

"No, boss," Liam said, looking at the floor. Mack liked that. Cowed was a good look on him.

"Mackenzie?" Xavier growled and Mack shifted his gaze away from Liam.

"Sorry." Mack respected Xavier. The man had given him a job even knowing he'd done hard time. It was a rare second chance in a world that didn't often give them. "No problems here."

"Good," Xavier bit out. "Better not be." With one more glare in both their directions, he turned and kept on his way.

As soon as he was out of ear shot, Liam just had to open his mouth again. "How about we let Calla decide who's the better man?"

Mack gritted his teeth, shaking his head as he turned to follow Xavier. The only way this wasn't going to end with his fist in Liam's face was if he left now. "You stay away from her. Stay away from me too if you know what's good for you."

"Sounds to me like someone's afraid he won't measure up."

This mother fucker was just begging for it, wasn't he? Calla was Mack's kind of people. He wouldn't let Liam fuck with her or fuck her over. Mack turned back to Liam and put his finger right in his face. "I don't play games with good women. But I can guaran-goddammed-tee you that if she's heading back to anyone's hotel room tonight, it'll be mine."

Shit. He hadn't meant to say that. If he really had Calla's interests at heart, he'd forget he ever met her. He might be a better choice than Liam, but not by much. Besides, Mack wasn't in the market. Calla didn't need him spreading his shit on her. The days of thinking he could change the cards he'd been dealt were long gone.

Liam grinned, obviously happy to be getting under Mack's skin. "We'll just see about that."

This time Mack turned and didn't look back. He had to get out of here before he did something he'd regret. Liam O'Neill would get what was coming to him eventually, and if there was any justice in the goddamned universe, Mack would be there to see it.

8

LIAM

LIAM STOOD near the bar that had been set up at one end of the hotel ballroom and watched the door for Calla.

The party had been in full swing for almost an hour but she and Mel had yet to make an appearance. At least Mack was staying well away from him. Liam'd only glimpsed him once since he'd been down here. Best move that wanker had made all year. Liam was surprised he'd showed at all. Mack wasn't exactly famous for being sociable.

Liam took another swig of beer. He had to give it to them, these people knew how to party—they poured Guinness by the pint.

He glanced around the packed space. A live band was set up at the far end of the room. The fiddler sawed away like the devil himself had lit a fire under his arse. Another line dance had broken out. Liam couldn't help watching on in amazement. All these grown damn men and women stomped and swung and clapped in almost perfect synchronicity as the music barreled on.

He'd just emptied his second pint as the song finished and a loud round of applause and whistling filled the room. The dancers broke off into couples or headed toward the sidelines as a slower tune started up.

And that's when she walked in.

Liam blinked, thinking his mind was playing tricks on him again. For the past half hour he'd been looking up and down every jean-clad, big shiny-belted woman.

So he was not prepared for the siren that walked in sporting a cleavage-bearing red dress with a giant slit up the side showing off so much leg it'd make a grown man cry. He might not have even recognized it was Calla if not for Mel walking beside her, holding her hand and urging her forward.

He was still blinking back his surprise as Mack walked right up to her and grabbed her hand from Mel, lifting it to his lips.

Liam's fists clenched. Where the fuck had that bastard been lurking? Liam jumped up from his barstool, about to make a beeline toward them, when his path was suddenly blocked.

Liam barely managed to stop from barreling into the woman in time. He was about to step around her and continue toward Calla when she put a hand on his arm.

"I thought I saw your name on the registry."

Liam looked down, frowning at the blonde who held his arm possessively.

Well shite, it was the betty from the bar last night.

"Looks like we'll be competitors. If you need any help with your mustang, I'd be happy to come out and we could work her together. And any time you want to practice your riding technique..." she smiled at him coyly. "I'm happy to oblige."

Aw *Jays*us. If he'd known she was the clingy stalker type, he never woulda feckin' touched her last night. Time to shut this down. "Look, Betty—"

"Bethany," she corrected, eyes flashing for a moment before she went back to batting her lashes.

"Yeah, well," he didn't hide his grimace. "Let's just call last night what it was. A mistake." He tried to pull away from her but she just giggled and latched onto his arm harder.

"Don't be silly. We were both just a little drunk. Tonight I'll *really* show you a good time." She tried to pull him toward the dance floor.

Now she was just pissing him off. She was pushy, had a face that looked the same as a million other girls, and he felt like he was choking from the cloud of hairspray from her overly puffy blond hair.

Add that to her stalker tendencies and she was one hundred percent not attractive. He was about to tell her just that, but a little voice at the back of his head whispered it might not be the smartest idea. It was a small community and she knew who he was. Letting his inner arsehole loose probably wasn't a grand idea, much as he was tempted.

Dammit, he hated this being a responsible lad shite.

"Sorry, miss." He pasted on a disingenuous smile and peeled her arm off him. "I'm not interested."

But she just kept smiling at him, leaning over to no doubt bare her cleavage in the little tube top she was wearing. "You can run now, but you can't hide, Mister," she said in a baby voice. "I'll be here when you realize just what you're missing." Then she tapped him on the nose with her forefinger and he jerked away.

Any of Liam's responses to that delusional statement definitely wouldn't count as gentlemanly. So he bit his tongue and walked away without another word. In his experience that was the only way to deal with crazy.

But when he looked for Calla, he couldn't see her anywhere. She and Mel weren't by the entrance anymore.

Shite. Liam scanned the ballroom for any sight of them. Okay, there was Xavier. Hard to miss a man who stood a head taller than most. The only way Xavier would be at a party like this was if Mel had dragged him. And where there was Mel, he'd find Calla. Time to get this night back on track.

Liam smiled and made his way around the edge of the dance floor until he came up to Xavier. Just as expected, Mel stood right beside him.

But Calla was still nowhere to be seen. He was about to ask where she'd gone when he heard a loud peal of laughter behind him.

Which was when he turned around and saw her at the edge of the dance floor. Apparently trying to teach Mack to two-step.

Son of a cunt.

At least from the clumsy way Mack was fumbling around it was obvious he was a shite dancer.

Small compensation, considering it only seemed to charm Calla more. She grinned as she yelled out instructions, her arm linked with Mack's as they stomped and then started forward again. Well, they were *supposed* to be going forward, but Mack was still backing up. Which just made Calla laugh more as she tugged on his arm to try to get him moving with the rest of the group.

Jaysus, Liam had only been caught up with that blonde leach for a couple minutes, and here Calla and Mack were already looking as chummy as if they'd known each other for years and not days.

Enough of that.

Liam was about to head to break into their little dance lesson when Mel suddenly caught his arm. Her face was serious so he stopped instead of just blowing her off. It was loud with the blaring music and noise from the crowd, but he leaned down to hear what she had to say.

"You guys need to take it easy with her. She doesn't have much experience with men."

Liam nodded and was about to pull away because every second he wasn't by Calla's side was another that Mack was wheedling himself into her good graces. Mel's grip just increased on his arm.

"I'm serious, Liam."

He paused at that. She did look serious. Deadly so. Was he missing something?

"I just want to show her a good time, that's all."

Mel's look didn't soften. "What I'm telling you is that she's not used to men like you." She leaned in so she was talking directly into his ear. "Or any man. You get what I'm saying?"

Liam pulled back sharply so he could look her in the face. Did she mean—

"Tell me you get what I'm saying."

Liam's gaze went to the lovely woman on the dance floor and then back to Mel. He leaned down, glancing around to make sure no one else would hear him. "Are you saying she's a virgin?" Calla had to be in her mid-twenties. Surely there was no way that she wouldn't have had—

"I'm seriously breaking the girl code by saying anything about it. But I've seen how you guys operate and—"

"I've never done anything with a woman they weren't fully on board with." Liam couldn't help his sharp tone and Mel winced.

"I'm not saying that you have. Or would." Mel huffed out a breath. "I don't know what I'm saying."

Liam didn't know what to do with this information. Staying away from virgins was one of Liam's hard and fast rules. He looked out over the dance floor at Calla laughing and leaning into Mack.

Jaw tightening, he bent back down to Mel's ear. "You tell Mackenzie this?"

She shook her head. "No chance. She let it slip while I was doing her make up and I probably shouldn't have even told you, but—"

"I'm glad you did."

She nodded, still looking uncertain.

He gave her arm a squeeze and then started through the crowd to get to Calla's side. If Mack hadn't been in the picture, he might have left well enough alone. Getting tangled with a virgin was usually the last thing he would have been up for.

But Mack *was* in the picture. He might not know her well yet, but the last thing she needed was to be seduced by some fucking ex-con. Liam was more determined than ever to get her away from the bastard.

9

CALLA

"Your RIGHT FOOT. No, your other right." Calla laughed even harder as Mack stumbled along to the line dance steps, his face an adorable mask of concentration as he stomped a beat after everyone else. At least he was finally moving back and forth *with* the crowd, even if he didn't seem to be able to catch onto the simple step-kick, triple step pattern of the dance.

"Step, kick, tri-ple step," she said, overexaggerating each syllable as she tried to demonstrate.

He seemed to finally get it, but then came the part where they were supposed to shuffle forward and he was still stomping and kicking. She grabbed his arm and dragged him forward, laughing so hard her stomach was starting to hurt.

God, she couldn't remember the last time she'd had this much fun. Maybe never?

She'd been so nervous while Mel was doing her hair and showing her how to apply some light make up. The dress alone had been so daring Calla hadn't been sure she'd be able to go into public in it. So she hadn't said no when Mel offered her a shot of tequila before they headed downstairs to the ballroom. She *might* have snuck a second while Mel went to the bathroom, barely able to hide her scrunched face before Mel came back out.

Calla was usually a strict beer drinker. But she couldn't say she didn't like the way the tequila heated her chest, burning all the way down. Then there was how, just moments later all her limbs went nice and loose and suddenly she'd been eager to get down to the party. To Mack and Liam.

Maybe it was wrong of her not to have chosen one over the other yet.

Then again, screw that. It wasn't like she was looking for marriage. She just wanted to have *fun* tonight without stressing over all the shit she usually did.

Mel had tried to get her into a pair of heels but it took about zero point three seconds to determine that nope, there was no way she'd be able to take two steps in the damn ankle breakers. In the end, Mel agreed that Calla's good cowboy boots—as opposed to her daily work ones—with the dress did look pretty cute. Cute wasn't a word that had ever been applied to Calla before, so with Mel's encouragement and one more shot of liquid courage, they'd come downstairs.

All her old anxieties came back the second they walked into the crowded ballroom. God, people she *knew* were going to see her in this get up.

Before she could start hyperventilating and running back to the exit, though, Mack had come up to her. It was impossible to miss the appreciation in his eyes as he looked her up and down. She was sure she'd gone beet red, but he pulled her out to the dance floor.

The song came to an end right as Mack started shuffling the right direction. She held onto his arm to hold herself up she was still laughing so hard.

"Glad I'm entertaining you," Mack said gruffly, but she could tell by the twinkle in his eyes he wasn't actually put off.

On impulse, she went up on tiptoes and planted a kiss on his cheek. She meant it to just be a quick peck but he wrapped an arm around her waist, his other hand slipping around to cup the back of her head.

His gray eyes were more intense than she'd ever seen as he leaned down. He wasn't aiming for her cheek, either. Calla dropped her eyes closed, waiting for their first kiss with bated breath. She'd only kissed one other boy her whole life and it turned out Tommy Shelton had been dared to kiss the class tomboy for five bucks.

But a hairsbreadth away from Mack's lips touching hers, a voice cut in loudly. "Can I have the next dance?"

Calla pulled back from Mack in surprise to see Liam standing right beside them, a broad grin on his face. He held his hand out toward Calla. Calla could feel Mack's body stiffen, they were standing so close.

But Calla could only smile back at Liam. He looked more handsome than ever in his tight jeans, black shirt and shiny black cowboy boots that had silver embellishments. He might not be from this country but damn, he wore Western well.

"Now the Sleazy Slide," the band leader called out and everyone around them hurried to line back up.

Calla stepped away from Mack but she grabbed his right hand. "Let's dance!" With her other hand, she took Liam's, then she pulled them both into the line, one on either side of her.

"Watch me," she squeezed Mack's hand and he looked at her with an expression that said, *help*.

"Left slide," she called out as the whole line started shifting that way. This one was more complicated than the Cotton-Eyed Joe.

Liam picked it up quickly and when he did the little shimmy along with the slide, she couldn't help appreciating his ass in those tight jeans. The next second, though, she was distracted by trying to help Mack figure out how to do the half-turns. She'd abandoned trying to get him on the beat a long time ago, but the whole crowd was facing a new wall and Mack was still trying to slide.

Mack stumbled his way through the song and Calla continued laughing harder than she ever had in her life. Liam was hamming it up on her other side, making sure to wiggle his ass in an overexaggerated manner.

When the song was over, Calla clapped and whooped as loud as anyone else. She fanned herself with her hands. With all the bodies in the room plus the dancing—not to mention the tequila earlier—she was definitely past comfortably warm.

She lifted her hair off her neck as the band started up the next song. Couples around them started pairing off for the two-step.

"May I have this dance?" Liam asked, taking hold of her hand and pulling her toward him. Calla glanced over her shoulder to see Mack glowering so she reached back and squeezed his arm. "Next one's yours!"

But then Liam had her pulled up against his body, one hand in hers and the other tight around her waist. And damn, it was like the man was born to two-step. He took command as he led her around the floor and Calla felt her body sinking into his. While she had plenty experience line dancing, she'd only two-stepped like this a handful of times—and when she had, she was usually standing in for the guy because there were too few of them at the dance. She'd certainly never been able to just lose her body to the rhythm and follow the lead of a man with a strong, firm grasp on her waist.

As they rounded the edge of the dance floor, Liam spun her out. She shrieked and laughed as the next second, he was spinning her back into him. Her hands rose to his chest as he pulled her snugly against him. Her breathing was erratic and not just because she was short of breath from the dancing.

Liam O'Neill had her in his arms. When had she stumbled into this alternate universe and when was reality going to come smashing back down like it always did?

Liam grinned and rolled his hips into hers before pulling them back into the whirling crowd of dancers.

When they got around to the side of the room where they'd left Mack, Calla looked around for him. She felt bad. It was probably bitchy to just leave him and dance off with Liam. She didn't know what the hell she was doing. She was just going with whatever felt good in the moment—probably a disastrous way to go about things.

When had she ever not thought out everything she did from ten moves back? That was the only way to run a ranch. She had to be on top of all the everyday tasks in addition to putting out whatever inevitable problem cropped up, whether it be a sick cow, a broken section of fencing, hiring and firing ranch hands, or the hundred other things that went wrong on any given day. She'd dropped into bed each night exhausted but unable to sleep because she was worrying about the list of everything she needed to see to the next day.

It was non-stop, dawn to dusk, seven days a week, three-hundred sixty-five days a year. A night like tonight, with no responsibilities and going out just to have *fun*? Unheard of. She hadn't been out dancing in years and tonight reminded her just how much she'd always loved it. The most she ever socialized these days was hitting Bubba's a couple times a week before evening chores so she could actually be around humans other than her ailing, taciturn father and the ranch hands she'd been in charge of.

Liam spun her again and her stomach swooped as he grinned at her and pulled her back into him.

God, every time he did that he drew her even closer to his body afterwards. Her chest bumped his in a way that made her nipples tighten and her sex clench. She gasped and Liam only grinned bigger. He knew exactly what he was doing to her.

And if she was living each day like it was her last, she damn well sure didn't want to head to the great beyond with her virginity intact. It'd be best to lose it to a man who knew exactly what he was doing, wouldn't it? There wouldn't be any awkward fumbling with a man like Liam. If the way he led her so confidently around the dance floor was any indication, he'd be right at home taking the lead in bed. Didn't they say how a man danced told you a lot about how he was between the sheets?

The second she thought it her cheeks burned but Liam was spinning her out again and banishing any other thought except what it felt like in his sure grip.

That was, until she glanced over and saw Bethany in Mack's arms.

Her ebullient mood popped like a balloon and her feet got tripped up with Liam's when he stepped into her and she didn't step back.

She yelped as she almost went down. Only Liam's hands gripping her waist saved her from toppling ass over head.

"Sorry!" Liam said, almost shouting to be heard over the music. Then he followed her train of sight to where Bethany was urging Mack into a two-step. The song finished and Calla stood there lamely attempting to get her breath while also forcing herself not to stare at Mack with Bethany. She tried to flash a smile up at Liam. Hadn't she just been contemplating losing her virginity to him? So why was she reacting so strongly to seeing Mack with her arch nemesis?

Was it just because it was Bethany or would she feel that way if Mack were dancing with anyone? Because as much as she'd admired Liam from afar, it was Mack who'd come up to her first. Him who'd she had the intense moment with at the kitchen sink last night. Him who'd said he wanted to explore things with her. *Sexually.*

Or maybe she was just stupid, reading far more into all that than he'd intended. Of course when he was presented with a far more tempting option like Bethany he'd jump at the chance.

"Hey asshole."

Calla's head jerked to Liam. He was walking up to Mack. Oh crap.

These two guys already obviously hated each other. She was just driving a deeper wedge between them, making everything worse.

She moved to grab Liam's arm, ready to tell him... What? That she had a headache and was heading to bed for the night?

God, what was she even doing here, wearing this ridiculous dress? It felt like a Halloween costume. She'd had fun playing dress up, but she was *not* this woman. What the hell had she even been thinking?

Mack's head swung to look at Liam and then Calla. He dropped his arms from around Bethany.

"You owe this beautiful woman a dance." Liam's voice was biting as he addressed Mack. He moved Calla toward Mack with a hand low on her back and it took all her wits not to stumble over her own feet again.

"I do," Mack said, stepping away from Bethany.

Calla didn't miss the way Bethany's eyes narrowed and then went wide with surprise, like she was just recognizing who Calla was. Fair enough. She'd barely recognized herself when she looked in the mirror earlier.

"That I do," Mack said, smoothly pulling Calla into his arms. The band had switched to a slow song and Mack urged her closer. Calla looked over at Liam even as she raised her arms around Mack's neck. What exactly was going on here? Was Liam passing her off so *he* could dance with Bethany?

But Liam turned his back on the other woman, still with a wide smile for Calla. Then he came up behind her until she was sandwiched between the two most gorgeous men she'd ever known.

Calla's breath caught as Liam's hands gripped her waist from behind, just above where Mack held her.

It wasn't until they both started moving in tandem that Calla completely lost the plot of what was going on.

Mack pulled her closer to him so that, like earlier with Liam, her breasts brushed his chest. And then there was Liam's heat at her back, his hands slipping around the front of her waist as he moved his hips forward until they made contact with Calla's ass.

Her eyes shot wide and she looked over her shoulder at Liam. There was a wicked gleam in his eye as he looked down at her. She couldn't hold his gaze and turned her face back toward Mack's chest. It wasn't a second until she felt Liam's breath hot on her ear. "Tonight is all about making you feel good, baby."

She blinked, feeling light-headed. Her arms tightened around Mack's neck. Then Mack's hand was on the back of her head, urging her to lay her cheek against his chest. Turned out she was wrong earlier when she'd thought Mack had no rhythm.

He had plenty, it turned out, when he was dancing in a way he was used to. And damn was he good at it. He notched his legs between hers until the red fabric of her dress strained at the slit. So close that it was almost like she was *riding* him.

And Liam was still just as tight at her back, his thumbs rubbing tiny circles on her waist as all three of them swayed back and forth to the music.

She swallowed hard and her fingers gripped the collar of Mack's shirt. Why were they—? What did this even mean? Were they trying to get her to choose between them? She'd just wanted to come have a night of carefree fun. Maybe join a few line dances. Try out getting drunk for the first time. But this felt like some game she didn't know the rules to.

When Mack danced back and forth with his leg between her knees, she couldn't help her breath hitching. Oh God. Did he realize that with their height differences, his upper thigh was rubbing against *that* spot?

Instead of Mack reacting, though, it was Liam's fingers who clenched on her waist. Almost like he could sense the spike of heat at her center and knew exactly how turned on she was. Which was so embarrassing she was glad her face was buried in Mack's chest.

"You're so hot, baby," Liam whispered in her ear.

Oh God, he knew. He knew and Mack probably did too.

She felt like the stupidest girl in the world to be getting so riled by a *dance*.

And suddenly, it was all too much. What the hell was she doing? All but grinding down and getting herself off on Mack's leg while they freaking danced? Right here in front of God and everybody else?

She jerked away from Mack, backing into Liam until he stepped to the side.

"What's wrong?" Mack asked, his face instantly registering alarm. "Are you okay?"

Calla lifted a hand to her forehead. "I'm hot." Then she realized just what she'd said and her eyes widened in mortification. "Like dizzy. It's so hot in here."

Liam joined Mack in a twin look of concern.

Oh God, she was being a total freak, wasn't she?

"I'm not feeling so good." And then, not able to stand their concerned expressions for another second, she spun on her heel and bolted for the exit.

"Excuse me," she said as she pushed through the crowd. "I'm sorry. Excuse me. Pardon me."

She thought she heard her name called from behind her but she didn't look back. If she hadn't looked like a crazy person before, she definitely did now.

Tomorrow she'd just tell them she was sick. That was all. And she'd wear her normal overalls and flannel and never try anything this stupid again. Who was she kidding? People never changed, she was such a goddamned *idiot* to even think for a moment that she could—

She finally made it out of the ballroom and then she was high-tailing it through the lobby of the hotel for the elevators.

"Calla. Cal!"

Okay, one of them was definitely behind her, calling her name. Calla cringed and moved from fast-walking to all out jogging.

"Hold it," she called out when she saw an elevator door closing. She *had* to get on that elevator or she would die in a puddle of embarrassment. The doors started opening again and she slipped inside.

It was only as she spun around and punched the button for the third floor that she saw both Liam and Mack closing in.

Oh God, if she had to face either of them right now she would absolutely die. She punched the *close door* button furiously until the doors closed right as Mack was reaching toward her.

10

MACK

"YOU FUCKING IDIOT," Mack spun right as the elevators shut on a freaked as hell Calla. He shoved Liam as soon as the bastard caught up with him, slamming him against the wall. "What the fuck were you thinking, dancing with her like that?"

"What was *I* thinking?" Liam shoved him back and stumbled away from the wall, still glaring. "You were the gobshite dry humping her in the middle of the fecking dance floor."

Mack got right up in his face again. "And you think coming up and double-teaming her like that wasn't going to freak her the fuck out?"

If he was honest, he felt like punching himself just as much as he wanted to smack Liam. Why had he asked Calla to dance? He'd only meant to go down to the ballroom to redeem the two drink tickets they'd given everyone doing the mustang makeover.

But then he saw Calla standing there in that bombshell dress beside Mel. Her face had been uncertain, though. She'd crossed her arms awkwardly, looking vulnerable and unsure of herself. So he'd asked her to dance. The smile that lit up her face was bright as the fucking sun.

He shoulda walked away right then and there. He wasn't anyone's knight in shining armor. But he'd ignored the voice of reason shouting in the back of his head and taken her arm.

Just like he was ignoring good sense now as he watched Liam look up at the numbers above the elevator doors. The elevator skipped the second floor and stopped at the third. Then it continued up to the fourth and paused again. The hotel was only four stories tall. Calla was either in a room of the third or fourth floor.

Liam must have had the same thought as Mack because he jerked open the door to the stairs right before Mack could reach for it himself. The bastard could run, Mack would give him that. He jackrabbited up the stairs and Mack had to push it to stay on his heels.

"You try the third, I'll check the fourth," Liam called over his shoulder as he hit the landing for the third floor and continued up.

Fine with Mack. He jerked open the door to the third floor just in time to see Calla's back retreating down the hallway. She stopped in front of her door. As Mack got closer he could hear her swearing.

"Son of a bitch, where did I—"

She must have heard Mack's footsteps because she whipped around to look at him, one hand down the top of her dress. She jerked her keycard out of her bra, then froze. Her cheeks were flushed a pretty pink.

She cringed before turning back around and dropping her forehead to her door like she was defeated. Mack almost reached for her but stopped himself just in time. Fuck, he didn't want to spook her more than she already was. It was another long moment before she said anything.

"I don't suppose we can all just forget the last half hour?" Her voice was so quiet, the only reason Mack heard it at all was because he took a step closer in spite of his determination not to make her any more skittish.

A racket behind him had Mack turning just in time to see Liam barreling through the stairwell door. "She wasn't on the fourth, did you find—" he cut off, obviously seeing Calla. "Oh. Hi."

"Oh my God," Calla whispered under her breath, hand going to her eyes. "I've never been more embarrassed in my entire life."

Fuck that. She had no reason to be embarrassed. She was beautiful and sweet. Having her in his arms downstairs had felt like the best thing that had happened to him since he got out of that fucking hellhole where he'd rotted for eight long years.

She'd made him laugh. He couldn't remember the last time he'd laughed like that.

So he reached for Calla's elbow and spun her to look at him. Her eyes were wide and if he wasn't wrong, almost teary. God-fucking-dammit if there was one thing he couldn't handle, it was seeing a woman cry. He'd watched his mother weeping over one bastard or another his whole life. He always swore he'd never be the kind of man that made women cry.

But here he was. Spreading his shit. Dirtying up a girl who was as poor as Mack had ever been but still hadn't let it turn her bitter or ugly. Fuck. He shouldn't have followed her. He shouldn't have ever touched her.

All these thoughts flashed neon in his brain but he proved yet again exactly how much a shit he was—because none of that stopped him from dropping his lips to hers and stealing the kiss that should have been his earlier.

Her lips were warm and trembling. And soft. So fucking soft. He couldn't help a low moan as he stepped into her, pulling her body flush against his as he kissed her deep, then deeper still. She was so much soft, warm, sweet woman, he went instantly hard.

When his tongue teased at the seam of her lips, she opened them on a gasp. Mack didn't hesitate for a second before dipping his tongue inside and kissing her in a way that made his intentions clear.

Because suddenly he had to have her. He felt like a starving man presented with a feast.

When she went pliant in his arms, he felt like roaring in triumph. She wanted to be claimed as much as he wanted to do the claiming.

"Why don't we take this inside her room?"

Calla jerked back at Liam's voice like she'd just remembered he was there. Ha. Take that, you Irish bastard.

But then he saw Calla's face as she looked toward Liam. Like she was stricken.

Mack's chest tightened. Did she look like that because she was worried about hurting Liam? Or because she wished it was him kissing her instead?

Before Mack could figure out one way or another, Liam was asking, "Where's your key, beautiful?" and running his hand down her bare arm.

Son of a bitch. Mack would make him regret ever—

But then he realized Calla was trembling at Liam's touch. From the look of longing on her face, it wasn't from fear, either.

She felt something for Liam. Mack's jaw tightened. Fuck. Double fuck. He should leave them to it.

But his insides rebelled even at the thought. And then he saw Liam looking at him, his eyebrows raised in question.

Mack hadn't missed how Liam had handed Calla over to him earlier on the dance floor. Sharing her. Because Liam had seen the same thing Mack was just now realizing—she wanted both of them.

And Mack wanted her.

Fuck but he wanted her. He hadn't wanted anything other than revenge in so long he'd forgotten what it could feel like. The feeling was such a revelation that, no matter how much he fucking hated the Irishman, Mack would make sure Calla got what she wanted. Anything she wanted.

Mack nodded to Liam's inquiring gaze.

"Let's go in," Liam said, lifting the keycard Calla had been clutching in a trembling hand and pressing it against the door censor. Calla looked confused for a moment until Liam said, "All of us."

Calla's eyes widened and her mouth dropped open slightly. But when the door unlocked, she looked back at Liam and then Mack. She pushed the door in and then kept going until she held it open wide. An invitation.

Fuck him. Mack felt it in his chest and his balls—the wanting. *She doesn't know what she's inviting in.*

Liam stepped right over the threshold, brushing his chest against Calla's as he passed in a way that was anything but unintentional.

Still, Mack hesitated. *Get the fuck out of here. You're a shit stain and you always will be. She deserves a million times better than either of you horny fucks.*

He was about to turn around and leave. He really was.

But then Calla reached over and took his hand. With her other, she reached out to Liam. When she started tugging them inside, Mack let himself be pulled forward.

He didn't know if he was heading into heaven or hell. But as the door closed behind him, Mack knew there was no other place he'd rather be.

11

LIAM

CALLA'S EYES were wide as she backed up against the closet door, looking back and forth between him and Mack.

Shite, had he made the wrong call here? Did he forget what Mel had told him not even an hour ago? Calla had zero experience with men.

And now, what, they were going to have a threesome? Jaysus, talk about running before you could fecking walk.

"Nothing happens in this room except what you want, gorgeous," Mack said.

Liam looked over at Mack, annoyed he'd said it before Liam could.

"He's right." Now there was a phrase Liam never thought he'd say in reference to Mackenzie Knight. "We can just stay up all night watching TV together if you want."

Time to take control and make sure that anything that happened tonight went at a pace Calla was comfortable with.

Calla's eyes flicked to the TV and then to the king size bed. Her eyes stopped on the bed. Then her tongue peeked out and she licked her lips.

Did she have any idea the kind of thoughts that gave a man?

Her eyes tentatively bounced between him and Mack. "I don't want to watch TV."

It was just a whisper but it was more than fecking enough. Liam had never been happier to not watch TV in his life.

He started but Mack blocked his path, stepping forward and taking her in his arms just like he had outside the door. He kissed her deep again.

The strangest combination of jealousy and arousal hit Liam. He wanted to taste those fucking lips. But watching the way Mack took control of the kiss so masterfully... fuck, it made Liam's dick jump in his jeans. For a second all he could do was stand and watch.

Mack ran his hands down Calla's arms until he grabbed hold of her waist and pulled her into his chest. Was he hard already too? Liam caught himself just as his gaze dropped to the front of Mack's jeans where he pressed into Calla.

He jerked his eyes away. Jaysus. Sure, he'd been open to all sorts of experimentation in his life, but *Mack*? For feck's sake, he hated the wanker.

Then again... some of the hottest sex Liam had ever had was hate sex. There'd been Sean, his mate from Uni. Sean had lost Liam's respect when he came wheedling for cash for some shite pyramid scheme. He was happy to prostitute himself, and his girlfriend, Brigid, for the money. Taking Brigid while she took it out on Sean's arse had been simultaneously one of the most satisfying and empty moments Liam had ever experienced.

It wouldn't be empty if it was with Calla and Mack, though. Liam didn't know how he knew it, but he was as sure of it as he was the fact that the sun would rise tomorrow morning.

Liam stepped toward the two locked in their heated embrace. It felt like the most natural thing in the world to lift the hair off the back of Calla's neck and start kissing her there.

Jaysus but her skin was soft. His cock got even harder as he leaned down and traced his tongue along the delicate shell of her ear. He could hear her and Mack's mingled breathing as they kissed.

Calla let out a gasp against Mack's lips when Liam sucked and then bit down lightly. That was right. He smiled against her skin as a shiver went down her spine. He'd play her body so well she'd be singing his name by the end of the night.

Mack too, the lanky fuck. Maybe this was where they were always meant to end up. Tonight it would be settled between them. Once and for all.

Liam pulled back just enough so he could unbutton his shirt and pull it over his head along with his undershirt. He needed skin to skin contact.

Calla turned to look at him and he'd swear her pupils dilated at seeing him shirtless. He kept his grin to himself. He was in better shape than he'd ever been in his life. Amazing what getting regular exercise and not living off a diet of whiskey and pub food could do for a lad. He'd been knackered every night for the entire first month he'd worked the ranch, but two years later and he was sporting a solid four-pack.

Mack urged Calla to turn her whole body so that she faced Liam. "Touch him," Mack whispered in her ear, taking over where Liam had left off kissing down the back of her neck. Liam frowned. That was supposed to be his line. He was the one directing this show.

But when Calla licked her lips again in the way that made Liam fecking crazy, he decided it wasn't worth making an issue of. She reached out a trembling hand toward his chest. Liam stepped in to her touch and he swallowed at the way her fingers felt like a blazing brand against his skin.

"Jaysus you don't know how good that feels, baby," he hissed out between his teeth, urging her other wrist forward so she was tracing down the lines of his pecs with both hands.

Calla's eyes shot up to his like she was surprised at his words. She was so innocent.

Liam's eyes flicked up to Mack but his face was buried in the back of Calla's hair. Liam could still hear the other man's low voice when he next spoke.

"Now reach inside his pants. Feel how hard he is."

Calla's whole body jerked as she looked at Mack. Jaysus, didn't the gobshite know she might need to take this slower?

He was about to remind her she didn't have to do anything she wasn't comfortable with but the next second her hands glided down from his chest to his stomach. He hissed out, totally mesmerized as he watched her hands jerk at his belt.

"That's right," Mack murmured in her ear. "Now reach in and feel how hard you've made him."

Liam almost couldn't breathe when Calla did exactly what Mack told her to. Her hand wasn't tentative as she slid it underneath his boxers. Her fingers closed around his shaft in a firm grip. Liam couldn't help thrusting his hips against her because, fecking Christ, that felt good.

Calla's eyes shot up to Liam as she gripped him and he'd have sworn he'd never been so hard in his whole goddamned life.

"You ever touched a cock before, baby?" Liam asked. He knew the answer, of course, but he needed Mack to know just how inexperienced she was. Because Christ, all the hard-won self-control he'd tried to develop over the last year and a half was flying right out the fecking window. He wanted to toss Calla back on the bed and bury himself hilt-deep inside her. To feel her virgin little pussy squeezing around him while he pumped in and out—

Her hand froze at the question. "No." Her answer came out whispered and she dropped her head like she was mortified to have admitted it.

"Don't hide your face, baby," Liam said, reaching one hand to her chin and raising her face. "You're perfect just as ya are. Christ, I'm hard as stone knowing me cock is the first one ya ever touched."

When Liam's eyes flicked up toward Mack he saw the surprise on his face. He'd pulled back from Calla's neck, eyes wide. But then, as Liam watched, Mack's nostrils flared and he shifted his hands to trace up her stomach from behind.

"You mean no one's ever held these sweet as fuck tits of yours before?" Mack asked.

Mack went slow enough that Calla could have stopped him if she wanted. Apparently she didn't want because she stood still while his hands finally reached her breasts. Mack's hands dwarfed her as he cupped her in his hands.

Mack swore as his fingers squeezed her little nipples between his thumb and forefinger until they were visible peaks through her silky dress.

"Let him know how good it feels, baby," Liam murmured.

Calla let out the hottest fucking moan Liam had ever heard. The next second she reached for the straps of her dress. Mack helped her shove them down, along with her bra.

Slow. You need to be taking it slower.

Liam's cock jumped as he heard the distinctive noise of a zipper being unzipped. Suddenly the front of Calla's dress went slack and with jerky motions, she pushed her dress down to her waist. Her breasts were only exposed for a second before Mack had his hands on them again. He squeezed them in a way that didn't look gentle at all, but had Calla reacting like she'd just been sparked with a live wire.

With one hand Mack guided her to look over her shoulder where he took her mouth as he squeezed those sweet as fuck little titties.

Enough. Liam hadn't even gotten a taste yet. He stepped into Calla and he lifted his hands to gently direct her face back to him. Mack let her go, though he did flash Liam a dark look he couldn't quite read.

Didn't matter because he was finally kissing Calla's soft lips. He shoved his tongue in her mouth. Maybe not the most suave kiss, but Jaysus she had him riled. He pressed his pelvis up and into her without qualm.

Virgin. She's a virgin, he tried to remind himself. *Slow the fuck down.*

But the next second her hand was between them reaching for

Liam's cock again. The second her hot little hand closed around him, he thrust into it.

"Get on the bed," Mack growled. Liam wasn't sure if the command had been issued to him or Calla, but when Calla pulled away from his lips with a gasp and started toward the bed, Liam wasn't going to be anywhere else except right by her side.

Mack pulled his own shirt off his head and threw it to the floor. Liam couldn't take his hands off Calla and he followed her onto the bed, crawling right on top of her and kissing her deep again. He kissed down her chin to her neck, then further down to those sweet as fuck little tits of hers.

She wasn't big, maybe a generous size B or a small C, but she had plenty to cup and squeeze and damn, that was all Liam needed. Better yet, she was all natural.

The next second he had his mouth on her little rosebud nipples. He sucked them and then teased the rock-hard tips with his teeth. She let out another one of those hot as hell moans and her legs opened to him.

Liam immediately rocked his groin into her hot center. There was too much material between them, though. The fabric of her dress kept her legs from falling open fully.

Liam's hand dropped down between them. He shoved her dress up. He had to touch her there. He had to be the fucking first.

But then another hand, not Calla's, knocked his out of the way.

"I'm gonna feel you now," Mack said. "You want me to stop, you just say so." And then Mack's hand slipped between Calla and Liam, brushing Liam's cock as it went.

Liam squeezed his eyes shut, not wanting to react and fucking resentful as hell that Mack got to touch her first.

But he didn't want to overwhelm her so he moved off her and watched as Mack's hand disappeared underneath the fabric that was now shoved all the way up to the top of her thighs.

Calla's back arched almost the second Mack made contact, pushing her breasts up into the air. She gripped the pillow behind her head as her pelvis moved against Mack's hand, her face screwing up in pleasure.

"Jaysus Christ." Liam's cock was painful still confined like it was in his jeans. He reached down and shoved his jeans off. The fecking things were so tight he had to lay back on the bed and wrestle to get them off his legs. He couldn't get them off fast enough. He finally kicked them to the floor and then he turned so he was laying sideways. He sucked Calla's nipple into his mouth again as he reached down to stroke his cock.

"Get your hand off your goddamned dick."

Liam was so surprised by Mack's demanding voice that his hand dropped off his cock. Mack seemed almost angry as he glared Liam down. "Only Calla gets to touch your cock. She's the only one who can get you off. Now get your ass up the bed and let her see it up close."

Liam laid there frozen for a moment. Who the fuck did that wanker think he was? Liam wasn't the one who got ordered about in scenes like this. He *did* the ordering. He wanted to grab Mack's balls and crush them in his fist until he dropped to the ground in front of him and offered to suck him off as way of apology.

But then he saw Calla's eager eyes searching down his body.

Damn, she was a total ride. And she wanted exactly what Mack said, didn't she? It turned her on to follow directions like that. Fuck that was hot.

So Liam crawled up the bed, cock jutting out toward her mouth.

Calla's hand immediately grabbed for him and he put one hand to the headboard to support himself while he hovered over her. At first she just held his shaft, lifting his cock and hesitantly stroking it while she looked him up and down. Was she trying to tell if his cock was manky?

"I'm clean," he assured her.

"Oh." Her eyes came up to his. "I wasn't even thinking about that..." She paused and blinked a couple times. "So if you're clean, then it's safe to do this?" She leaned up on one elbow to get even closer. And then the very tip of her tongue peeked out to lick just the very tip of his cock where his little slit was.

"Jayyyyyysus," he groaned. Was she trying to fucking kill him?

"Did I do it wrong?" she asked, worry clear in her voice.

"Oh no," Mack answered for Liam, "I think you did it very, very right. Taste him some more, gorgeous. Suck on his cock while I explore this sweet little pussy down here."

Mack pulled Calla's dress the rest of the way down her legs, tossing her underwear and bra to the floor.

And then she was just laid out naked on the bed like a sacrificial virgin set out for the monsters to devour. And devour her they would.

Mack bent over her lower body, his thumbs pulling her folds apart to expose her wet, juicy pussy. He wasn't trying to just jam his cock in her. Liam would have ripped the fucker off her if he'd tried that. She needed to get used to the feel and idea of sex—what it felt like to have a man's hand on her body. Or rather, *hands.*

Calla's eyes were wide as she looked down her body, gaze flicking between Liam's cock and Mack's head descending to her sex. She bunched her legs together and Mack looked up, eyes meeting hers.

"Open up for me, honey." He slid a hand down her thigh, nudging her legs back open. "Focus on Liam's cock. I like seeing it in your mouth."

Liam's shaft jumped at Mack's words. Shite. He was usually the talkative one in situations like this, but he had to say, it was fecking hot with Mack narrating.

"What do you like about it?" Liam asked, his eyes meeting Mack's for the first time since they'd come in the door. He felt stupid the second it was out of his mouth. His focus should be entirely on Calla. He was only putting up with Mack's presence because he was following Calla's direction. He'd give her whatever she wanted without making her feel bad for her desires, no matter—

"I like the way she's fascinated by your big dick. That's right honey, move your hand up and down and pop just his head in and out of your mouth. See how he responds each time?"

Jaysus.

Calla nodded almost imperceptibly, her mouth still around Liam's cock.

Liam hissed and his fingers gripped the headboard. Mack kept his gaze locked on Liam's even as he kept talking to Calla. "That's one of the most sensitive places on a man's cock. We love it when we get friction over the head. How's it feel, honey?"

Liam's breath caught. Because he wasn't sure if the honey was addressed to Calla or him. He blinked hard a couple times as Calla came up for breath. "It feels good." She obviously thought it was meant for her. Christ, of course it was. Liam shook his head.

"Am I doing okay?" Calla asked, her clear hazel eyes coming to Liam's. And there was such... openness there. Hope for approval, but also excitement, and lust, and energy. The mix of emotions from the past minute and a half made Liam feel knocked on his arse.

"You're doin' perfect, baby." He cupped her cheek and she smiled brilliantly. Then offered him a devilish wink and sucked his cock back into her mouth.

"Jaysus," he swore, shifting forward as she tugged him closer. Then she lifted off the bed the last few inches and took the crown of his cock in between her lips.

Liam dropped a hand to her head. Her hair was soft. But the second her mouth closed around him she started sucking like a goddamned vacuum. Liam's eyes dropped closed as he thrust ever so slightly forward.

She let out a startled cry and Liam looked down to see Mack's head buried between her thighs. Christ, he was eating her out. What did she taste like? Sweet? Bitter? Sweet mixed with salty?

Goddammit, he needed to know. Besides, what the hell was he doing waiting for direction from Mack? He wanted to taste Calla, he was going to taste Calla.

He pulled his cock out of her hot mouth, but only for a second as he crawled down her body, arranging them in a sixty-nine position.

"Suck me in again, baby." He grabbed his shaft and directed it back toward her mouth. Her tongue eagerly swirled around his tip the second he made contact and Liam had to clench his jaw against the impulse to blow his load right then and there.

But no, he was going to take his time. For a lad who'd always been given whatever he wanted growing up, it was a hard lesson learning that things were so much sweeter when you earned them. But goddammit, he had learned it.

"Bob up and down on his cock," Mack said. "That's right baby. Really pop those lips around his ridge every time he goes in and out."

Fuck, Calla was a fast learner. He squeezed his eyes shut as he kissed down her stomach. Until his head banged into Mack where he was eating at her pussy.

Mack looked up sharply and Liam took the opening. "Make room," he grinned.

Then he latched onto Calla's clit. It was already swollen and glistening from Mack's attention. He was sucking on the flesh Mack just had his mouth on. His cock jumped in Calla's mouth at the thought and he drew on her little bud with even more suction.

He expected Mack to try to shove him away, but instead Mack just started kissing down Calla's thigh.

Liam smiled into her pussy. Good. He'd put the wanker in his place. He didn't know what had happened with that weird moment earlier, but he and Calla were doing just fine without Mack thinking he could call the shots. Sixty-nine was a two-person position. No third wheels need apply.

He'd barely had the thought before Mack's head started moving back up Calla's thigh. Then before Liam even registered what Mack was doing, he licked a long line up her inner thigh all the way to her dripping cunt.

If Mack thought he was getting back in the driver's seat, he had another thing coming. Liam suckled Calla's clit, nipping it with just the edge of his teeth. Her suction on his cock stuttered and Liam growled with satisfaction.

He pulled back to lick the tip of his tongue all around her clit.

And that was when Mack dove back in, forehead bumping into Liam's.

What the— Did he think he could just knock Liam out of the way?

Okay, so sure, that was what he'd done to Mack. But that was just him establishing the proper power dynamic. The world worked a certain way. There was a particular pecking order. And if Mack thought he could have Calla's pussy back, he had another thing coming. This clitoris was fucking his.

So when Mack's rough cheek scraped against Liam's as he ate at Calla, Liam barely even flinched. No way was he giving up his ground.

That was when he heard a wet slurping noise. He blinked and looked Mack's direction. His face was so close it was hard to even see what he was doing. He could just make out Mack's tongue before it plunged into Calla's wet opening. *While* Liam was sucking her clitoris.

Liam was about to draw back and tell him to move the fuck off but Calla's hands lifted to grip the backs of Liam's thighs that were braced on either side of her head. She groaned a long, low rumble around Liam's dick.

Fuuuuuuuuuuck. That was— Jaysus Christ, maybe she'd just been pretending to be an amateur at all this. Because that felt like a fucking pro move.

Mack repositioned his head so he was eating Calla out so close to Liam that again, their cheeks grazed one another.

It was just because he didn't want Mack to have control over Calla's pussy that he didn't pull away at the repeated contact. That was all. It didn't have anything to do with the way his groin tightened every time their faces brushed.

If Mack thought he could intimidate Liam with a game of chicken —seeing which of them would pull away first the nearer their faces got—Liam would just show him. Liam couldn't count the number of men he'd been with in his life. His preference usually ran to women, it was true, but there'd been more than a handful over the years to break up the monotony.

Liam tilted his head sideways and then licked down the inch and a half from Calla's clit to where Mack was tonguing her sex. Liam didn't pull away when his tongue made contact with Mack's.

Mack jerked back and Liam buried his grin of satisfaction by shoving his own tongue up Calla's opening.

Liam thought that would be it.

Surely Mack would back off now.

Or... not. Because the next second Mack moved his face even closer and his tongue clashed with Liam's, tangling as they both tried to get at Calla's slit.

Fuck.

Fucking *fuck*.

Liam's breath got shorter and shorter the more he battled Mack's tongue to drive in Calla's cunt. The way they were angled, mouth's fighting it out over the same hole... it was almost like they were...

Kissing.

Liam's stomach tightened and he shut his eyes hard. But fuck, when he thrust his tongue forward and felt Mack's mouth kissing and slurping, he—Jaysus Christ but that felt. So. Goddamned. *Good.*

And when Mack grabbed the back of Liam's head, urging him back up to Calla's clit, Liam didn't fight it. Mack didn't let up his grip, though. He kept a firm hold on Liam's neck, pulling him back so that they took turns licking and sucking on Calla's clit. Mack directed it all, pushing Liam's head into position and yanking him back when he wanted his own turn.

Taking turns was good. Far better than his mouth being so fucking close to Mack's.

They repeated the move until Calla's legs shook crazily, the little whimpers coming from her throat growing louder and louder.

"She's almost there," Mack murmured, then he dug his fingers in the back of Liam's short hair and dragged him down at the same time shoving his own face into Calla's pussy. The sides of their faces cemented together and Christ, when Mack's tongue darted in and out of his mouth to lathe at Calla's clit, it felt— Shite, that was *so* fucking hot—

Liam abandoned himself to it. He didn't flinch when his tongue touched Mack's. And when the tip of Mack's tongue accidently encountered the tip of his, he lost it.

He pulled his hips back from Calla's mouth because fuck— He was gonna—

He reached his hand down and jerked at his cock while he and Mack kept up their assault on Calla's slick flesh. Mack's tongue touched his again and again and—

"Jaysus." He jacked himself even faster and his orgasm hit so hard it felt like an electrical jolt slammed into the bottom of his spine. His tongue stuttered but Mack just seemed to go even crazier, his grip on the back of Liam's neck never letting up. He was French kissing Liam and Calla's cunt at the same time.

Liam grunted hoarsely as cum pumped out of his cock and sprayed all over Calla's tits. Once. Twice. Fecking *Christ*.

His hand stayed on his half-hard cock and he rubbed it in the slick trail he'd made between Calla's breasts. He pinched her nipple and exhaled into her pussy.

When Mack's hands came to his shoulder to shift him off to the side, Liam didn't have any strength to fight him. He fell sideways onto the bed and watched with a sort of haze over his eyes as Mack kept eating Calla out for several more long moments until she was quivering again and her cries reached a high-pitched fervor.

Jaysus, she was about to come. Again. It had been so long since he'd been with a woman even half as unfettered with her pleasure.

His hand still on his cock started stroking even though there was no way he could go again any time soon. As he watched Mack crawl up over Calla's body, his cock stirred back to life. Well Jaysus, if they kept this up, maybe he'd be back at full mast sooner than he thought possible.

He was so lost in the idea of trying to come again, he missed Mack's intention until he heard him ask, "You ready?"

Ready for what? *Shite*. Liam tried to scramble to shove Mack off. "No, wait, she's a—"

But it was already too late. Mack jerked his hips forward and he thrust his condom-covered cock into Calla's sopping pussy with one quick push.

12

CALLA

OH GOD. Mack was inside her. That pressure deep inside her was his cock. She was having sex. She was actually having *sex*. With Mackenzie.

"Get off her, she's a fucking virgin," Liam yelled, shoving at Mack.

Mack's eyes shot to her and widened in sudden horror.

"No, don't," she said.

"You heard her," Liam said. "She said fucking *no*."

"No!" Calla wrapped her legs around Mack's waist when she felt him withdrawing. "Don't go."

Mack's cock pulsed inside her and her eyes dropped shut as she tried to memorize the feeling. Being stretched like that—God, she didn't even know how to describe it. It didn't hurt. She'd expected there to be pain. But there was the slightest pinch as Mack's cock pushed in. How big was he? As big as Liam? Liam had felt huge in her hand and even bigger in her mouth.

God, she'd had Liam O'Neill's cock in her mouth. He'd been so hard. Like, obviously he was hard. She wasn't that dumb about sex.

She'd even watched porn a couple times out of curiosity. But in the videos she'd seen the sex had been rough. Nothing like the exquisite care Mack and Liam had taken when their mouths were both on her driving her to the edge of sanity. She shuddered both at the memory and the way Mack's cock felt inside her when he slid out a little further and then pushed in again.

"Are you okay, Calla?" Liam asked, his voice concerned.

Calla swallowed and reached out a hand for him. Liam clasped her fingers and came close so that his face was only inches away. It felt like the most natural thing in the world to prop herself up on her elbow so she could kiss him. She wrapped her arm around his neck and pulled him down with her when she lay back.

"That's right, sweetheart," Mack said, his tone gentler than it had been all night. "You're doing so good. Do you know how good it feels to be inside you? I've never felt anything so fucking good." He hissed through his teeth as he pulled out and then slowly pushed back in. Achingly slowly.

His groin made the barest contact with her clit as he moved and she shifted restlessly against him. Nice that he was being a gentleman and all, but dammit, she needed him to *move*.

"I'm okay," she said, breaking from Liam's kiss to look at Mack. "You're not hurting me."

Mack's face was ruddy with color and she saw a vein straining at his neck. Calla reached out and traced it with her finger. "I'm not going to break."

"We know," Liam dropped down to kiss her deep again. "You're our strong girl."

Our.

Why did her blood race at hearing him say that? *Theirs.* She wanted to be theirs. God, she hadn't even known such a thing was an option, but now that she'd glimpsed it, she wanted it bad.

Which was ridiculous. This was just one night. They were obviously so much more experienced than her. If she had any space left in her head to question things, she'd probably be freaking the hell out right now. Two guys at once? She didn't even know people *did* that.

But it had just felt so natural when they were both at her door. They'd looked at each other and apparently shared some unspoken signal because the next thing she'd known, they were both kissing her and she was shoving down the straps on her dress.

"Does me fucking you feel good?" Mack asked, his hips shoving up against her pelvis.

Liam let up from kissing her long enough for her to nod and manage a shaky, "Yes."

"I can make it feel even better," Liam said, blue eyes flashing. He snaked a hand down between her and Mackenzie's body until his middle finger was strumming her right where they'd had their mouths earlier.

"*Oh*," she gasped, one hand clutching Liam's shoulder, the other holding onto Mack. Mack leaned down and kissed her. Gentle at first. And then harder and harder as the rhythm of his thrusts picked up.

"She's so fuckin' tight," Mack murmured.

"I bet she is," Liam responded. "Is she clenching on you?"

"You have no fuckin' idea." Mack twisted his hips, grinding into her and bearing down on Liam's hand between them. Did Mack feel him there? When he slid his cock out, did Liam's hand brush his length? Why the hell was that thought so arousing?

Mack's tongue thrust deep in her mouth, echoing the movements of his hips. Oh God, she'd never— She didn't know it would feel so—

Her eyes squeezed shut as her back arched into Mack's chest. Oh God, it was hitting. So much deeper and harder than before. Her toes curled and she buried her hand in Liam's hair as he swooped down, sucking on her neck while Mack kissed her.

Her high-pitched cry pierced the air as the blinding wave inside her went up.

Up.

Up.

UP.

And then all the weight of gathered pressure released in one heart-stopping crash of pleasure. Like every ounce of her being was fulfilling its purpose perfectly, stretching out to the edges of her toes and out to her fingertips as she hovered at the apex for—one heart-beat. Two heartbeats. Three—

And then the breath swooshed out of her as she collapsed backward on the bed as the wave finally receded.

Her eyes drifted open only to see Mack's exquisite face as it contorted in pleasure. His mouth was dropped open and his gray eyes burned as he looked down at her. Then he thrust his hips forward and planted himself so deep she knew she'd never forget the feel of him. Ever. Not until her dying day and probably not even then. She'd remember this feeling for eternity.

Mack collapsed on top of her, holding his hands on either side of her so he didn't crush her. She looked down at the top of his head, wondering what he was thinking. And Liam. She reached for him again and drew him down so that he was lying in the crook of her arm. Then she ran her hands through Mack's dark hair and he bowed his head into her collarbone.

The room was completely quiet except for the noise of all of them catching their breath. And Calla thought there hadn't ever been a more perfect moment in all of existence. She'd never felt more connected to a human being, or more fully alive than she did right at this moment.

Until Mack pulled off her. The next second, he rolled so that his feet were on the floor. Calla blinked up in surprise to see him walking away from the bed. He didn't look back at her. He turned only enough so that his face was in profile, his gaze fixed on the door. His voice sounded raw when he said, "Get her cleaned up."

And then he slammed out the door.

13

MACK

Mack skipped the elevator and went to the stairs. He had to get the fuck out of here. It wasn't until he was down the stairs and out the front hotel doors that he stopped to even breathe.

"Fuck," he yelled, grabbing both sides of his head. What the hell had he just done?

She'd been a virgin. A fucking *virgin*. She had no clue what she'd been getting into. But he'd pulled her into it. And then, ordering Liam around, just like he had with B—

Fuck. He slammed the brick wall closest to him with his palm. Several people walking by on the sidewalk jumped and then held their purses tighter once they got a look at him.

Calla had never looked at him like that. She'd never once seemed scared of him. Her eyes had held complete trust. Even when he was taking her fucking virginity.

She'd been an innocent.

Until him.

He shut his eyes and immediately he saw Ben. It was seven years ago and his new cellmate was looking up at him just like Calla had.

Ben was no innocent though. No, Ben's innocence had been stolen the first night he was in lock up.

"You got me away from him." Ben had looked at him reverently.

Mack had turned away, not able to take the way the kid was watching him. "It was nothing." He said it in a tone meant to discourage further conversation.

Ben made an incredulous noise. "Nothing?" Mack could feel him take a step closer even as Ben's voice dropped to a whisper. "That monster raped me every night, sometimes twice a night, for nineteen months, three weeks, and two days. When I was told I was changing cells, I thought it'd just be more of the same."

Mack spun around at that. "I'm *nothing* like that fucker."

Ben didn't flinch at Mack's shout. "I know. I been your cellmate for a week and you ain't even looked at me sideways." He took another step closer. "I thought I just got a lucky break. Till I ran into Bone in the yard this afternoon."

Bone. Mack's back went rigid at the name. Danny 'Bone' Jones. The sadistic fuck who had been Ben's previous bunkmate.

"He said you must have traded in all your markers to get me reassigned to your cell."

Mack's jaw went rigid. "What else did that fucker say?"

"A bunch of other shit, but for the first time in nineteen months, he didn't lay a finger on me. 'Cause of you." Awe was clear in the kid's voice. "He's afraid of you."

"He's afraid of Pres," Mack quickly bit out.

"Same thing," Ben said, and he wasn't wrong.

Mack had spent the first two years in lock up working out and bulking up until he was the biggest, baddest motherfucker on the block. The President of the Devil's Spawn MC had noticed. Offered him protection in exchange for pledging.

Considering his only other option were those Aryan motherfuckers, Mack had agreed. He spent every day of the next year enforcing for the Devils. Well, at least he did when he wasn't in the hole for fighting. No one knew it but he looked forward to his time in solitary.

Meant he didn't mind busting up whatever motherfucker Pres aimed him at. Gained him the nickname Torpedo. Pres pointed and *boom*, whoever it was wished they'd never gotten in the Devil's shit.

Mack had never asked for a thing in return. Until last week when he requested Pres make Ben's transfer. Pres hadn't even blinked. Even though as vice president, Bone was way higher up than Mack, and Pres had to know that stealing his favorite toy would piss Bone off, he still made it happen. Mack asked for the transfer last Tuesday and by Wednesday night, Ben, skinny, shivering, and eyes full of terror was escorted to his cell.

"What I don't get is *why*. You ain't even looked at me sideways," he repeated, shaking his head.

"Ever heard the saying don't look a gift horse in the mouth?"

Ben's eyebrows furrowed. "Naw, I ain't heard that."

"It means just be happy and don't question shit."

Ben went quiet at that. Mack turned toward his bunk and yanked down the ratty blanket.

"You could, ya know."

"Could what?" Mack looked over his shoulder.

"I wouldn't mind if ya... *ya know*." Ben's head lowered but he kept his eyes on Mack. "If ya wanted somethin' in return. Like I said, I'm real grateful. I can tell you's a different sort than Bone. I wouldn't mind it if ya wanted to—"

"I don't." Mack's voice was sharp.

But over the next weeks and into the second month, Ben didn't let up. He'd take any opportunity to touch Mack he could. He stayed right on Mack's heels whenever they left the cell. Tried to give him half his food every day.

"Everyone already thinks you're husbanding me," Ben said one night, sitting on the edge of Mack's bunk.

"Well I'm fucking *not*," Mack bit out, not much passion behind it. He was tired. So goddamned tired of all of it.

"I wish you was," Ben's voice sounded wistful and Mack glared at him.

"Plenty folks go wolf when they're inside. Don't mean you're gay or nothin'. Just that you got needs." His voice dropped even quieter. "Everybody got needs. Even you. I hear you at night taking yourself in hand when you don't think anyone else's awake."

"Get the fuck off my bed," Mack said, shooting to his feet.

It was already lights out but he could see by the dim glow from beyond the cell when Ben dropped to his knees in front of him.

Mack shoved him so hard he toppled backwards, head cracking on the concrete.

Shit. He hadn't meant to hurt Ben.

He stopped himself right before he could apologize. Maybe Ben would finally get the fucking message.

Still, Mack listened anxiously and only breathed out in relief when he heard Ben shuffling across the floor to his own bed.

He thought it would be done then. He'd made his position more than clear.

So when he jolted awake in the middle of the night to a hot mouth sucking his cock, Mack assumed he was still dreaming.

He pumped his hips back and forth because *fuck*, it was one good dream. Brianna had come and begged for forgiveness. She'd even bribed the prison officials in order to get a conjugal visit to show him just how sorry she was.

Mack reached a hand down toward his cock. And his hand landed on a head that wasn't fucking Brianna's.

As soon as he realized that, *shit*, he was awake, and *double shit*, Ben was giving him a blow job, he jerked his hips back. He had to grit his teeth against the pleasure firing down his spine when there was an audible *pop* as he came out of Ben's mouth.

"Get the fuck off me," Mack growled. He was about to reach down and shove him off when Ben said six words that had Mack freezing.

"You was Bone's before I was."

"Shut up," Mack hissed. He grabbed Ben's shoulders and took him to the floor in a headlock. "Don't you ever fucking say that again."

"It's true though, ain't it?" Ben gasped, hands going to Mack's arm at his throat. "You was his for two years. I hear you shoutin' in your sleep. You're still there back in his cell. In your head. I know 'cause I am too." Ben's voice got high and thin, like he was just holding back tears. "He tried to break ya but he can't. You're too strong to ever break."

"You don't know what the fuck you're talking about." Mack gripped Ben's throat even tighter. Anything to shut the fucker up.

"I do," Ben wheezed. "And more than anything I wanna help you." Ben stopped struggling underneath him. "Help... us... both."

Mack dropped him and moved away, backing into the wall.

Ben didn't say anything else. The sound of him gasping, trying to get his air back, echoed around the cell.

"Fuck," Mack whispered, kicking the wall. Which hurt like a bitch. Everything fucking hurt. All the fucking time.

Because goddammit, Ben was right. No matter how long he was free of Bone. Some part of him would always be locked in that cell with the sadistic motherfucker.

Two and a half years. Every night. No matter how big Mack got. No matter how hard he fought. Every *night*.

Till one day he stopped fighting. He'd barricade himself inside his head and let Bone do what he was going to do.

Two weeks after that, he was transferred to cell block D where the Pres and most of the Devil's lived. At first he thought it was because he'd finally proved himself. Things had been heating up between the Devils and the Mexican Mafia. Mack took every opportunity to back the Devils, trying to show how useful he could be.

Then he saw the young guy shrinking and following at Bone's heels. Ben. Poor bastard hadn't even turned twenty yet. The large black eye and way he walked with a limp told Mack everything he needed to know.

Mack hadn't gotten moved to D block because he'd proved he was worth something to the Devils. Bone had just gotten tired of him and replaced him.

Not two weeks after he'd stopped fighting back.

Mack had barely made it to the trashcan to puke up the entire contents of his stomach. He hadn't known which was worse—

knowing he could have gotten out from under Bone months, maybe even years earlier if only he hadn't fought him every night. Or how fucking happy Mack was that it wasn't him locked in a cell with the monster anymore. Even though the only reason Mack was free was because some other poor fuck had taken his place.

Every day he saw Ben for the next year and a half, the guilt ate at him. Till he finally made his play to get him free of Bone. Knowing even as he did it that Bone would just start up again with some other kid. Fresh meat arrived each week.

But it wouldn't be him. And it wouldn't be Ben anymore.

"Please," Ben cried in the dark. "I need you. He made me— and I can't—" Ben's voice kept breaking off with sobs. "You saved me. You're all I can think about. Just pretend I'm a girl. One hole's as good as another. *Please*. I'll make it good for you. I love—"

Before he could finish that fucking sentence, Mack went for him. He lifted him up off the floor and then shoved him face down into his bunk. "You want it?" he asked furiously.

"Yes," Ben cried. "I need it. I need you." Ben's hand reached for him again but Mack knocked it out of the way.

Then he yanked Ben's pants down, spit on his hand, rubbed it over his cock, and shoved home up Ben's ass.

And just look how that had turned out. Just like all those years ago, Mack kicked the wall. And just like all those years ago, pain spiked through his foot. He didn't fucking care. Mack kicked the wall again.

People walking by jumped back and scattered. The hotel wasn't downtown, but there were still a few restaurants around.

"Fuck!" Mack shouted, kicking the wall one last time. That was when he saw a couple cell phones come out, their bright screens illuminated. Shit. Just his luck they were calling the cops. The last thing Mack needed was to get in trouble with the fucking law.

So he turned and limped as fast as he could down the sidewalk, hopefully in the direction of a fucking bar.

14

LIAM

"HE'S A TOTAL ARSE," Liam said as he washed Calla's chest with a warm washcloth. "Forget about him."

Calla's eyes moved from the door Mack had slammed out of and then back to Liam. They were wide with bewilderment. And hurt.

The next time Liam got his hands on Mack, he'd fucking kill him. It was Calla's first time. And then for him to just fuck off like that— Liam gritted his teeth.

"Did I do something wr—?"

"Fuck no," Liam said, throwing the washcloth to the floor and gathering her in his arms. She was shaking.

"Shh," he said, holding her head against his chest and rocking back and forth. "Shh, it's all right. Don't cry, baby."

"I'm sorry," Calla said, swiping at her eyes and trying to pull away from him. "I'm being stupid."

"No ya aren't," Liam said, running his hand through her hair. "Come on." Liam moved to the edge of the bed and tugged Calla with him. "Up we go." He stood and pulled Calla to her feet.

She clutched for the bedsheet but Liam gently pulled it away from her and tossed it back on the bed. "You've a beautiful body. Be a shame to hide it."

Calla's cheeks went pink as she held one arm over her breasts to cover them. Cute. Didn't she remember how not very long ago he'd had the nipples she was covering in his mouth?

He just shook his head at her, then took her arm in his like they were entering a movie premiere and led her to the bathroom. He didn't let her go even when he reached to turn on the shower.

He eased her into the shower and then stepped in behind her. She swung her head around and looked at him with wide eyes, water beading on her lashes. Damn she was a striking woman. He felt like even more of a gobshite for not seeing it sooner. Then again, he was usually just looking to dip his mickey in easy pussy. Calla was a lot of things, but easy pussy wasn't one of them.

Which made Mackenzie even more of a bastard, to use her like that and then leave.

Liam laid his hands on Calla's shoulders as she faced the shower spray and started massaging. She sank back against him and his chest tightened. She was so goddamned trusting. Didn't she know she'd get flattened in this world if she kept that up?

Not if you protected her.

Liam blinked against the thought. He'd sure as fuck never been anyone's protector. All his life he'd only taken care of number one —himself.

He frowned as he reached for the small bottle of hotel shampoo. "Close your eyes," he said to Calla softly. He barely recognized his own voice. When he looked over Calla's shoulders, he saw she'd listened and shut her eyes.

Liam angled her forward so the water soaked her hair. He turned her by her shoulders so that she was facing him. Her eyes were still shut. As water sluiced down her face, she looked like the most perfect, pure thing he'd ever seen. That clear, creamy skin. Her long neck and softly rounded shoulders.

When she reached out for Liam, he stepped into her. "I'm here." There went his voice again, sounding all odd and strangled.

He turned to the side and squeezed shampoo into his hands. Then he worked his fingers into Calla's hair. He couldn't remember the last time he'd done this for a woman. If ever. He'd had shower sex before, sure, but he didn't think he'd ever washed a partner. The intimacy of it had his chest squeezing again. Especially when Calla dropped her face so that her forehead laid on Liam's chest.

She let out a contented sigh as he continued working the shampoo through her hair. After he'd finished soaping up her hair, he ran his hands down her back. All the way to her buttocks, which he couldn't help squeezing.

Calla giggled and turned her face up toward his, eyes still closed since her hair was foamy with shampoo and some of it had slid down onto her face.

"You ticklish, baby?" Liam grinned.

She shook her head.

Liam glided his hands back up to her waist. He pinched her and she let out a giggling little shriek, pulling back from him.

Liam wasn't having that. He stepped with her, pulling her into his arms as the shower spray started rinsing the shampoo from her hair. She kept her eyes squeezed shut but she had the most gorgeous smile on her face.

Liam could only stare for a moment. He wanted that beauty. He wanted to taste it. To breathe it. To own it.

He leaned down and kissed her before all the suds had washed off. Her lips tasted like shampoo. He didn't care.

Calla gasped in surprise when his lips made contact, but then she wound her hands up around his neck, fingers burying in his hair. With her leaning against him like that, her breasts thrust right up to his chest. Liam broke from her mouth only long enough to draw one of her nipples in his mouth. It was warm and wet and immediately went hard as his tongue flicked back and forth across it.

His cock went hard against her stomach. Calla gasped again, and

Liam didn't know if it was from pleasure or surprise because she'd just felt his cock too.

He kissed up her neck, drinking the water that dripped down her throat as he went. Most of the suds had washed from her hair and Liam wanted to drink her in, every single bit of her.

His arms around her crushed her closer. "I want you," he growled against her lips, even knowing as he said it that he shouldn't. She'd just lost her virginity for Christ's sake.

But it hadn't seemed to pain her much when Mack had taken her. And there wasn't any blood. Liam had glanced down to see, wanting to know if Calla would be hurting or not. She rode horses—didn't they say horse riding could break a woman's hymen? Then she wouldn't be *that* sore if he—

"Then take me," Calla said, blinking her eyes open in spite of the shower spray.

Liam shook his head at the same time his cock jumped against her belly. "I don't want to hurt you."

She smiled like she was amused at him. "You won't." Then she bit her lips like she was embarrassed. Her eyes dropped as she murmured. "I've um, you know, used a..." She waved a hand in the small space between them. "I have a BOB."

"A beeyobi? What's that?" Liam asked. Was this some American term he didn't know?

She laughed again before clapping a hand over her mouth.

"What?" Liam smiled but pulled back, searching her face. "What is it?"

"A B. O. B. Like the letters." Her eyes dropped again before meeting his gaze. "It stands for battery operated boyfriend."

Battery operated— Did she mean, like—

Liam arched an eyebrow. "You've got a vibrator."

Her eyebrows scrunched like she was waiting for some sort of judgement.

"Baby, that's sexy as hell." And it meant he could have her without hurting her. As soon as he thought it, his legs flexed, his hips seeking her entrance.

"Shite, you've got me so hard." He hissed through his teeth, pressing Calla against the back wall of the shower. He gripped the back of her head and dropped his forehead to hers, struggling for control.

"Are you... um. Clean?"

Liam pulled back, startled at Calla's question. "Yes. I get tested twice a year. Just got the results and I'm clean as a whistle."

"I'm clean," she said. "Well, obviously. But you know—"

"You on birth control?" Fuck, he was getting harder and harder with every word that came out of her mouth.

"No," she shook her head, "but I only get my period every few months and it just finished so—"

Liam's hips dropped and he grabbed his cock, rubbing it through her folds. "Are you saying you want me to take ya bare?"

Her eyes shot to his and she nodded. "I want to know what it feels like." Her eyes searched his. "I want to feel you."

Well fuck Mackenzie fecking Knight. He might have gotten *one* first, but Liam was taking this. He'd never gone without a condom with any woman. Ever. It was crazy for him even to consider. Even when using condoms, he'd had that woman try to claim her baby was his.

But Calla wasn't those women. She didn't know how rich he was. She wasn't wanting this for any other reason than she wanted him. Wanted *him.*

Liam didn't shove in like Mack had. He went slow. She'd feel every inch of him. Since he had her against the far wall, the spray of the shower was hitting his back. And sinking into Calla while steam spun all around them, it was sexy to the point of fucking magical.

He lifted one of her legs for better access and then groaned as the head of his cock passed through her lips. Jaysus she was tight. She might have already been fucked that night, but she was still tight as a fecking drum.

And this wasn't fucking. Liam had fucked a lot of women. He wasn't a complete manwhore but he had a fair handful of partners each year.

None of them had felt like this. The only other woman he'd even considered going bare with was Brigid. He'd considered a lot of things with Brigid, until she'd turned out like all the rest.

Calla lifted a hand to his cheek. "Are you with me?" Her eyebrows were furrowed. Like she could see him dwelling on the past. Screw that. He wasn't going to let his shite history fuck up this moment with Calla. He put his hand over hers, then flipped her palm to kiss it. His other hand dropped under her ass, clutching her as he slid in another inch. And then another.

Calla's eyebrows went high and her mouth dropped open. She was the goddamned picture of ecstasy.

He'd take her there. Jaysus Christ but he'd take her there, and then follow her over. He pushed the last of the way inside her until their hips were flush together. He rocked his pelvis so his groin rubbed her clit. That might not be enough. It wasn't with some women.

But before he could even think about dropping his hand between them to ensure, Calla's own hips rolled into his, rubbing just the spot she needed. Liam could tell because her eyebrows arched further up each time she ground against him. They'd be at her hairline soon but fuck, he loved how expressive she was.

He dragged his cock out and then in again and she clenched around him. "Baby," he hissed out.

"Is this real?" Calla whispered, dragging her cheek across his before kissing him again. "Is any of this real? Earlier, with... And you." Her eyes were bright with wonder as she looked at Liam. "You're *you* and I'm just the town tomboy." She clenched on him and bit her lip.

But Liam's stomach had soured. "What do you mean I'm *me*?" Did she know who he was? How much he was worth? Fuck. Was she playing him like everyone had his whole life?

If she was then she was one hell of an actress. But Jaysus, hadn't he overheard Xavier talking to Mel about how Calla had just lost everything? She was totally broke and then here comes the rich billionaire—fucking Christ how was he stupid enough to be bare-backing with—

"Liam?" Calla's voice was colored with concern. "I lost you again. Where are you?" Her eyes searched his back and forth.

"What did you mean by sayin' you're *you?*"

She blinked like she was confused. "You're Liam O'Neill. The whole town knows you."

What? He knew that witchy little blonde had found him out, but—

"Everyone talks about you guys at the ranch. And you," her shoulders lifted in a small shrug. "Well, you're the fun, sexy one. You're always making people laugh. I'd see you, at the bar sometimes. And whoever was with you was always laughing." Her eyes scrunched and she tilted her head. "You've just got this *shine* about you."

Shine. He had a *shine* about him? Him? Not his money or the gold and diamond jewelry she thought he'd shower her in?

But the more he looked at her, those eyes of hers so open, the more he believed her. She wanted him. Just him.

She thought he had shine.

He covered her mouth with his. Christ, she tasted sweet. The instant the tip of their tongues made contact, she started writhing against him crazily. Like she couldn't get enough of him. Like she'd never felt anything so good in her life.

Liam pulled out and shoved back in, hiking her up by both her legs and pinning her against the wall.

Her features went soft with lust and he leaned in to nip her gorgeous throat with his teeth. She clutched his head and held him to her, all the while making little high-pitched gasps. The octave seemed to rev higher and higher the more he thrust.

And then she let out a keening wail as she shuddered around his cock. Liam leaned over and drowned the noise with his mouth on hers. His balls drew up—it was coming. Jaysus fuck it was coming. The tip of his cock— Fuck, it was so insane without a condom. He could feel everything. Fucking *everything*.

His cock bottomed out and he kissed her crazily as his cum

spurted deep inside her. Holy fuck. Holy— He pulled out and thrust back again, spilling the last of his load. Still he kept moving. She felt so fucking amazing.

He dropped his head to her chest, breathing like he'd just run a marathon. He felt her lips on his temple and her arms and legs clenched around him tighter than ever. They stood there for one breath. Then another. Until finally his legs started shaking from holding her up.

She laughed as he awkwardly set her down. But he pulled her back into his arms as soon as her feet touched the shower floor. The spray was still hot around them. The beauty of hotel showers. If they were back at the ranch, there would have been pounding at the door for using up so much hot water at once.

He kissed her again, a short, sloppy press of lips. He couldn't decide if his body felt light or heavy. The moments after orgasm always left him feeling emptied out. Not just physically. There was a coldness that usually stole in the second he recovered from coming.

But having Calla in his arms, the way she clutched him back... He looked down and her features were relaxed and happy. Satisfied.

And damn if that didn't have his cock hardening all over again.

Liam pulled away from her reluctantly. "Come on," he said, running his hand through his wet hair to get it off his forehead. "Let's get you cleaned up."

He soaped his hands and caressed down her stomach and then between her legs. She grabbed hold of him, her whole body shaking. He needed to get her to the bed. He hurried at his task and soon they were both stepping out of the shower.

15

CALLA

"Dad, have you seen these statements from the bank?" Calla chased her father down as he walked to the barn. She shook the papers from the envelopes she'd uncovered from the very back of Dad's filing cabinet. "Why didn't you tell me the ranch was having money problems?"

"'Cause it's none of your concern," her father bit out as he leaned on his cane and took another step. The tremors that had started out in his hands a couple years ago had worsened until his whole body now shook. Which made even simple tasks like walking the uneven dirt lane out to the barn difficult.

"None of my concern?" Calla's mouth dropped open. How could he— She'd cut her sophomore year at college short to come back and help with the ranch. She'd only known the ranch was in trouble because Harris, her dad's ranch manager, called and told her what was going on. About how her dad's condition was worsening more rapidly and about all the debt. Harris had been working at reduced wages for six months out of loyalty to her dad since he'd been with them for almost a decade. But he had a family and couldn't afford to keep it up.

When Calla got mad and asked Harris why he hadn't called her earlier, he said her dad forbid him to.

So she came home and was doing her damndest to save the legacy that had been her family's for three generations. Four, counting Calla.

"That's right," Dad turned around and snapped at her. "I didn't ask you to come back here. I've run this farm for twenty-two years. Then you come home from your one year of college—and suddenly you think you know everything about *my* business? Tryin' to tell *me* what to do." He pointed one trembling finger at Cal. "We just hit a spot of bad luck. Happened before and it'll happen again. Us Carters always come out just fine."

Calla breathed out heavily. "You levied a second mortgage on the ranch." Why wouldn't he just listen to reason? "And you can barely pay back the *interest* on the loans each month, much less start chipping away at the principal. Dad," she pleaded, "the bank's gonna take the ranch unless we—

"You don't know what you're talking about!" her dad yelled, his face going red as he spun toward her. He lost his balance as he did it. He took one stumbling step forward to try to stay up but it only sent him crashing to the ground with more momentum.

"Dad," Calla cried. She'd tried to lurch to catch him but wasn't able to get to him in time. She leaned over to help him up.

He just swatted at her hands.

"How many times I gotta tell ya to leave me be. The ranch was fine before you got here. *I* was fine."

His legs jerked back and forth in the mud with the uncontrollable shakes. He tried getting to his feet by propping his cane and hefting himself up. But his cane slipped in the mud and his butt hit the ground with a splat.

Ignoring his protests, Calla got her hands underneath his armpits and lifted him up. Until he started shouting in her ear, "Don't need no help getting to my damn feet!"

He pushed her away even though he was collapsing back to the mud by doing so.

Calla finally pulled back, heartbroken as her father glared her down. "Get on," he waved a hand toward the barn that was still half a field away. "Animals won't feed themselves."

He didn't really mean for her to just leave him there, did he? "They can wait a few more minutes." She reached for him again. "Just let me help you—

"Dammit girl, am I not speaking English?" He jerked his tremoring arm away from her. "Get on your damn way."

"Daddy, just—"

"GET!"

Calla turned away and jogged toward the barn, tears stinging her eyes.

"Calla. Calla, it's just a bad dream. Shh, you're here with me, baby."

Calla blinked and startled awake.

There was a warm body at her back. Arms around her. Holding her.

"Liam," she managed, swallowing and swiping at the tears running down her cheeks.

"Shh, gal, I've got ya." Liam rolled her so that her face came against his chest. Calla hid her face from him. Dammit. She hated crying.

The dream had felt so real. Probably because it wasn't just a dream. It was a memory.

Dad never would listen to reality when it came to the ranch's finances. He'd gotten more and more distant every time she'd tried to talk to him. She didn't know if that was because he just didn't know what to do about the debt or if it was because of the Huntington's.

Getting less communicative was one of the symptoms. Memory loss, too. It about broke her heart when her dad would repeat something he'd said just a few minutes earlier. Even when she did manage to get him talking, it was like he wasn't tracking the conversation in real time. He'd respond to something she'd said five or ten minutes before as if she'd just said it.

Heart. Breaking. Like a machine had come in and bulldozed little sections, one chamber at a time. She'd left little pieces of her heart all over that ranch.

One piece with Prissy. Another chunk lost the day she had to drive her dad to the nursing home. More when he refused to speak to her the whole way except to point a tremoring finger at her. "I'll never forgive you for this."

Another tear crested and fell down her cheek. She swiped at it angrily.

"Baby, what's wrong?" Liam asked.

"Nothing." She gave what was probably a weak smile and tried to pull away from Liam. He didn't let her go.

"It's not nothing. Talk to me. I know I'm usually just a pompous asshole, but I swear I can listen."

Calla balked. "I've never thought of you as a pompous asshole."

One half of Liam's mouth quirked up. "What can I say? You bring out the best in me."

His words made Calla's chest warm. She still pulled away and Liam let her. She swallowed and looked at the ceiling the moment her back was to him. How much more of her heart had she lost last night? How long before there was nothing left of her to lose?

"Calla?"

She felt Liam sit up behind her. She tried to shake off the dream. She'd just spent the night with Liam O'Neill. *Her*. Calla Carter. She'd woken up in his arms. And last night, with Liam… and Mack. Where had he gone when he tore out of there like a bat outta hell? Would it be awkward the next time she saw him?

Pretty sure, yeah, it would be. *He had his cock inside you.* She didn't know how you just smiled and pretended that never happened.

"I'm not sure how to do this morning after thing," she murmured. She'd been serious but Liam laughed, his arms coming around her waist. He dropped a kiss to the top of her spine in between her shoulder blades and she shivered.

"What time is it?" she asked. She looked back at Liam and he leaned over to grab his phone off the nightstand.

"Seven-fifteen."

Calla jerked her feet to the edge of the bed. "Shit. Xavier's gonna be pissed. He wanted to get out before morning traffic."

She looked around for her clothing, leaning over and snatching up her bra from the ground beside the bed.

"Shit," she said again, stubbing her toe on the frame of the bed and jumping up and down.

"You're fecking adorable, you know that?"

She glared at Liam. "Did you hear the part about how we're gonna be skewered like breakfast sausage if we don't get our butts moving?"

Liam just continued grinning at her with that wide smile of his.

She rolled her eyes and hurried over to her suitcase, dragging the sheet with her to cover herself.

She pulled on a fresh pair of panties and then pulled her sports bra overhead. "Dammit," she swore, the bra getting stuck on her face as she tried to wriggle into it.

This was met with a loud chuckle.

She was about to snap at Liam again but then his hands were on her. He helped get her bra over her head and down over her breasts. He also used the occasion to give both her breasts a good squeeze before letting her go and smacking her ass.

"Get going, woman," he said. "What do you think? We have all morning for me to spend ogling you and inspecting your assets?"

She spun around and pretended to be annoyed. "You're one to talk. I actually have my underwear on. You're still—" She gestured up and down his body. His naked body. He stood there for her and God to see, completely unabashed. Wow. Was his cock always that size or was he aroused right now? What did dicks look like when they weren't—

Suddenly Liam swooped down on her and landed a kiss. A leisurely, lingering kiss. All thought of them needing to hurry flew from her head.

There was only Liam, his hands in her hair, the heat of his bare chest as it brushed hers. When he finally pulled away, she felt dazed.

Never in her life had she felt such crazy joy. Happy to the point of silly. It was too much. Too fast. She was gonna come down hard from this and the crash was gonna be *brutal*. But for at least one more minute, she basked in everything that was Liam O'Neill.

"You keep staring at me like that, woman," Liam growled, eyes dark, "and we won't get out of this hotel room before noon."

Calla knew she was definitely lingering in an alternate universe when all she wanted to say was, *Yes, screw it, let's lay here and make love all day.*

There was today. Today, today, and only today.

Exceeeeeeeeeept, what about her *job*? And Xavier? And the mustang that even now was waiting to be trailered?

With a sigh of reluctance, she gave Liam one last peck on the lips and then pulled out of his arms.

"I hear reality is waiting for us outside that door," she said ruefully and gestured toward the door.

Liam frowned, eyes scrolling up and down her body like he was trying to memorize what she looked like without clothes on.

Then he strode forward, eliminating the small bit of distance she'd put between them. When he pulled her into his arms again and she heard his growled, "Fuck reality. It can wait another half hour," she didn't even put up a token resistance.

All she could do was shriek with laughter when Liam picked her up in his arms and carried her back to bed.

"Wow, you're the last one I would have thought would turn out to be the town slut." Bethany's shrill voice cut across the parking lot and Calla froze in her tracks. After she and Liam had finished one last energetic round of sex—seriously, she'd heard of doggie style and reverse cowgirl, but she never thought she'd ever have an adventurous enough sex life to experience them firsthand. Well, after this morning, those were another two bucket list items she could cross off.

Then she'd checked her phone and found a text from Mel saying Mack was too hungover to drive and would Calla mind driving the last trailer back? Mel would be driving Mack's.

Calla's heart had hiccupped at reading it. Mack was hungover? He'd been perfectly sober when he joined her and Liam in their hotel room. Was the experience with her really so bad that he'd had to go out and get drunk? *Really* drunk if he didn't even feel well enough to drive home.

Calla hurriedly texted Mel back that it was no problem. She'd been hauling trailers since she'd gotten her driver's license at sixteen.

Mel immediately messaged back: *Great. Keys will be at the front desk. We're heading out, see you at home.*

Calla had just pulled the truck and trailer into the BLM's holding facility where they were picking up Liam's horse—the one they'd be hauling. Liam had jumped out to go in to see about the mare's status in the lineup and Calla was out double checking the rigging and lights on the trailer when Bethany's words stopped her cold.

"Guess you never can tell about a person. But really, taking both of them up to your room?" Bethany made a tutting noise through her teeth.

Calla turned around and barely stopped her hands from clenching into fists. Bitch said *what*?

Bethany stopped right in front of Calla. It was eight in the morning but Bethany was in full make-up and hair, skintight jeans and a halter top that exposed her midriff. She cocked her head at Calla. "Then again, your mom was the town whore, so I guess it's not that surprising. But not even she had two at once. Tell me, did they fuck you at the same time or did you make them take turns?"

It wasn't premeditated—Calla genuinely had no idea what she was doing until her fist connected with Bethany's face. Her nose, more specifically.

Bethany howled and stumbled back, grabbing her nose. Calla

could already see it was bloody. Wow, it was a sight that really *shouldn't* feel so goddamned satisfying.

"Usually I'd say violence is never the answer," Calla said, for once in her life giving the devil on her shoulder full reign, "but in this case, I gotta say—red looks good on you."

In the distance, Calla saw Liam waving his hands at her. His mustang must be up next for trailering.

And with that, Calla climbed back in the cab of the truck, ignoring the slew of expletives pouring from Bethany's mouth. And for once, she had the rare joy of doing and saying what she felt, exactly when she meant to. Seize the fucking *day*. She'd never felt more liberated in her life.

"You'll pay for this, you whore! You broke my nose! I'm going to file assault charges. You're going to be sorry you ever—"

Calla turned the engine over then held a hand over her ear when it roared to life. "What's that? I can't make out what you're saying."

Bethany screamed and gesticulated wildly. Calla genuinely couldn't hear her over the engine though she thought she made out a couple words. "... sue... arrested!"

Calla glanced around the lot. She didn't see any cameras. "Good luck with that," she called out her window, then revved the engine and left Bethany in her dust.

16

MACK

MACK CLUTCHED HIS HEAD. "Jesus, can you turn down the music?"

Xavier just swung his head to look at Mack, then his eyes were back on the road. He didn't say a thing, just reached a hand over and turned *up* the volume on the blaring country station.

"What the fu—"

"Watch your tone in my truck," Xavier said low, eyes cutting briefly back to Mack. "I had half a mind to leave your ass back in Denver. The one thing I asked was that none of you embarrass me or the horse rescue. You think I named the rescue after my *wife* so my employees could start a fucking bar brawl at last call? Or that I came all the way down here just so I could get up at two in the goddamned morning to smooth things over so you didn't end up with another strike on your record? You trying to make me sorry for taking a chance on your ass?"

Throughout Xavier's tirade, Mack's head sunk lower and lower. This must be what it felt like to get chewed out by a father. The way the pain in his head spiked with every angry syllable, he was actually glad he'd never had a dad. He hated feeling like an errant fucking schoolboy. Then again, he'd fucked up last night. He knew he deserved this and far worse. Plenty of folks woulda cut his ass loose after the shit he'd pulled last night.

"No," Mack said quickly. "No sir. You know I appreciate everything you and Mel have done for me—"

"Do you?" Xavier cut in, hard eyes glaring at him again. "'Cause you sure got a funny way of showing it."

Mack swallowed and looked out the passenger seat window. "It won't happen again."

"It better fuckin' not," Xavier muttered. Then his hand moved to the dial for the music again. He turned the volume up even louder.

Mack groaned and slumped further down in his seat.

THAT DAY and the next were not fun ones for Mack. Xavier had let up on the radio, turning it off an hour outside of Denver when the signal started failing. Too bad the raging headache Mack was sporting had grown to epic proportions during the hour-long high-volume blast.

And he'd swear, every time his hand went to his aching forehead, Xavier smirked.

Suffice it to say, it was a long six and a half hours.

Then when they'd gotten back to the ranch, he was supposed to start training his mustang. Right away. From the second the horse stepped out of their trailer into one of the round pens.

After a year and a half on the ranch, Mack wasn't clueless about what needed to be done. He'd watched Xavier break two mustangs the previous year.

But after almost seven hours in the cramped cab of the truck, paired with the worst hangover he'd swear he'd ever had in his life, all that training flew out the window.

Patience. That was what Xavier always instructed them when dealing with a new horse, wild mustang or not. You had to listen to the horse. That's what he was always saying. *Listen to the horse. They'll speak loud and clear if you let them.*

Well all Mack heard when he finally got Torpedo to step out of the damn trailer was a whole lotta pissed off horse. Didn't seem like Torpedo had enjoyed the ride any better than Mack. He was twitchy, nervous, wouldn't stand still long enough for Mack to even put his hand near him, much less to touch him.

Meanwhile, in the circular paddock in the distance, he saw Calla up and *riding* her horse. The first day. *Riding.* What the fuck type of juju magic did that woman have?

She'd certainly had him under her spell. When he wasn't cursing his killer hangover, the night he'd shared with Calla and Liam kept coming back to him on endless loop.

The look on her face when he breached that tight little pussy of hers—Christ, there hadn't been an ounce of fear on her face. How the fuck was he supposed to have guessed she was a virgin?

And then you just fucking left her there.

He cringed every time he thought of how he'd stormed out of there like the world's biggest asshole.

He felt the shame of it even as he slammed the hotel door behind him and all but ran down the hall. He did shot after shot at the bar in an effort not to feel it. Not to feel anything. And when that dumb redneck got up in his face near closing, well, it was the perfect opportunity to take out some of his fury. Punching the bastard in the face did feel good. At least until two of the guy's buddies joined in and Mack was dodging fists from all sides. He could have handled three guys back when he was at his prime. But three years of working with his hands instead of his fists plus a shitload of tequila and they got in several hits.

He made them regret it, at least. Until Xavier showed up to pull him off the fuckers and they got out of there right before the cops were called.

Just one more thing he owed to Xavier. It chafed. He didn't like being in debt to anyone.

After spending the day failing to make any progress with his mustang, he grabbed his dinner and jogged up the stairs to eat in his room. He'd felt Calla's eyes on him as he went. Liam's too.

He ignored them and spent the rest of the night in his room. He felt on edge as he got in to bed that night.

Sleep didn't come.

His ghosts were too restless.

Ben. His mother. His years spent as Bone's bitch. The feel of Ben's slim body slipping onto his bunk each night.

Ben was always too skinny. He'd have skipped meals if Mack hadn't been there ordering him to eat.

Sometimes Mack had resented Ben's neediness. There were days Ben would go all but catatonic unless Mack was there giving him commands. Near the end, there was a six month stretch where Ben only came alive at night when they were alone together in bed.

"Master," he'd whisper as he reached for Mack in the darkness. "How do you want your slave tonight?"

It was a game Ben liked to play. Mack balked at first until he felt Ben's distress when he refused. He didn't know why Ben liked it that way. His devotion to Mack was probably unhealthy. Then again, they were in a fucking super max prison—healthy wasn't really an option on the table. So Mack played along.

"On your knees," Mack ordered, swinging his legs over the side of the bed as he sat up. "Suck my cock."

Moments later, he felt Ben's trembling hands reaching to pull his cock from his pants. Then a hot mouth sucking him in.

Mack's hands went to Ben's head. He always kept his hair so short it was almost shaved. Mack massaged Ben's scalp as Ben went to town on his cock.

"Deeper. I want to come down your throat," Mack growled.

Ben pulled off just long enough to whisper, "Yes, Master. Whatever you say, Master."

Mack hissed out through his teeth as Ben swallowed his cock. He could deep throat like no one Mack had ever met.

He had to fight from coming right there on the spot.

"Fuck your hand while you suck me off."

Ben's head shook back and forth on Mack's cock. Mack gripped Ben's head harder.

"Fucking do it. Master will punish you if you don't."

Ben moaned and Mack leaned over until he was whispering close to his ear. "You don't do what I say and I'll take your ass, little slave. I'll fuck you so hard you'll feel me into next week. Now grab your fucking cock."

Ben lifted both his hands to rest them on Mack's thighs.

Mack's cock swelled at his refusal. Some nights Ben was only up for giving him a blow job. More often than not actually, these days.

Maybe him wanting more meant that he was coming out of whatever funk he'd been in lately. Mack hoped so. He hated seeing him so listless.

Mack grabbed Ben's shoulders and pushed him back. Ben's mouth made a loud *pop* noise as his lips slid off Mack's cock.

Mack didn't hesitate. He dragged Ben up onto his bunk bed, shoving him face down into the mattress.

"On your knees."

"No, Master. Don't. I swear I'll be good. Don't fuck my ass."

"I told you the consequences if you didn't suck my dick." Mack gripped Ben's hips as he positioned himself behind him.

"No, don't," Ben said, getting on his knees and shoving down his pants in the same motion. "Don't, Master. I can't take your big cock." He leaned back, brushing his ass back and forth against Mack's dick. "You're too big and hard."

"Spit," Mack said, shoving his hand in Ben's face. Ben obeyed and Mack rubbed it up and down his cock. Then he positioned his crown at the entrance of Ben's anus. He paused there a moment, listening in the dark for the sound of Ben whispering his safe word or snapping his fingers. But there were only Ben's heaving breaths.

Mack pushed inside Ben's ass and *Jesus*, it felt good. Ben's little whimpers only drove him forward. But not too fast. Or too hard. No matter how riled up he got, he never lost himself so much that he didn't remember he always had to be careful with his little Ben.

Mack pushed in inch by inch until he was finally seated all the way up Ben's ass. He leaned over his back and kissed the nape of his neck. "Look at you gripping my cock like such a good little slave. Are you hard yet? Admit it. You love being fucked by Master."

Ben shook his head back and forth but the more Mack kissed along his neck, the softer Ben's body went.

"You dream about it all day long, don't you? You were hard at dinner, weren't you? Thinking about how Master was going to bury himself inside you."

"I'm your slave," Ben whispered, his back moving up and down with each heaving breath. "I have to do whatever Master says."

Mack pulled out and then shoved slowly in again. Ben trembled underneath him. "Don't lie," he whispered, his voice harsh. "If I grab your cock, I'd feel just how much you love it. Your eyes have been begging for me to fuck you all day long."

"No," Ben started but Mack reached around and grabbed his cock, rubbing his thumb across the precum that was beaded on the tip and massaging it up and down Ben's shaft.

Ben's breath hitched and he bucked back against Mack, driving Mack's cock further up his ass.

"That's too bad." Mack let go of Ben's dick and he immediately whimpered. "Slave boys who don't do what they're told don't get treats."

"No, Master. I'll be good, I swear."

"Too late. Fuck your hand. Show me how much you want to please me. Make me believe it."

Mack dropped his lips back to Ben's neck, kissing around to the side and then sucking hard enough to leave a mark. Ben loved being marked. He said it showed everyone who he belonged to.

"You're mine and you'll do whatever I say," Mack rasped into Ben's ear before latching onto his neck again.

"Yes, Master," Ben gasped, his voice reedy with need. "I belong to you."

Mack felt the moment Ben gave in. This was the moment every night built toward—Ben resisting until he finally consented out loud. Only then would he see to his own pleasure. For whatever reason,

Ben needed it that way. Every time. Mack suspected it had everything to do with that fucking bastard, Bone, but he never said that out loud.

"Then show me," Mack said. "Fist your cock. And tell me who you belong to."

"I'm yours," Ben gasped, and even though Mack couldn't see, he knew Ben was jacking himself off. "Forever."

Mack's cock surged and he grabbed Ben's hips while he tried his damndest not to fuck Ben as hard and quick as he wanted.

Especially when Ben moaned his name. "*Mackenzie.*" Not Master. In the last moments it was always Mackenzie.

Mack felt it hit his balls.

"Come," he ordered harshly. Ben squeezed on Mack's cock and bucked before letting out an agonized gasp. Mack forced himself to keep fucking Ben slowly.

He'd learned how to come this way. Slow and steady. Feeling the moment of Ben's pleasure and his cock inevitably responding. He felt the cum lighting up his cock and he grunted as he shoved to the hilt again. Then it hit and he pumped in and out. Once. Twice.

Ben all but collapsed beneath him and Mack rolled them so they were on their sides, spooning.

Mack yanked the sheet over them. Nothing made him sleep better than coming hard. He was almost asleep when he heard Ben's voice.

"I'd die in here without you."

Mack stiffened. "Don't fucking say that."

"It's true," Ben said. And then quieter. "I love you. More than I've ever loved anyone. I'll love you to my dying day."

Mack's stomach clenched. "Stop talking about dying."

Ben went quiet after that.

Mack felt the words left unsaid. He knew Ben did too, though he never complained that Mack never told him he loved him back.

Mack snaked his arm around Ben's stomach and pulled him close.

Not knowing how much he'd come to regret not telling Ben he loved him that night.

Because the very next day, Ben was shanked in the yard.

By Bone's newest cellmate. Mack had been inside on assigned

kitchen duty. He had to hear secondhand about how Ben had bled out right where he fell in the dirt. All alone in his last moments. He was dead before the medic even got on the scene.

The day following, Bone grinned at Mack from across the room. It was then Mack decided that if it was the last thing he ever did on earth, he'd put that motherfucker in the ground.

17

LIAM

"Come here, horsey horse." Liam held out his hand and approached his mare for what felt like the hundredth time in the past few hours. "Come on. You can do it."

Just like every other time, the horse watched him sideways as he came toward her. Then, right before he got within touching distance, she bolted to the opposite side of the circle pen.

"Fecking Christ!" Liam took off his hat and hurled it at the fence. And immediately his da's voice was ringing through his head.

"How is a son of mine so goddamned worthless?" his da shouted, storming into his bedroom with some shite gossip magazine in his hand.

Liam had been nursing a hangover and grabbed his pounding head. "Can you keep it down, da? I'm still langered somethin' awful."

Well that just seemed to set his da off. "I will not keep it down. You're a twenty-four-year-old man still living with his father. You barely graduated and only because I donated an extremely generous endowment to the university your senior year. You have no skills, no ambitions, and are an embarrassment to the O'Neill name! Look at this." His father pointed at the headline on the front page above the picture of Liam being hauled away in cuffs by the Garda. "Playboy Billionaire Arrested for Brawling...Again." Then he opened the magazine and began reading. "Liam O'Neill, son of Prism Media Group mogul Ciarán O'Neill was yet again caught brawling in the streets of Dublin, this time outside a pub in the—"

Liam flopped back on his bed and pulled his pillow over his head to muffle the sound of his father's voice.

The next second his da had ripped the pillow away. "You listen to me when I'm speaking to ya, ya useless, poxy little shite. I pulled meself up from nothin' to give you everythin' you could ever want—

"Don't give me that shite," Liam said, launching off the bed and getting in his da's face. "Everything you've ever done in your life has been for yourself. Not for me or ma. Christ knows you scraped her off quick enough so you could go scuttle women half your age. Not that I imagine havin' a ring on your finger stopped ya from gettin' your knob polished by skanks all around the world on those business trips *you took all the time even when ya were married."*

That was when his da punched him so hard he was knocked to the floor.

"Hey there."

Liam spun around and put his hand to the back of his neck as he saw Calla standing just outside the fence behind him. Shite. The only thing worse than failing so bad at this was having a witness. Especially Calla.

"Xavier mentioned you were having a little trouble with her." She gestured behind him in the direction of his mare.

"It's been two days and she won't even let me touch her." Liam shook his head, squinting in the setting sun at the mustang. "She's banjaxed, I'm telling ya. The organizers have to recognize that some horses are just too far gone. If I had meself a nice foal from a reputable breeder, well, I know I'd really be getting somewhere. But this one—" He shook his head again. And realized that, shite, he was rambling. Like an insecure idiot. He was never insecure around women.

They'd barely had time to spend more than ten minutes together alone since driving home from Denver. The last two days, Calla had spent almost all her time not doing morning chores with her mustang. Yesterday he'd hoped to have some time with her after dinner, but when he got downstairs after cleaning up, Mel told him she'd borrowed their truck to go visit her dad in a nursing home.

He hadn't known her dad was even sick. Then he realized exactly how little he actually knew about her. Which made him feel like a selfish scumbag. It was an uncomfortable sensation. He wasn't used to all these... *feelings*.

Wanting to shag a girl, sure. But, like, comforting someone with a sick da? He'd considered staying up to see Calla when she got back. But then he tried to imagine how that would go.

Sucks about your da... So, wanna go up to my room and let me make you feel better?

That was something the old Liam might have done. And now that he was trying to be a better version of himself?

Staring at Calla now, trucker's hat on her head, in a loose tank-top and jeans—obviously not concerned with primping or showing off her figure to its best advantage to lure him in—well, he still didn't have any fucking idea what to say to her. In the circles he'd lived in most his life, appearance and status were everything. Calla broke every rule he'd always lived by.

Calla just smiled and leaned over to slide through the fence posts and into the pen with him and the mustang. "I've been watching a little while. You've been really patient."

"Oh." He lifted his hand to the back of his neck again. The last thing he'd expected was a compliment. He felt like a huge fuck up. "Thanks." And then he blurted, "I heard about your dad yesterday. I'm really sorry."

The smile faded from Calla's mouth and she looked into the distance. "Yeah." She was quiet a moment and then seemed to shake herself out of it. "So. About the mare. What'd you name her?"

"Satan's Mistress."

Calla laughed. "Aw, poor baby."

Liam didn't know if she was talking about him or the horse.

She came a little closer. "You're doing good but maybe I can share a little technique that will help."

Liam held out his hands. "Please. Anything." Then his eyes narrowed as he looked across the pen at the mustang. "Not that it will do anything." He hadn't been joking about her being defective.

Calla just laughed and shook her head. "Come on," she gestured for him to come with her. She walked slowly toward the horse.

"Make sure you always stay on her left side so she can keep an eye on you as you approach."

Satan's Mistress was looking in their direction as they made it halfway across the pen. Liam was about to take another step when Calla held out her arm to his chest.

"Now back."

Liam looked at her in surprise. They weren't anywhere near the horse.

But when Calla backed up, her front still toward the horse, Liam mirrored her movements. "Just keep taking deep, calming breaths."

Again, Liam wasn't sure if she was talking to him or the horse. But he stayed quiet and did as Calla did.

Once they got back to the fence-line, Calla stood there a second before heading back in the horse's direction. This time they took a step or two past the center of the paddock before backing up again.

"Like boiling a frog," Calla said. "You gotta go slow. By small degrees or she'll bolt."

Liam nodded even though he wasn't sure about it. Calla didn't know *this* horse. The only time he'd gotten close in the past couple days after getting her home, she'd almost taken off his fingers. And she had big damn teeth.

It took another fifteen minutes before they came within five feet of the horse. "See how she's tensing up? Watch her ears." Calla said, nodding at the mare. Liam observed her ears flicking back and forth.

"She's telling us back up, she's not comfortable. Horses have a herd mentality. They want to be dominated. You just have to show them who's boss, but at the same time you can't force it." She took several steps backward and Liam followed suit. "It's a dance between you and her to establish your dominance."

Calla held one hand out as she started approaching the horse again. "You find the line..." They reached the same spot they'd been in a moment before, about five feet away. "Then you take one or two steps over it." Calla took another step closer. Now that Liam was watching more closely, he saw Satan's Mistress's ears twitching and the way she shuffled back and forth at their nearness.

"Then we reward her by taking the pressure off again." Calla started backwards and again Liam followed.

It was an infuriatingly slow process, but to his shock, fifteen minutes later, Calla was reaching out her hand to the mare's nose for her to sniff. Calla still didn't make contact. She just took another step closer and blew lightly at Satan's Mistress's nose.

"This is how horses greet each other in the wild. Let her get to know your scent." Satan's Mistress shifted uneasily and Calla pulled slowly back. "Then you reward her by stepping away again and leaving her alone for a little while."

"Like playing hard to get. Are you sure this isn't dating advice?"

Calla laughed softly, still never taking her eyes off the horse. "Can't say I know much about that." Her eyes flicked his direction and Liam wasn't sure, but he thought her cheeks reddened.

After retreating to the fence again, Calla gestured at him. "You try saying hi to her this time."

She stayed by the fence while Liam headed toward Satan's Mistress. He felt his heartbeat thudding in his ears. Ridiculous. It was just a fecking horse.

Worthless.

Useless poxy shite.

"Remember to breathe," Calla said from behind him. "She's reading your body language. So make sure you're giving off calm with every step you take. You might not make it all the way on the first pass. That's okay. Find her line and take just one step beyond it."

Liam stopped and watched the horse. She leaned down and took a bite of grass but the way her head was cocked, it felt like she was still watching him.

He took a step forward. When she just kept chewing grass, he took another. Then another. Her head came up and she shifted nervously a few steps.

Liam backed away just like Calla taught him. And to his astonishment, the next time he approached, Satan's Mistress let him come all the way up to her. Liam had only made it this close a couple times before—both of which had ended with Satan's Mistress snapping at him with those big teeth of hers.

Liam took a deep breath in and out and held out his hand toward her nose. But unlike in the past, he didn't keep pushing to try to touch her. He left his hand about a foot away from her. Then, when she didn't move, he took another step in. Her ears flicked at this.

One step past the line. Okay. Liam took a tiny step closer and then blew at the horse's nose. Which felt frankly ridiculous.

But instead of snapping, the mare nosed a little closer to him. Like she was curious. A thrill shot through Liam's body.

He was doing it. He was actually doing it.

"Now back," Calla said.

Liam wanted to take that last little step so he could touch the mare. Maybe even try seeing if he could get her to take the bit.

Then he considered his failure rate before Calla had shown up. Baby steps. He backed off.

When he got back to Calla, her eyes were shining as she beamed at him. "You're doing so good. You're a natural at this."

His chest flushed with warmth like he'd just had a shot of whiskey on a cold day. "I don't know about that."

Calla scrunched her eyebrows together. "Wait. What's that?" She bumped him on the shoulder before looking up at the sky. "Did I miss the pigs flying? Is Liam O'Neill actually being modest?"

Liam barked out a laugh. No one ever took the piss out of him. And everything was just so natural with her. They'd had sex—not just that, but she'd lost her *virginity*, maybe not technically to him, but as good as. And yet here she was, not making a big deal about it or pressing anxiously for more.

He'd been joking earlier when he said the tactics she was using on the horse would work for dating but maybe there was something to it after all.

He wrapped her in his arms, lifting her up off the ground and spinning her around. She shrieked and hugged his neck. He set her back on the ground and nudged the bill of her cap back until it fell off her head. Damn she was pretty. Those flushed cheeks. The adorable freckles sprinkled across her nose. The way she looked at him like he was the most exciting thing that had ever happened to her.

He leaned down and kissed her hard. He probably should have taken it slower. But for once he was letting go of all his normal calculated moves and just going with what felt right.

From the way she kissed him enthusiastically back, he'd say it was the right way to go.

At least until she pulled back. She was still grinning at him as she pulled out of his arms, though. "I still want to work with Painter a little more and get him groomed. See you at dinner."

"You bet your arse," he said. Then, before she could turn to go he stepped forward and kissed her again.

She was laughing as she pulled away. "I'll see you." Then she turned and slipped back out through the fence. She walked away but looked back at him a couple of times, that radiant smile still on her face.

He frowned. What if she *was* playing him? This innocent, not immediately available, hard to get act could just be that—an *act*.

It wouldn't be the first time a woman had tried games to capture his attention. There was nothing he hated more than people trying to fecking manipulate him. For a long while there he hadn't thought there was any other way to interact.

Wasn't he the guy who believed no one ever gave anything without expecting something in return? So what was Calla's angle? If she didn't want him for his money, what *did* she want? Maybe his body. She'd certainly seemed to enjoy everything he'd done with her.

He stared in the direction Calla went long after she'd disappeared around the corner of the barn.

Jaysus, he couldn't remember the last time he'd felt so in over his head. With a horse or a woman.

"WHAT DO you think happened with Mackenzie?" Calla asked. They were sitting on the porch swing after dinner, her in his lap with her head nestled in the crook of his shoulder.

Usually when he had a woman in this position, he'd be quickly shifting her other leg over him and hiking up her skirt so they could get on with things.

But he and Calla were just... talking. Well, occasionally they'd make out for a while, but then it would calm down again and she'd just curl up into him like a contented kitten.

Liam paused from where he was running his fingers through her hair, finally registering her words. "Um. He's an arsehole?"

Calla shoved his shoulder lightly. "I'm serious."

Liam had been serious too. Mack was a bogger arsehole and that's all there was too it.

"Have you seen him the past couple days?" Calla lifted her head from his chest to look at him.

Liam shrugged. "Just the back of his head after he's grabbed his food and heading up to his room."

Calla sighed. "Exactly. I think something's going on with him." She dropped her head back to Liam's chest but she pulled away moments later to look at him. "Do you not want me to talk about him? Is that..." she glanced down. "Is it not okay to bring him up?" Her eyes were anxious.

Liam squeezed his arms around her. "You can talk to me about anything. I don't want you holding back." He was just starting to trust that she wasn't a fake. He certainly didn't want her to think she should put on a show of any kind.

She swallowed and smiled tentatively. "I've just never done

anything like…" she waved a hand. "You know." She lifted and dropped her eyebrows significantly. "And he was part of it with us."

Liam felt a flare of pain in his chest. Was he not enough for her?

It faded quickly at seeing the distress on Calla's face, though. "Do you still want him?" His tone was more even than he'd expected it to be.

Calla glanced down again before taking a deep breath and meeting his eyes again. "I don't really know him. But I didn't know you either. And then… that night." She pursed her lips and shook her head. "It felt, I don't know…" she looked around like she was trying to find the right word. "*Important*. Like all three of us were connecting in this really special way." She turned her head to look out at the dark night. "That's probably stupid and naïve. I don't know what I'm talking about."

"Don't say that." Liam's arms tightened around her. "Don't doubt your instincts." It might not be his favorite thing to hear that she was still thinking about Mack, but here she was, telling him up front. Being real with him. No matter what she was feeling, it was right there on her face.

"What did you think about that night?" she asked. "Did you like it when he… When you two were…"

"Sure," Liam said, then he felt Calla stiffen at his clipped tone.

"I'm sorry," she said. "I shouldn't have ask—"

"It wasn't the first time." Liam took her hands so she didn't feel like he was cutting off her line of questions. He wasn't used to being open with people, but if she could do it, so could he. Well, he could try, anyway. "I've done things like that before. With both a man and a woman."

"Oh." Her eyes widened as she looked up at him. "Like, both at the same time or, you know," her cheeks went pink.

Jaysus she was cute. So innocent. He smiled, enjoying her reactions. "Both. Together and individually. Does that shock you?"

"I don't know," she blinked. "So are you, what do they call it? Bisexual?"

Liam shrugged. "I don't put a label on it. I usually say I'm a trysexual."

Her brow furrowed.

"As in, I'll try anything once."

She chortled out a short laugh at that but then sobered again. "Do you like one better than the other?"

Liam traced his fingers along the back of her neck underneath her hair, liking the way she shivered at his touch.

"I've slept with more women than men. But I didn't really expand me horizons until college."

She propped her hands underneath her chin as she looked up at him. "So how do you know?"

"Know what?"

"How do you know if you're attracted to someone? Like, what makes the difference between a guy or girl you're just friends with and someone you want to, you know, sleep with?"

Liam laughed. "There's no science to it. I'm either attracted to someone or not."

She tilted her head. "So how long have you been attracted to Mack?"

Liam choked. "I'm not," he hurried to say as soon as he could speak again. "Not to him."

"Oh." She frowned. "But I thought you just said—" She squinted her eyes at him. "And with how the two of you were—"

"I was just going with the situation as it presented itself." He shook his head so violently Calla had to pull back. "But Jaysus, I'm *not* attracted to that wanker."

"Oh." She sounded disappointed.

Shite. Why? Did she want a repeat of what happened in the hotel room?

Liam had been doing his best to block it from his memory. When he replayed that night, he only focused on the time after he got Calla into the shower.

"I just..." she trailed off again before continuing, her eyebrows scrunched, "I think he's really lonely. And I know what that's like.

Feeling like you're all alone in the world." She shook her head, her eyes going distant again.

Liam didn't know what to say to that. Whenever he thought about Mack, it was usually just to cuss him out. In his head or out loud if the occasion warranted.

But then he focused on the rest of what she'd said. About feeling lonely. "Yeah," he swallowed. "I know the feeling too."

Calla's eyebrows went up as she looked back at him. "You? But you're always so," she waved a hand. "You're so good with people. Everybody loves you."

His chest went tight. That was how she saw him? "I don't know if I want you taking off those rose-colored glasses, beautiful."

She scoffed at that. "Hardly. I just call it like I see it." Then she paused, her brows lowering. "Tell me about it. How does a guy like you feel lonely?"

Liam shrugged. He wasn't going to play the poor little rich boy card. If there was anything he'd learned the last year and a half, it was how fucking entitled he used to be. He wasn't about to start whining about how hard he'd had it.

Calla lifted her hand to his face. "Tell me. I want to know everything about you."

"Me da and I weren't that close. He worked constantly. And Ma was checked out most the time. Drinking and pills. They got divorced when I was nine. The nanny raised me. She's still the one who calls me on me birthday and Christmas."

Calla tilted her head, her eyes going soft.

"Don't do that." He couldn't help his voice going stiff. "Don't look at me like that."

"Like what?" Her eyebrows went up again.

"Like you pity me."

Her eyebrows met her hairline. "I'm not pitying you. Believe me," she huffed, "I know how shitty that feels. I was just thinking about you when you were a kid. I wish I could have been your friend back then."

Liam laughed. "You would have hated me. I was a complete shite.

I'm shocked Mrs. Owens put up with me as long as she did. None of the nannies before her lasted six months."

"Oh no, don't tell me you were the kind of kid who would snap girl's bra straps?" Calla groaned.

Uh. So now probably wouldn't be the time to admit that from the ages of fourteen to seventeen his opening line when he met a pretty girl was to tell them to blow him. Or the fact that, more often than not, they'd actually done it.

"What?" she asked, obviously seeing something on his face.

He shook his head, not wanting to meet her eyes but doing it anyway. "I wasn't a nice person. For most of me life, actually, I was a complete—" *bastard*. He stopped just short of saying it and instead finished, "—arsehole."

Her brow scrunched up. "So what changed?"

Liam shifted her in his lap. He'd had a hard on for most of the half hour they'd been snuggled up together, but it was quickly deflating at this conversation. "I don't know. I guess I grew up."

That was a copout and he knew it. But he couldn't tell her the truth. Not if he didn't want things to change.

Calla was the first woman who wasn't with him just because of his money or what he could give her. Well, apart from orgasms. He hoped to give her plenty of those in the near future. But if she knew who he was, it would ruin everything before it even had the chance to really start.

Calla's brow was still narrowed. Like she could sense there was more to the story. She didn't press it, though. "Well, I guess I'm glad I met you now and not then."

"Me too, baby," he whispered, then leaned down and kissed her. "Me too."

Those were the last words they said for a long while. Jaysus, she tasted sweet. His cock quickly re-inflated but he didn't push for anything more than kissing. For once in his life, he wanted to do the right thing by a girl.

Which wasn't to say when Calla finally pulled away, her pupils blown, and asked, "You wanna go upstairs?" he didn't jump to his feet and all but drag her in the house and up to his room.

She giggled the whole way. At least until he closed the door behind them in his room and he pressed her up against it.

"Liam," she whimpered between kisses. Fuck but he liked the sound of his name on her lips. Right then and there, he made it his mission to have her gasping it all night long.

18

MACK

IT WAS the third day since Mack had gotten home with Torpedo and it wasn't going any better today than it had yesterday or the day before. He wasn't making any progress with the mustang. If anything, he felt the horse was getting jumpier around him.

He finally gave up for the day and went in the house to take a leak. After he went to the bathroom, he stopped in his room to check his phone messages before he went back out for evening chores.

Bone's parole hearing was today. It had him on edge, he couldn't lie. Xavier always said horses could sense your mood. If the way Torpedo had bolted away from him all day was any indication, Xavier was spot on.

Mack grabbed his cell and saw he had one voicemail. His throat got tight even as he shook his head at himself. Stupid to be so fucking anxious about it. Of course Bone wouldn't make parole.

Still Mack felt his heartbeat in his ears when he listened to his old friend Sammy's voice come over the line.

"Hey bro. Hope everything's good out there in the prairie. Still can't imagine you ridin' a fuckin' horse."

Mack smiled. He and Sammy had gotten to know each other during a nickel Sammy had spent on the inside. He'd joined up with the Devil's Spawn for protection just like Mack. Mack had tutored him and helped him get his GED and he was doing good now that he was out. Had a good job in customer service, a wife, a new baby. Living the fucking dream. He always said if there was anything Mack ever needed, to consider it done. Mack never thought he'd cash it in. Till he realized how helpful having someone with their finger on the pulse would be in keeping tabs on Bone.

"Yeah, so, bad news about Bone. I know you ain't gonna want to hear this, but he's gettin' out. He made parole. Good behavior or some shit."

Mack's hands clenched into fists.

Parole?

What the *fuck*?

"I guess it takes two or three weeks for all the paperwork or whatever to go through. But yeah. By the end of the month, he'll be out. Sorry, man. I'll keep an eye on him for you and give you regular updates."

"Fuck!" Mack barely stopped himself from throwing his phone across the fucking room.

He raked a hand through his hair and stood up, pacing across his room. The Devils must have paid someone off to get Bone out early. Motherfuckers. Bone had been in for a double homicide he'd committed when he was nineteen. Sentenced to twenty years. And they were gonna let the bastard out after sixteen?

Mack kicked the frame of his bed and it screeched as it moved across the floor. It wasn't enough. He felt like ripping apart the whole damn room.

He leaned over with his hands on his knees. Calm down. He needed to calm the fuck down. So he thought he'd have a few more years to prepare. So what? Nothing had changed, not really. He'd gone over his plan a million times in his head. He'd just have to act sooner rather than later.

And in the end, Danny 'Bone' Jones would still be dead.

In the meantime, Mack needed to smash the fuck out of something. He leaned over and yanked his boxing gloves out from underneath the bed. Then he jogged down the stairs and toward the back barn where Xavier had let him set up a bag.

He wailed on the bag for half an hour or more. Instead of releasing his tension like it usually did, though, each hit only seemed to make his blood burn hotter. In two or three weeks that murderous, raping bastard would be back on the streets. Mack slammed the bag again, immediately pulling back for another punch.

"I saw you training Torpedo earlier."

Mack startled at the soft voice. He jerked around and saw Calla standing a few feet away, leaning against the wall of the barn.

"You've got a gentle touch. You were good with him."

Sweat poured off Mack's brow and down his chest. He leaned over and grabbed his shirt from where he tossed it earlier to mop himself off. He didn't look Calla's direction again.

"Can we talk?" she asked.

"Got nothing to say." He tossed the shirt back down and reared back for another swing at the bag.

"Well I do." She sounded impatient. "I didn't like how you just left like that the other night."

Mack didn't respond, just let loose a series of jabs.

"Liam says you're a coward and we should forget about you."

Mack's hand fisted tighter in his gloves. Of course that's how that fucker would spin it. Mack stretched his neck to try to ease some of his tension. Still he didn't look at her. "Guess he's right," he said.

"Bullshit." Her voice was like a whip and he felt her take another step toward him. "I was there that night. At the dance. I saw you laughing. Having a good time. Then it's like some switch flipped. And I haven't seen the guy I first met that night in the kitchen since."

Finally he turned to her. She was back in her overalls with a skimpy little tank underneath. She'd tried to tie her hair back but it was escaping all around her face. Her cheeks were pink, probably from the heat. Mack's cock twitched remembering how her cheeks had looked the same when he was burying himself inside her. And the look on her face—that mixture of shock and pleasure, everyone of her reactions playing out on that expressive face of hers.

Mack clenched his jaw and he swung for the bag again. "So now you want to stand around and talk about feelings? We had fun the other night. Then I moved on. End of story."

"Is it?" She took a step toward him and put her hand on his forearm to stop his next jab. "Because that guy I first met? The man I danced with? I really liked him. He was someone special."

Mack felt her words in his gut. Special? She didn't know what the fuck she was talking about. The only special he had in him was being especially good at kicking the shit out of people. He glared at her. "I was trying to get laid. That's all."

Calla shook her head as he talked and he could see the stubborn written all over her face. It was a familiar expression. Ben used to look like that when he wanted something. "It was more than that," she said. "I don't know much but I know that."

Mack turned back to the bag. Fact was, he couldn't look at Calla now without seeing Ben.

Just one more reason to shut this shit down. "Oh yeah?" he sneered. "And why do you think you know anything? You were a goddamned virgin. Fuck, most teenagers have more experience than you. Besides, three months from now, I'm outta here. Right after the competition." It was the conclusion he'd come to about fifteen minutes into wailing on the bag. He respected Xavier enough to finish what he'd committed to with training the mustang. But after that, he was out. The grim reaper was coming for Bone, and Mack would be the one to introduce them. "I don't need any complications between now and then."

Calla put her hands on her hips. "I don't have to be a complication. I'd like to be your friend."

"Already got enough friends." He swung at the bag again. The impact went up his arm and into his chest. He punched again, even harder. He hadn't wrapped his hands with tape before putting his gloves on, and if he kept it up this way he'd find his knuckles bloody when he pulled them off.

Calla scoffed. "You don't have any friends."

"Exactly." *Punch.* "And that's how I like it." *Jab, jab, punch.*

"Everyone needs friends. I'm just starting to realize that. I lived most of my life lonely and thought it would never change. I was wrong." Her voice went soft. "You're wrong too."

"Look, little girl," Mack spun on her and pointed a glove her direction. "You were an okay fuck, but shit, I never would have touched you if I knew you were gonna get all clingy and shit."

Calla's nostrils flared and her hands clenched. "Maybe Liam's right. Maybe you're nothing but a bully."

He wished she'd stop bringing that fucker up. He hadn't missed the way Liam was always finding some way to touch her whenever the two were in the same room. Like a dog staking his fucking claim.

After several more long moments of him not responding, Calla threw her hands up in the air. "I give up."

She spun and walked away. Mack forced himself not to watch her go. If she looked back, he didn't want her to see him looking after her like a lost fucking puppy.

No, better for everyone involved if he took out his frustrations on this goddamned punching bag rather than pulling a sweet girl like that into his fucked up sphere.

He'd been a selfish fuck to ever look for distraction in her soft arms in the first place. But that was over.

Bone was out of prison. His purpose was clear now. He'd train up to peak condition again. Make himself a machine. To do the only thing a savage like him was good for.

"She didn't want to listen when I told her you were a lost cause."

Mack gritted his teeth at hearing Liam's voice behind him. What, suddenly the back barn was Penn fucking Station? Why couldn't they just leave him the fuck alone?

"People want to deny it but breeding matters. Just take the mustangs. Maybe we get them trained to follow a few commands so we can sell them as a work horse at the auction. If we're lucky. But they'll never be anything more than what they were born as." His lips twisted in disgust. "And nothing compared to a purebred."

Mack sneered, turning to look at Liam. "I take it you're the pure-bred in this little metaphor?"

Liam shrugged, a superior smile on his face. "Just calling it like I see it."

"Yeah, well no one fucking asked you." The mood Mack was in, Liam better shut his goddamned mouth and run away with his tail between his legs if he knew what was good for him. "You should be happy. You're getting the girl. That should satisfy your ego." Mack couldn't help adding. "Even if it's just 'cause I'm letting you have her."

The vein on Liam's neck stood out as he took a step toward Mack. "She feels sorry for you. I'm sure I can convince her to give up on her little charity project without too much trouble. Your mongrel arse doesn't deserve her and you know it. Not that it stopped you from getting your dick wet though, did it?"

Fucker pushed it too far. Mack had been itching for a rematch ever since Liam had gotten in those hits that night in the kitchen. 'Sides, if he was gonna take on Bone, he could use all the practice he could get.

Mack shook his head and feigned like he was gonna walk away. Then he spun on his heel and swung at Liam.

Liam's eyes went wide with surprise and he ducked out of the way of Mack's glove at the very last second.

"Oh, ya want to batter me? Fine." Liam raised his fists. "I'm happy to settle once and for all who's the better man. I was light-weight champion for three years running at Exeter. Woulda been four," he smirked, "but I got thrown out for fighting."

This time it was Mack's turn to smirk. "Think you know how to fight because you could beat up some other pansy assed rich kids?" He shook his head and pulled off his boxing gloves, cracking his fingers as he went. "This is gonna be fun."

He faked a jab and then reared back, letting loose a punch that would have smashed Liam's face in. If the little fucker hadn't danced away at the last second, that was.

"Boxing is all about footwork," Liam said, doing more of that stupid bouncing around bullshit.

Mack was almost too busy laughing at him to dodge when Liam let out a left-cross. He barely managed to knock Liam's hand away mid-air.

But Liam was ready and came back with his right, landing one right on Mack's jaw. Motherfucking piss ant son of a—

Mack roared and ran full speed into Liam. He caught him off guard and took him to the dirt floor. Liam grunted in pain as Mack landed on top of him but Mack didn't waste a second pinning him and then trying to get his arm around the fucker's neck to choke him out. Right before he could, though, Liam grabbed Mack's shoulder, jerked his arm across, and then rolled out from underneath him. Slippery little fuck—

Next second he was jumping on Mack's back and slamming him into the ground. Then he did some fucking ninja move, grabbing Mack's arm, putting a hand around the back of his neck, and then ramming into him from the side until he flipped Mack on his back.

Mack struggled but the bastard still had one hand around Mack's neck and his knee on Mack's other arm.

Liam grinned in Mack's face as Mack wriggled and fought to get free. "Did I mention I also dabbled in wrestling?"

Superior piece of shit. Mack might not know any fancy fucking wrestling techniques, but he knew the basics of getting out of a tight spot. He reached behind his head and grabbed Liam's hand, jerked it down with pure force, then jammed his elbow into Liam's body. He used the momentum to flip Liam so he was on his back.

Liam hit hard and his chest moved up and down as he breathed heavily underneath Mack's body. His teeth clenched. "So you know how to get out of a half nelson. Good for you."

"I know how to get a mouthy little shit on his back, if that's what you mean." Mack ground Liam into the floor, chest to chest.

The more Liam jerked and tried to get out of his hold, the wider Mack's smile got. "Guess brute strength wins out over breeding."

Liam's face went red and he tried to knee Mack in the kidneys from behind. Mack just shifted so he pinned Liam's entire body and not just his upper half. Which meant his pelvis came into contact with Liam's.

He almost jerked back at what he felt.

Liam had a huge fucking hard-on.

Liam's eyes flashed and he yanked to try to get away from Mack. All that accomplished was rubbing his cock more against Mack's. Liam was wearing jeans but Mack only had on athletic shorts and he felt every inch.

When his own cock stiffened in response, again Mack almost pulled back and let Liam go. But then he saw the way Liam's face had gone cherry with embarrassment.

"So I'm white trash not worth the shit on your shoes," Mack sneered, "but you still want to fuck me."

Liam's nostrils flared as he glared back at Mack, jerking again to try to dislodge him. With the same results—he wasn't going anywhere.

Mack lifted up slightly but only to get enough momentum to slam his body back down on Liam's. The move had their cocks grinding together even more.

"Sure, I'd fuck you," Liam shrugged, pretending nonchalance. "Or have you chauffeur me around. Or wipe down the table after I eat." Liam's eyes went flinty even as one side of his mouth lifted. "There's all kind of uses for the help."

Mack laughed. "You got one thing wrong there, little boy." Keeping Liam's arms pinned at his sides, he rolled him until Liam's chest was smashed into the ground. "I don't get fucked," he hissed in Liam's ear from behind. "I do the fucking."

Then, moving to hold both of Liam's wrists behind his back with one hand, Mack reached underneath Liam, jerked the button of Liam's jeans free, and shoved them down to expose his toned ass.

For a second neither of them said anything. Until Liam bit out, "Condom. Back pocket."

Holy shit. Mack was bluffing. He'd just meant to put Liam in his place. He didn't expect him to...

Mack shoved his hand into the back pocket of Liam's jeans. He yanked out the condom. Stared at it for a moment. Then he ripped the packaging open with his teeth.

He'd show this Irish motherfucker once and for all who was in fucking charge. They'd get it out of their system. Then Mack would be done with him.

Mack shoved his own shorts down and rolled the lubed condom down his cock.

"Grab your ass cheeks," Mack bit out, finally letting go of Liam's wrists. "Open for me." Again there was a moment of hesitation. But it wasn't even two seconds before Liam reached back and separated his ass cheeks. Exposing his little puckered hole.

Mack's cock lunged almost of its own fucking accord. His hips did the rest.

The head of his cock pressed at Liam's entrance.

Mack swore. This part always made him fucking crazy. Would he be able to get in there? How much struggle would his partner put up before submitting? Because he suddenly very much wanted Liam to submit. More than anything else he'd wanted in a long time, apart from Calla.

"Relax," Mack ordered, putting his hand on the bottom of Liam's spine. "Open up more."

Liam pulled his cheeks even further apart and Mack thrust in at the same time. And fuck, *yes.* The crown of his cock breached the tight ring of muscles. Liam's body spasmed underneath him.

"On your knees."

Mack kept pressing forward with his cock as Liam pushed back against him, struggling up to his knees.

"That's right," Mack said, grabbing Liam's ass hard. "Look who can't wait to take it up the ass. How long you had a hard-on for me?

How many nights you slept in the wet spot after coming to the thought of me? Come on," he lunged deeper. "Tell me.

Liam turned and glared over his shoulder. "Fuck you."

Mack laughed. Shit but this felt good. So goddamned good. "No, fuck *you*." He shoved his cock all the way in to the hilt to emphasize his point. Liam's mouth dropped open and his face contorted. Pleasure or pain, Mack couldn't tell. He suspected both.

"Show me how fuckin' hard you are for me." Mack reached around Liam's waist and grabbed for his cock. It was a good size. Fucking *thick* too.

"You stuck this cock in Calla? You two fuck after I left?"

Liam's eyes opened again and he smirked. How he had the nerve to smirk at Mack while he had his cock up his ass, Mack didn't know.

"I fucked her so good she couldn't even remember your name by the time I was through."

Mack jerked his hips back and then he rammed back in. Liam grunted as his body jolted forward. Mack grinned.

"You ride her as hard as I'm riding you?"

Liam's eyes narrowed in challenge, his head still swung back to look at Mack over his shoulder. "You call this hard? I barely even feel your mickey. That a pencil back there?"

Oh he was fucking in for it now. Mack growled in determination as he pulled out and shoved back in. All the way. No fucking mercy. And Christ, the way Liam's body clenched on him.

Then Liam shifted, shoving back against Mack's thighs as Mack thrust forward. Mack grabbed one of his shoulders and then started pounding the fuck out of him.

And for the first time since Mack had read that fucking email earlier, his mind cleared. Christ, he'd forgotten how a good lay could do that. Make all the other bad shit go away.

Ben had known. And he'd known Mack needed it just as much as he had. But Mack had always had to be careful with Ben. He couldn't take him hard. Not after what Ben went through. No matter the dominance games they played, Ben was only comfortable with certain positions. Certain role play. Slow and easy, that's how it had been between them. Every inch Mack gained he had to coax from Ben, even though it was Ben who'd pushed them being together in the first place.

But Liam apparently wasn't in the market for slow. And pile driving his ass like a mad motherfucker seemed to turn the guy on even more. His hips bucked as he rode Mack's cock, faster and faster until the slap of their flesh echoed around the barn.

That was when he heard a high-pitched yip of surprise. And it didn't come from Liam. Both Liam's and Mack's head swung to the barn door and Mack froze.

Fuck.

It was Calla.

19

LIAM

SHITE. Liam stared at Calla. This was bad. What the hell had he been thinking?

"Calla, I—" Liam started but then broke off. Because what could he really say while Mack's cock was buried up his arse?

Her eyes were wide as saucers and she had a tall glass of lemonade in her hand. "I thought you might be thirsty, working up such a sweat," she whispered, eyes flicking to Mack.

A heavy silence fell around them.

"After all the shit I said to you, you came back with fucking lemonade?" Mack's voice was half-strangled.

Calla gulped and looked down.

"I'll just go—" Calla started but Mack cut her off.

"You aren't going anywhere. You're gonna sit your ass down right here," Mack pointed to a bench beside them, "and take off your overalls."

Liam swung his head to glare at Mack over his shoulder. "Don't you fecking talk to her like that."

Mack's nostrils flared. "So you're the only one I can order around like my little bitch?"

Goddamned bastard. Liam didn't know what to say to that. He didn't know why he'd spread himself when Mack asked. Not thinking had been the whole damn problem. When Mack had him pinned, so easily taking him down…

Jaysus. Liam's cock just got harder and harder with every ounce of force Mack used to hold him to the floor. When Mack had pulled his jeans down, Liam's cock went fucking stone.

He'd had the condom in his pocket in case things got hot and heavy with Calla again. How screwed up was it that it was now on another man's cock—one that just happened to be buried in his arse?

And yeah, he'd been with men before, but was always the top. Every single time. Sometimes he used toys in his arse, sure—prostate stimulators were fucking magic if you knew how to use them.

But he'd never let anyone else in there. Ever.

He took power.

He didn't give it.

So why today, of all fucking days? And why Mack, of all fucking people?

"Sit." Mack looked back at Calla, jerking his head again at the bench.

Calla came forward and sat.

"Take off your overalls and finger yourself while you watch us fuck."

Jaysus Christ, did he have to be such a crude bastard? Then again, maybe that was part of what was making Liam so hard. Liam had often been just as much of an arsehole with the people he screwed, back in the day. He didn't know why it was so different with Calla. Maybe because he actually respected her?

Calla's breath hitched, but the next second she undid the straps of her overalls.

"Take your shirt off."

Liam could see her hands trembling as she reached down for the bottom of her shirt and pulled it off over her head. She was wearing a sports bra that all but flattened her breasts. She covered herself awkwardly with her arms.

"You're beautiful," Liam encouraged but Mack just snapped, "Bra too."

Mack pushed back into Liam's arse as Calla's bra came off. Liam let out a low hiss and his hand dropped to his own cock.

"See how bad he wants it?" Mack asked Calla. "He loves getting his ass fucked." Mack gave Liam's arse cheek a smack.

Liam glared over his shoulder at Mack, his hand still moving up and down his own shaft. "You're fecking pushin' it."

Mack lazily sawed his cock in and out and oh Jaysus— He was hitting that spot just right and— Jaysus, Mary and *Joseph* that felt good.

Liam's head tipped back, mouth slack. He jerked himself harder.

Calla's quick gasps filled the barn and Liam glanced over at her. Her hand disappeared into the pool of denim at her waist and her back arched, thrusting her pale breasts out.

"Pinch those pink little nipples," Mack ordered.

The hand not massaging herself pinched one nipple than the other. She obeyed each of Mack's commands so eagerly. So it wasn't only Liam that responded to Mack being a jackass.

And watching her at the same time Mack thrust in again. Liam worked his cock quicker than ever. "I'm gonna c—"

"Don't you dare." Mack's hand came down hard on his arse. The stinging bite of it mixed with everything else he was feeling. Liam's hand fisted around his cock, squeezing the tip roughly. Shite. He didn't know how much longer he could hold off.

Mack grunted with effort as he drove mercilessly into Liam. Liam watched Calla as Calla watched them.

She'd leaned over like she was trying to see the exact spot where Mack entered Liam. Shite. It was all good, so, so good.

"Hands and knees," Mack said to Calla. "Crawl over to us."

Liam clenched on Mack, angered and even more turned on by his every word. Calla blinked and then she dropped down to the ground.

At least she still had the pants of the overalls on so her knees wouldn't get dirty.

And then, shite. She actually crawled toward them, her breasts full and swinging as she came.

Mack reached for her when she got close, taking her arm and urging her up. Liam looked over his shoulder and watched as Mack kissed her hard. Never once did he lose his rhythm pounding away at Liam's arse.

It was only when Liam said, "I want her too," that Mack pulled back and pressed his forehead to Calla's for the briefest moment. Then they stared at one another. Liam couldn't read the emotion on their faces. Whatever it was, it was intense. Jealousy growled through his stomach. He wasn't sure if it was for Calla or for Mack.

"Kiss him," Mack said, eyes breaking from Calla's only long enough to nod to Liam.

Calla leaned in and gave Mack another quick kiss before she dipped down to Liam. Liam twisted his head toward her and met her lips. They were warm and wet from where Mack had just kissed her. Liam's tongue thrust inside. He wanted to claim her. To take her. To own her.

"Sit," Liam said. "Here." He gestured for her to sit close to him, right beside where he was on his hands and knees. "Touch me."

He took the hand she'd been pleasuring herself with and dragged it underneath him to his cock. Her hand squeezed around him and he almost choked. He reached for her center.

"Jaysus, she's wet," he hissed before leaning over to kiss her again even as his forefinger slipped inside her.

She let out a quick moan before kissing him back. Her tongue danced inside his mouth, out to tease at his lips, then back in to tangle with his tongue again. It was like she wanted everything at once, she was so fecking eager.

There were no games with her. No façades. She was just beauty. Just sweetness. Innocent in spite of all the ways they wanted to debauch her. His thumb circled her clit and she gasped, eyes dropping closed as Liam worked her.

But suddenly that wasn't enough. He hadn't put his mouth on her since the first night. He didn't just want to touch her. He wanted to taste her.

Mack leaned over his back and Liam's eyes shot open. Jaysus, that angle. Mack's cock brushed Liam's prostate with every thrust.

Shite, he wanted to taste Calla before it was too late. He wanted to be buried in the scent of her when he lost it.

"Lay back," Liam managed between gulping breaths. He moved his hand from Calla's pussy to her hips to help urge her down in the direction he wanted. She crab-walked backwards a little bit and Liam tugged her overalls down, exposing her slick cunt.

Behind him, Mack put his hand on the back of Liam's head and shoved him down into Calla. Liam didn't have any qualms about taking this unspoken order. And just knowing Mack wanted the same thing, shite, it made it even hotter.

Liam licked up Calla's center and then latched on her clit. He wasn't wasting any time. He wanted her right on the edge with him. Liam leaned down to steady himself on one elbow, clutching her hip with one hand while he dropped the other back to his cock.

He glanced up Calla's body and saw her eyes flicking up and down between Mack and Liam like she couldn't decide who she wanted to look at.

What was on Mack's face? Some superior smirk? Or was he as lost in pleasure as Liam and Calla?

And why did Liam want the second to be true so desperately?

Calla's legs started shaking underneath Liam's mouth. She was about to come. Liam could feel it. Taste it. He focused in on her clit, moving the tip of his tongue back and forth across her swollen bud.

Right as her legs stiffened and she started coming, Mack suddenly pulled out of Liam and with his hands on his hips, rolled Liam onto his back.

Calla let out a little whine at her denied orgasm.

"What the—" Liam started, but then Mack came forward, chest to chest, and shoved up his arse again.

Liam's eyes shot open.

Holy *fuck*.

Mack's cock had only been grazing his prostate before. But in this position, the head of Mack's cock hit the nail square on the head.

"Up," Mack growled and Liam blinked, trying to see through the haze of pleasure. Did he mean—

Calla got to her knees, then to her feet. Mack grabbed her hand and tugged her over to where he crouched on his knees, cock up Liam's arse. Then he jerked her overalls all the way down.

"Step out."

Calla stepped free of the pile of denim and then Mack's hands were on her hips, positioning her so she straddled Liam's body, her pussy right in Mack's face. Her hands landed on Mack's head as he dived in.

Son of a bitch wanted her pleasure for himself. Mack had stopped thrusting while he'd arranged Calla, but then he started up again.

And all the breath left Liam in a great whoosh because Jaysus fucking Christ— His spine lit and he grabbed his cock, jacking himself furiously while Mack thrust so that his cock hit the jackpot every single time.

"Oh God," Calla cried and Liam felt like shouting along with her. It. Was. Hitting. So. Fucking. Hard.

Cum spurted all over Liam's hand and he tugged himself even harder. Prostate orgasms were usually intense but this went beyond the—

He groaned in pleasure as he milked the last of his cum from his cock. He looked up at Calla's soft round arse as she grabbed Mack's shoulders and trembled against him, her whole body taut a long moment before relaxing.

Only then did Mack shove himself in and out of Liam's ass more brutally than ever until finally he thrust in and stopped, then pulled out and pushed in again one last time. Liam clenched around him, imagining Mack's cum filling the condom.

When Liam looked back again, he saw Mack had collapsed into Calla, his arms going around the back of her thighs in an embrace.

And in that moment, as Mack's cock slipped from Liam's backside, Liam felt horribly disconnected to both of them. Like he was just a prop in the Calla and Mack show. Useful to be, well, *used*, but not for anything else.

It was a position Liam had found himself in far too many times before. People had used him for his money all his life. Occasionally for his body *and* his money—or rather, they used his body as a means to get at his money.

He didn't even know why he was being such a pussy about it. He'd just gotten laid. What the hell was there to complain about? Well, other than the hard-packed dirt of the floor underneath him and shite, his back was getting scratched to all hell by the hay scattered on the ground. So it was just another hard and dirty fuck. So what? He'd had plenty of those in his life. What was one more?

He crawled out from between Calla's legs.

But before he got very far, she turned and dropped to his side. She wrapped her arms around Liam's waist, her forehead to his chest. She clutched him hard.

She was warm. For a second, that was all he could think. Her skin was soft and so, so warm.

She wanted him. He was more than a prop to her.

And Mack?

Liam's eyes flicked over to him.

Mack was jerking up his athletic shorts and stumbling away from them. Calla's head turned until both of them were watching Mack. Waiting to see what he would do next.

20

CALLA

"Oh no you don't." Calla sprung up to her feet. "You aren't pulling a runner again." She marched over to Mack and got in his face. A voice in the back of her head was screaming, *oh my God, you're naked!* But the rest of her was too pissed to care.

"You wanted what happened here just as much as we did." Calla crossed her arms. "Don't even try denying it."

Mack's eyes followed the action of her arms and then paused there. Was he seriously checking out her boobs right now? *Men.*

"Just proving my point here, pal." She snapped her fingers in front of her breasts to get his attention.

Mack's eyes jerked guiltily up to hers and then his jaw went hard.

"Let me guess," Liam stood up, pulling his jeans on as he went. Yeah, that was probably the dignified way to go in this situation. Clothes. Still, she wasn't about to give up her ground now.

"This is the part where you tell us we're just good for a fuck but that's it?" Liam continued. "Or some other equally arseholish remark?"

Mack's eyes cut to Liam. "And if it is?"

"Bullshit." Liam took a step toward them. "Why can't you just admit it? There's something here but you're terrified of it."

"I'm not afraid of anything." Mack glared at Liam.

Liam smirked. "He says as he runs away with his tail between his legs."

Mack took a step forward like he wanted to punch Liam again. "You don't know what the fuck you're talking about."

Calla stepped between them. "So tell us." She placed a hand on Mack's chest, which glistened with sweat and little bits of dust and dirt from their vigorous activities. She didn't want to think what a mess she must be. She focused in on Mack's eyes.

"Liam's right. There's something here between us. All of us." She glanced Liam's way before moving her eyes back to Mack. "Something special. Something good." It was an echo of Mack's words that first day and she hoped she was getting through to him. "Life's too short not to grab ahold of something good before it's gone."

By the way the hard lines of Mack's face went soft, she could tell he remembered. His eyes were full of pain, though. "Not sure I got any special to give." He stepped forward and ran his thumb down her cheek. "This ain't where my road is headed, sweetheart. I meant it when I said I'm leaving in three months."

He was wrong about the special, Calla was sure of that. Calla had known a lot of folks in her life and never come across special the likes of Mackenzie Knight or Liam O'Neill. Still, Calla nodded. "So give us three months."

It just popped out of her mouth. She hadn't thought it through. But Mack was right about grabbing hold of good before it was gone. God knew it was the way she ought to be living her life. She never knew when life as she knew it could be over. And it would be cruel to ever get in a real relationship without telling the person there was every chance she was a ticking time bomb just waiting to explode their lives. No, even the damn fortune cookie knew it was smarter to live life the way Mack was suggesting.

No future. No tomorrow.

"We take it a day at a time," she said, reaching out for Mack's hand. "But we live the hell out of every moment while we've got it."

"You don't know what you're asking," Mack bit out, his hands balled into fists. Calla grabbed hold of it anyway. Liam's head was swinging back and forth, looking to her, then Mack. Calla grabbed Liam's hand in her other one, connecting the three of them.

Mack just stared down at their hands for a moment. And then, with a full body sigh like he was giving in against his will, Mack interweaved his fingers with hers.

Calla pulled both of their hands to her chest over her heart so Mack and Liam's knuckles touched.

"So we're all in?" She looked back and forth from Liam to Mack.

Liam's eyebrows wagged up and down. "Ménage with benefits till we get sick of each other? Count me the fuck in."

Mack rolled his eyes but nodded.

Calla grinned brilliantly, pulling both of them close and hugging them at the same time. Her heart raced with a happiness so full she felt high with it. She was elated. Ecstatic. Euphoric.

And when it ended?

And if the test results came back positive?

And if she slowly lost her mind? With no family? No money? Nothing to live for?

She shook her head and let all the negative thoughts go with it. She kissed first Liam and then Mack.

Live each day like it's your last, motherfuckers.

21

MACK

Mack didn't know why he hadn't immediately said hell no to Calla's ridiculous proposal that day in the barn two weeks ago. He ought to be focused only on his training. Every minute spent hardening his mind and body so he'd be ready when he came face to face with that evil fuck.

But then he'd think about what Calla was offering and, well, if there were no strings... He could still leave in three months. No harm, no foul. Friends with benefits, that's what Liam called it, right?

Except Mack didn't have friends. So what the fuck was he doing?

Well, for one, he was standing in Liam's room just like he did almost every night, watching Calla slip through the door.

Liam had the biggest bed so his room had become the unofficial fuck pad. It wasn't every night—sometimes after a day of hard work, one or the other of them fell asleep while waiting for the rest of the household to go to bed. But more nights than not, they'd meet up in Liam's room by the light of Liam's dim nightstand lamp.

"Shirt off, gorgeous," Mack said to Calla, his throat dry. This was the moment every day that Mack lived for. Watching Calla's jeans or overalls fall to the floor. Or on a day like today when she'd showered before she came, watching her strip her oversized sleep shirt off over her head. Mack's cock stiffened at the sight of her full, pert breasts.

This was what it always came down to, wasn't it? Strings or no strings, he didn't fucking care. He was a selfish piece of shit. He wanted this. Wanted it bad. Some part of him whispered, *you deserve to be happy in the time you have left.*

Which just proved what a son of a bitch he was. It was attitudes like that driving all the entitled fucks he hated. Using other people for their own pleasure or gain. Stomping all over anyone in their path to take what they wanted.

Liam got up from the bed where he'd been lounging and took a step toward Calla. He was in sweats and a shirt.

Mack glared his way. Speaking of rich entitled assholes. "You too," he said. "Strip."

Liam smirked at him. Then he stepped out of his sweatpants and boxers and tossed them to the ground, revealing his fully hard cock. When Liam moved to Calla and wrapped one arm around her, his shaft bobbed against her hip and she shivered, her gaze lifting to his.

Rebellious, stubborn little fuck. Liam hadn't taken his shirt off and Mack knew it was on purpose. He was always finding little ways to avoid doing what he was told. Mack stretched his neck and cracked his knuckles.

Liam drew Calla toward the bed. They slipped underneath the covers and he began kissing and caressing her. Mack pushed down his boxer-briefs and then got in on Calla's other side. He rubbed his hands down Calla's back, grabbing her ass and flexing his hips forward to grind his hard cock between the cheeks.

Calla gasped into Liam's mouth and pressed her ass back against Mack. Mack reached around to tease her with his fingers and found Liam's hand already there. He growled as he nipped at Calla's shoulder.

Then he rolled her so that she was facing him, her breasts against his chest. Liam immediately tugged so she was on her back, though, and he moved on top of her. Mack's jaw set when he glanced down and saw the other man already had a condom on.

So he thought he'd be the first to have Calla tonight, did he?

This was the routine they'd fallen into. Calla in the middle with them on either side, seducing her until they took turns fucking her sweet little cunt. Occasionally one of them would take her mouth while the other fucked her. Either way, she usually came three or four times each session. Sometimes they could tease her into one of her mega-orgasms that seemed to last for minutes with multiple peaks. She was fucking magnificent.

But Mack knew there was so much more to explore. Like they'd begun doing in the barn that day. A hundred combinations and ways of seeking pleasure. If only Liam weren't such a proud little shit. He was depriving Calla of all the experiences she deserved.

It was time to put it to an end.

"Sit up for me, honey," Mack said, grabbing Calla's waist and tugging her up the bed even though he could tell Liam had been about to thrust inside her.

Calla scooted up the bed. She was always so eager to listen and explore. Fucking beautiful.

Liam glared Mack's way and he smirked.

"I want to teach you something tonight," Mack said, then leaned in to drop a quick kiss on her lips. He got distracted for a moment by her little tongue darting out and he couldn't help deepening the kiss.

Then she moaned into his mouth, her lips going slack in the way they did when she was nearing the brink. Damn, Mack knew he was a good kisser, but he'd never made a woman come before by just kiss—

Wait a second. Mack looked down Calla's body and sure enough, there was Liam, eating her out like she was his last fucking meal.

Goddammit. Mack kept on kissing her. He wouldn't deny her the quick orgasm Liam was bringing her to. But it could be so much better. This constant grab for power between himself and Liam made for sloppy scenes that didn't have the careful build-up and release that would be so much more satisfying for all of them.

And he wasn't going to sit around allowing this bullshit to continue.

After Calla clenched and cried out, one hand grasping Mack and the other reached down to Liam's head, Mack pulled her up and into his arms where he sat.

"Like I said," Mack glared Liam's way, "I want to teach Calla something tonight."

"What?" Calla asked, eyes bright, only a little breathless from her orgasm. Her first orgasms of the night were usually short, quick little affairs like that one that got her primed. It was the second and third that really had explosive power.

Liam rolled to his side to look at them. Mack didn't miss the resentment in his eyes at having Calla pulled away from him.

"Usually you're at the center, gorgeous. But tonight I want to try a little something different. I want you to feel what we feel. Taking you there. Making you ride that edge."

Her eyebrows furrowed. "How?"

Mack's eyes went to Liam. "By Liam being the center tonight. I want to teach you how to worship him."

Calla's eyes dilated as she looked to Liam and she bit the bottom corner of her lip like she did when she was aroused.

Liam obviously recognized it too because he didn't automatically reject the idea outright. His eyes flicked between Calla and Mack. "How? What do you mean?"

"You'll see," Mack said. "Lay down in the center of the bed."

Liam looked uncertain. "Why don't we just—"

"Lay down."

Liam's nostrils flared. "Fine." His movements were jerky as he threw back the covers and laid down in the middle of the bed.

"Take his shirt off," Mack instructed Calla.

Calla licked her lips as her hands dropped to Liam's waist. She started to just pull it up but Mack dropped his hand to her wrists to slow her down. "Slowly. Tease him."

He demonstrated, inching Liam's shirt up and dragging the tips of his fingers across Liam's abs as he went. Calla's eyes flashed with heat when Liam let out a low hiss. She mirrored Mack's actions, caressing up and then down Liam's stomach. She teasingly ran her fingers down his happy trail to where his cock stood at rigid attention.

"You won't be needing this right now." Mack gripped Liam's shaft and tugged the condom off in one swift pull. Liam's whole body jolted at the touch.

Calla leaned over and gave the crown of Liam's cock a kiss, licking around the head. Her eyes went to Mack, seeking assurance. His whole body vibrated with the rightness of it. Yes. This is how it should have been between them all along.

Mack nodded and ran his hand down Calla's spine as she continued teasing Liam's cock with her tongue.

"Not too much now," he said, pulling her back after a few minutes. Calla stopped sucking and let Liam free from her mouth with a little *pop.*

Mack reached inside the nightstand and pulled out a tube of lubricant.

"What's that for?" Liam asked, rising up on his elbows and staring at what Mack had in hand.

"Lay back."

"Fuck you. What's that for?"

Mack handed Calla the lube. "Coat your first two fingers with that, honey."

Then he bent with his forearm across Liam's chest, forcing him back down to the bed. "You're gonna take what we fuckin' give you, you got that?"

"Says who?" Liam struggled against Mack's hold.

Mack grinned evilly. "Says me."

Then he said to Calla, his face softening. "Stick your finger in his ass, honey. Just one at first."

Calla's eyes flicked to Liam. His jaw was clenched but he nodded to her. Again Mack felt that roar of satisfaction in his chest.

"I can't— It won't go in," Calla said.

"Relax," Mack whispered to Liam.

Liam glared murderously back and Mack grinned again. Then he moved down the bed to where Calla was crouched.

Liam was on his back with his legs up, his long, thick cock laying against his stomach.

"Stroke him," Mack said. He squirted lube on his own fingers.

Calla obeyed, reaching up to pull on Liam's cock. Fucker was built like a horse. Mack's cock was just as long but not as thick. Even Mack had to admit—impressive.

"Now keep massaging all around his anus," Mack said softly. Watching Calla's small fingers pressing at Liam's ass was fucking hot, that was for sure. "Don't be afraid of hurting him. He can take it."

Mack pinched Liam's ass. Liam let out a gasp of angered surprise, but the next second, Calla's finger had slipped inside him. His head fell back against the pillow and he breathed rapidly in and out.

Calla's finger couldn't feel like that much of an intrusion. More likely it was the thought of what they were doing to him that had him on edge. Which just thrilled Mack to no fucking end for some reason.

"Now stretch him. Really ream him out," Mack instructed. Christ, Calla was beautiful, naked and bent over Liam, finger up his ass and jacking him off with her other hand.

Mack couldn't help but reaching down to give his own cock several long pulls. Fuck yeah.

Then he moved his own finger he'd coated in lube to join Calla's. He wasn't shy about wiggling his thick forefinger right in beside hers.

"Shite," Liam cursed, looking down at them.

"That's right," Mack said, stretching Liam's ass as he tugged on his own cock. "Loosen him up. You want to get two, maybe three fingers in here. I'm gonna show you where to massage a man to make him feel so fucking good, he'll fall at your feet."

Calla tongue flicked out to wet her lips as her eyes rose to Mack's. "I don't know about the falling to my feet part." She looked up to Liam. "But I do want to make you feel good."

She rubbed her thumb over the tip of Liam's cock, collecting precum and then massaging it in as she tugged up and down on his shaft.

"That's right," Mack whispered. "We want his pleasure to override every other single thing in the universe. You can do that. You have that power, gorgeous. We're getting him good and stretched now." Mack swirled his finger around inside the hot glove of Liam's ass one more time before pulling out. "Add two more fingers and then I'll tell you what to do, honey."

Calla nodded. She slipped a second finger in beside the first.

Mack's chest pumped up and down as he watched. "Now a third."

Christ, his mouth was dry watching her.

She edged a third finger up Liam's ass. Liam groaned but it wasn't in pain. His cock was rock hard in Calla's hand.

"About three or four inches in, feel along the front wall." Mack tapped right above Liam's cock to indicate which wall he meant. He dropped his hand down to play with Liam's balls while Calla bit her bottom lip in concentration.

Liam cried out, his whole body going tense. He threw his forearm over his mouth and groaned into it, hips thrusting his cock rapidly up and into Calla's hand.

"I'd say you found the spot."

Mack reached and took over masturbating Liam. But instead of jerking him off, he squeezed the head. Liam's face was pained when he looked down at them.

"Don't come yet," Mack warned. "Not until I say so."

He could tell Liam wanted to balk—most likely to tell him to fuck off. Mack squeezed his dick harder. "We're trying to teach Calla how to give and receive the most pleasure. And that means showing her how discipline can lead to even higher climax."

Liam's mouth went into a hard line but he finally dropped his head back to the pillow, eyes squeezing shut.

"Good boy," Mack murmured with a smile.

"He's gripping me so tight," Calla whispered, eyes wide and excited.

"You like that?" Mack asked.

She nodded.

"Is it making you hot?"

She nodded again.

"Show me. Open those legs wide. I want to see you dripping you're so wet."

A little shudder went through her as she went up on her knees, one hand on Liam's upraised knee to brace herself, her other hand buried up his ass.

"You can touch yourself, Liam, but stop if you're getting too close."

Liam didn't open his eyes, but he nodded and his hand dropped to his cock.

Fuck, that was a hot picture. Finally they were both under his control. Exactly where they were meant to fucking be.

Mack moved behind Calla, so close to the edge of the bed that he put one foot on the floor. He slid a finger to her pussy to see if she was ready for him and Christ, she was fucking sopping.

"I want to feel you, honey. You know I'm clean. You trust me to pull out?"

"Yes." She nodded, leaning over to lick the tip of Liam's cock as he jacked himself. The move only had her exposing her pussy to him further.

He didn't hesitate lining up his cock and pushing inside her. Fuck. Fuck. She felt so good. Squeezing on him like that. So hot. And tight. Fucking *tight*.

He looked on as she moved her finger in and out of Liam's ass and his face was just absolutely fucking destroyed with pleasure.

And Mack almost forgot to follow his own goddamned advice and spilled right that second. But he got hold of himself and forced it back. No. Not yet. He wanted this feeling to go on forever. To fucking live in Calla's cunt.

He'd never get tired of watching her finger fuck Liam's ass. Never lose the high of knowing they were both at his fucking mercy.

Shit. The idea had him so fucking hard. He grabbed Calla's hips and started jackhammering away.

"Oh," she cried in the breathy way she did right before she was about to come. Angle he was taking her at, he knew he was hitting her G-spot and it would be a big one. "Mackenzie. Oh. *Oh!*"

She was getting so loud he had to wrap a hand around her mouth to stifle her cries as he fucked her through her orgasm.

"Can I come?" Liam asked, voice hoarse as he watched them, hand working his cock hard and furious.

"No."

Liam groaned and writhed on the bed at being denied.

Calla's screams reached the highest pitch. Even muffled by Mack's hand, it was still clear enough she was hitting her peak.

His spine lit on fire and everything in him wanted to fucking explode.

No. Not fucking yet.

Calla finally went limp after long seconds of climax.

Mack didn't waste any time. Right as she came down, he pulled out of her and moved around the bed.

"Open," he demanded, fisting his cock and positioning it right in front of Liam's face. "Suck her juices off me."

There was only the briefest flash of opposition in Liam's eyes. Mack smacked Liam's cheek with his cock at the hesitation.

"Suck her off me or you don't get to come."

Liam's nostril's flared but he opened right up.

"Massage him good, honey," Mack called to Calla. "We're gonna make him feel better than he ever has in his whole fucking life."

"Yes," Calla said, sitting back on her haunches but narrowing her eyes in focus on Liam's hole. So fuckin' hot.

Mack fed his cock into Liam's waiting mouth. As soon as the tip of his cock hit Liam's tongue, he almost fucking lost it again.

Fucking Liam in the barn that day had been good, but this felt like it would finally put Liam in his place once and for all.

"Eyes on me," he snapped.

Liam's eyes lifted. Mack had expected more rebellious defiance. Instead, he saw... vulnerability. Liam's blue eyes were so wide and clear. Mack had called him boy before just to put him in his place. But suddenly he seemed like he was. Much younger than his twenty-seven years. And Mack felt the oddest protective sensation.

Which was just...

Mack shook his head at the sensation. He focused instead on his desire to simply dominate the fuck out of him. He wasn't gentle when he grabbed the back of Liam's head and shoved his cock to the back of his mouth, into his throat.

Liam's blue eyes went wide.

But he didn't choke. Or yank away. Instead he relaxed and took everything Mack had to give him.

And suddenly Mack was the one fucking breaking.

"Come," he growled, and like the order had been issued at himself, he immediately climaxed. It hit like a fucking freight train.

His cum shot down Liam's throat. Liam swallowed convulsively and his eyes stayed on Mack's even as his whole body arched.

They were coming at the same time. At the same goddamned time.

And then Mack heard Calla's muffled cry. When he glanced her way, he saw that she had her hand buried in her sex. She was coming with them, even as ropes of cum spurted from Liam's cock all over his stomach.

Fuuuuuuuuuuuuck. Mack clenched his teeth to hold back his roar as he mastered the whole fucking universe. Because there was nothing else in the world except his girl and his boy. And they were fucking *his*.

It was perfect.

Everything was fucking beautiful...

...

...

...

And then all his cum was spent and Bone's face flashed through his mind. Then Ben, lying lifeless in the yard under the bright noonday sun. He hadn't been there to witness it but he'd imagined it enough times for him to know just what the scene must have looked like.

He jerked back from where Liam and Calla had collapsed on the bed. Calla had crawled up so that she was cradled in Liam's arms. She looked toward him, a contented satiated smile on her flushed face.

Little beads of sweat dotted her forehead and she'd never looked more beautiful.

She held out her arms for Mack.

So innocent. So pure.

"Stay tonight." This from Liam who usually couldn't boot him from the room fast enough. "Please." Liam swallowed and Mack could see how much it cost him to ask it. Whatever had happened between them tonight, Mack wasn't the only one who'd felt it. "Stay," Liam repeated.

And that was when Mack knew he had to shut this shit down.

One night didn't change reality.

He was the shit from the wrong side of the tracks that people like Liam barely even glanced at or acknowledged as they passed by. He was the dumb fuck who couldn't even do the job right when he went to punish the fucker who'd been beating on his mom. He was the ex-convict who'd let himself become a victim in prison. And he was the sad sack of shit who got Ben killed. Never able to protect the people he cared about.

So even though he wanted more than anything to go curl up behind both of them and sling his arm across both their waists, he took a step back instead.

He was allowing himself the escape of being with them, but it could only ever be sex. Sex the way he dictated. He was aware it made him an asshole to want it both ways—control in the bedroom but no attachment beyond that.

Maybe if he stepped back, Liam and Calla could really have something. If he weren't in the middle complicating the hell out of things. They looked good spooned together there on the bed. Like they fit with each other

His back stiffened at the thought. He wasn't sure if he was more jealous for Calla or Liam.

Fuck it. They were both his for now. But that didn't stop him from turning his back on them.

"Got an early morning tomorrow," was all he said before he turned and left the room.

22

CALLA

"ALL RIGHT, Paint, let's show 'em what we can do." Calla smiled as she opened the back of the trailer to let Painter out. Today were trail trials, a laid-back competition at a wilderness park just outside of Casper. People came from all over Wyoming to try out their newly trained horses in public for the first time.

Calla could hardly believe two months had passed since she'd gotten Painter.

Then again, they said time flew when you were having fun. And the last two months had been the best of Calla's entire life. She spent her days doing chores and training Painter. And her nights... she blushed. Well, suffice to say, as much as she'd fallen in love with Painter, she spent the daylight hours counting the minutes until she got to be alone with Liam and Mack.

She shook her head. She couldn't be thinking about all that right now, though. This was her first chance to try Painter in a competition setting and prove to herself and everyone else that she had a real shot at that hundred thousand dollars next month.

She took a deep breath and closed her eyes. Alright. She didn't want to get cocky. But there was nothing wrong with being confident.

Today in the trials, riders would be judged on a series of ten to twelve obstacles all along a trail in the woods. The obstacles could be anything from logs in the path to navigating around a group of noisy campers to having to open a gate while astride your horse. Calla had never been on this particular trail but she'd been training Painter on dealing with unfamiliar situations and the mare caught on quickly to everything Calla threw at her.

Not to brag or anything, but Calla basically had the best, most genius mustang of anyone in the whole dang makeover. Facts were just facts.

Calla grinned, then clicked her tongue while she held onto Painter's lead. Painter stepped calmly down from the trailer.

"Good girl," Calla praised, rubbing down her withers. "What a good girl you are."

In the trailer beside hers, Mack tugged on his lead several times until finally his horse poked his nose out the back end of the trailer. Mack held an apple in his hand to coax Torpedo all the way out.

Several more trailers behind her, all she heard was Liam's loud cussing. "You stubborn donkey, move your arse."

Calla laughed and walked Painter around the trailer. "Good girl," Calla said again, running her hand down Painter's long neck.

And then Calla froze. Her head jerked to look down at her leg.

Her thigh muscle was spasming crazily underneath her jeans.

She blinked, her breath catching. She flexed her leg and the muscle stopped jumping. She breathed out.

Then it started up again.

Calla shook her leg and jumped up and down. She grabbed her foot from behind and pulled it toward her butt to stretch her quads.

After a few seconds stretching, she let go and stared at her thigh.

Painter shifted and snorted beside her, nosing at Calla.

"Hush," Calla muttered, shooing Painter away as she glared at her leg. Would it spasm again? If it did, did that mean—? Was this the first sign that she had Huntin—?

"Well look what we have here. The tomboy slut shows her face in public."

Calla squeezed her eyes shut at the voice coming from behind her. "Not now, Bethany."

"What'd you have to do to earn the gas money to get here? There are five guys who work out there, right? Do they each like, have a night? Or do they just fuck you whenever they want? Or all at once? Jesus, that's be a five-some. Or a six-some if you count that mutant-freak giant who runs the place. I'm surprised you're still walking upright."

Calla spun around, ready to let Bethany have it when she heard someone beating her to the punch.

"I've met some real bitches in me life," Liam said from behind Bethany, his horse in tow. "But don't think I ever met one as maggoty as you."

"Wait, no," Bethany sputtered, spinning around. "I was just— That was out of context." She laughed and waved a hand. "Calla and I just joke around like that sometimes. Crude, but you know—" She waved her hand again, eyes wide and desperate. "It's just a joke. Calla knows that."

"That true?" Liam asked Calla.

Calla glared at Bethany. "No. She's just a bitch." She clicked her teeth at Painter and led her away from Bethany, who kept sputtering about how it was all a misunderstanding.

But Calla didn't feel any vindication at finally having a witness to Bethany's true character.

Her leg. She kept sneaking glances down at her thigh as she walked. She didn't think it was spasming anymore. It was hard to tell while she was walking.

People get muscle spasms for all kinds of reasons. Dehydration. Not having enough magnesium in their diet.

"You all right, baby? Don't let anythin' that slag said get to ya."

Calla nodded jerkily. "Oh, I'm fine."

"Are you sure?"

"Just got us all signed in." Mack came over to them. "We're up in fifteen with the second group. I've just got to get Torpedo from where Xavier's holding h—" He paused, looking between Liam and Calla. "What's wrong. Did something happen?"

"Yeah, some blonde skank came around telling Cal—"

"Nothing," Calla cut Liam off. "Just some trash talking. That's all." She narrowed her eyes at Liam. "Let's just focus on the competition. Clear heads."

Mack's eyes softened. "You got this, babydoll." He reached out and tucked a stray hair behind her ear. "Nothing to worry about."

"Hell yeah, she's got it. Now, second place is a different story. Hopefully there are enough police nearby to hold back the rioting when an Irishman walks away with the trophy."

Calla rolled her eyes while Mack scoffed. "I'm shocked you managed to get that animal off the trailer. Look at her." Mack gestured to Liam's horse. "She looks like she's gonna bolt any second."

Calla glanced Mistress's way and Mack wasn't wrong. The way her eyes were wild and searching, it was obvious all the noise and fuss of the field where everyone had parked was putting her on edge. Calla kept telling Liam he needed to do more desensitizing training with her.

Liam's eyes narrowed at Mack. "Sometimes it's all about the superior rider."

Calla shook her head. Seeing them today, she'd hardly believe these were the same two men who'd been caressing each other and sharing such intimate experiences as little as three nights ago. Calla had been going to bed early to get ready for the trials but the boys were always like this. Everything a competition. But when they stepped in the bedroom, it was like they became different people. Or maybe that was the *real* them and all this bluster was the façade.

Calla glanced down at her thigh again. It was still.

Okay. It was just a false alarm. Right? Her throat went dry.

Today. Today is all that matters.

And today she was going to show that she was training up a prizewinning mare. Time to get her head in the game. "Where's the starting area?"

The guys stopped glaring at each other long enough for Mack to gesture behind him toward a cluster of people and horses.

Twenty minutes later, Calla, Liam, Mack and a group of about five others that unfortunately included Bethany grouped together near the start of the trail.

"Ready," the trail master called out, "Set. Mount up and go!"

Calla put her foot in the left stirrup and smoothly hiked herself up into the saddle. She only spared one glance behind her to see Liam get his foot in the saddle and then his horse started forward before he could get his leg over. He jumped back to the ground and tried again with the same result. He didn't give up and drop back down this time, though. He held on, standing with one foot in the stirrup as Mistress turned in circles, teeth snapping in Liam's direction.

Calla turned forward, trying to choke back her laugh. She clenched her thighs around Painter to get her moving, noting both Bethany and Mack and a couple others already had their seats too.

"Stand still, you manky mongrel," she heard Liam growl as Calla urged Painter into a trot down the trail head. She was third but the path was wide for a little while and she quickly passed a man and headed for the leader. Bethany's long blonde ponytail bobbed ahead in the distance.

"Let's go, Paint. We got this."

They were almost on Bethany's heels before she looked over her shoulder to glare at Calla. Her mouth dropped open and she looked infuriated before her long ponytail whipped around as she looked forward again.

Just in time, too, because they were coming up on the first obstacle. The trail narrowed slightly and several downed trees had been laid across the trail. Bethany barely stopped in time for her horse not to trip but Calla had plenty of time to transition Painter from a trot to a walk.

Bethany had brought out a crop and was smacking the back of her mustang's rump, finally urging her over the first log.

Ignore her. Painter was all that mattered right now.

Calla clicked her tongue and made sure Painter could see the obstacles. Then, just like they practiced every day at home, she led Painter to lift her legs and feel her way over the objects in her path. Out of the corner of her eye, Calla could see the judges standing off in the trees. Probably the only thing that kept Bethany from cussing her out.

Because by the time she'd led Painter over the last tree trunk, she was in the lead. Calla allowed herself a brief smile before tightening her thighs to send Painter on down the trail. She heard noise behind her—Bethany had probably gotten her horse over the logs and more riders had arrived at the first obstacle—but she tried to block it out.

Next came a willow tree with sweeping branches that she had to guide Painter through blind. It was an exercise in trust and Painter came through brilliantly.

She didn't pause to celebrate though because even though she only looked over her shoulder a couple times and only glimpsed Bethany once, she knew Bethany would be pulling out all the stops to beat her.

She and Painter had to be perfect.

They had to be nearing the end of the trail. They'd been through nine or ten obstacles already. Calla had lost count. She'd just finished with the gate obstacle and her entire focus was on finishing strong.

The next obstacle was a rocky embankment that led down to a stream. Calla led Painter down slowly, letting her get a secure foothold with each step. By the time she was at the bottom, she heard voices behind her and rocks tumbling as other riders made it there.

Crap. She knew she'd lost time on the gate. On the stupidest thing, too. She'd had to fiddle with the damn latch because it wouldn't catch the first few times she tried it.

Calla urged Painter into the little stream at the bottom of the embankment. Her impulse was to rush but she tamped it down. Painter's safety was always primary. While the first part of the stream was shallow enough that she could clearly see the bottom, white water rushed on the far side.

It probably wasn't deep. They wouldn't make it too risky for a competition like this, but still. There weren't any streams around the Kent ranch and this was one thing she hadn't been able to train Painter for directly.

But when she gave Painter her head, she strode into the water confidently. About five feet in, it went from ankle deep to about a foot and a half, but Painter didn't even falter.

"All right, girl. Now for a little deeper." Calla leaned back in the saddle as Painter took a step into the deeper white water. Her hoof slipped and she scrambled, letting out a short squeal.

"That's all right," Calla said calmly, letting Painter come to a stop so she could feel sure-footed. Calla reached forward and rubbed her neck. "You're all right. You're all right." Then she clicked her teeth and kept her thighs firm around Painter to keep her going forward. "Just a little bit more and we're done."

She knew her staying calm and keeping on would help Painter do the same and they were closer to the far shore than the one behind them.

The clatter of rocks and voices got even louder behind Calla, followed by splashes, but she didn't look back.

Painter took an uncertain step forward. "That's right, girl. You're doing so good. Such a smart, good girl."

Calla kept talking her through it and only moments later, they'd made it to the shore.

Clapping sounded in the distance and when Calla looked ahead, she realized the end of the trail was just ahead. They'd made it. She grinned as she nudged Painter up the muddy embankment, about to urge her into a trot toward the finish line when—

A roaring horse scream from behind her had her whipping around to see what happened.

Torpedo. He was reared up on his hind legs and—

"Mack!" she screamed. Mack struggled for a moment to keep his seat on Torpedo but the horse was too spooked. Both horse and rider fell backwards into the water.

"*Mack!*" Calla dismounted and ran back into the water.

Torpedo rolled to his side and got back to his feet but Mack was still down. Bethany and her horse ran by at the same time.

"Mack!" Calla screamed again, slogging through the knee-high water to get to him. Oh God, if anything had—

She reached him at the same time he sat up, sputtering and spitting water.

"Oh my God. Mack." She flung her arms around him. She was immediately soaked but she didn't care. He could be hurt. Oh God. She yanked back and looked at him. "Are you okay? Oh God. Does anything hurt? Can you feel your toes? Follow my finger with your eyes."

She raised her forefinger and moved it back and forth in front of his face.

He grabbed her hand and pulled it out of his face. "I'm fine."

Then he winced. Obviously *not* freaking fine.

"Is he okay?" Calla looked up to see Bethany on her horse, standing in the rapids and looking back at them. Since when was Bethany human?

"I'm fine," Mack muttered, hefting himself to his feet. Water sluiced down from his body but thank God, he didn't seem to have broken anything.

"What happened?"

"Is he okay?"

More and more riders were arriving and seeing Mack unhorsed. Several of the judges had come to the edge of the stream as well.

Out of her periphery, Calla noticed Bethany take off. In the direction of the finish line. Calla rolled her eyes. So much for human.

"Are you okay to walk?" Calla asked Mack. "I'll get Torpedo."

Mack nodded, wincing again as he took a few steps into the deeper water.

"He's okay!" someone behind them called out and there were cheers and clapping.

Calla got Torpedo's lead and he walked through the stream, no problem. Mack was standing on the shore, hands on his knees.

"Are you sure you're okay?" Calla asked when she got to him.

He immediately reached for Torpedo and the horse nosed toward him like he too wanted to make sure Mack was all right.

"What even happened?" Calla asked, staring at Torpedo in bewilderment.

"Fuck if I know. He must have got spooked by that blond chick's horse when she went past. We were doing fine until then."

Bethany. Calla glared open-mouthed toward the finish line. But no. Surely she wouldn't try to— Not just to win a piddly little competition like this?

Calla shook her head, dismissing the thought. Not even Bethany was that twisted. More likely it was something in the stream that had spooked Torpedo. He hadn't been exposed to a stream like that any more than Painter had. Some horses were bound to spook easier than others. It'd be something they'd have to focus on training him with when they got back to the ranch.

Other riders streamed past them toward the finish line. So much for showing what she and Painter could do.

Then she shook her head at her thoughts. God, what if something *had* happened to Mack? It had been a nasty fall. It was only by the grace of God he was all right. It had looked like Torpedo landed right on top of him.

"You want to just walk Torpedo in?" Calla asked. "It's not too far."

Mack glowered. "The saying is literally get back up on the horse."

Calla held up her hands. "Whatever you say boss."

"That's the right attitude." He smacked her ass and she yelped. "Stop slacking. If we're not careful, Liam's gonna beat us and neither of us will ever live that down."

"Speaking of." Calla nodded over Mack's shoulder as she grabbed hold of Painter's saddle to mount up again.

Liam and Mistress had finally gotten to the stream. Where she'd stopped to take a leisurely drink. Liam's curses could be heard clear across the stream. "Come on, you poxy cow! Move!"

Calla laughed as she readjusted her seat. *Ugh*. Nothing like the feel of wet jeans on a damp leather saddle.

"He's gonna kick her flank," Mack observed, not yet up on Torpedo.

"No," Calla said. "He knows better. She's ticklish there."

Liam kept nudging Mistress with his thighs to get her moving forward, but she ignored him as if he were little more than an annoying gnat.

Mack just shook his head. "He's gonna do it."

"He wouldn't—"

Liam kicked at her flank.

Oh, Calla winced. Mistress leapt forward into the stream. Leaving Liam behind. He popped right off the back of her rump. And landed hard on his.

Ow.

"Wild-eyed bitch threw me!" Liam jumped back to his feet, holding his backside.

"Calla and Xavier have both told you a hundred times not to kick her flank," Mack called out across the stream.

Liam looked around like he was searching for the voice. When he finally located Mack, he flipped him off.

Calla groaned. "Xavier's gonna be so proud of how we're representing him today." She shook her head and turned Painter toward the finish line as more and more riders rode past. Her shoulders shrank.

People from the group that had started ten minutes *after* theirs were passing them now. So much for showing she was a contender. Calla was pretty sure she, Mack and Liam would be coming in last place.

Her future had never been less secure. She thought about her leg tremor. If she had a future at all.

Still, as Liam and Mistress came up and she saw the goofy grin on Liam's face, her heart clenched with emotion for him.

It was like this every time she felt any moment of happiness or joy. There was always the accompanying terror. It was always there. Whispering this was the best she'd have it and soon it'd all be gone.

Enough.

Calla clicked her teeth to get Painter moving as Mack and Liam started bickering about who did better in each obstacle. She looked back and forth from one man to another.

She was terrified of all the things she wanted with them. Of all the things that might never be. *Enough.* She was done living her life in the shadow of fear.

It was time to know.

It was time to get the test done.

23

CALLA

"I WANT to get the test. For Huntington's." Calla sat up straighter on the exam table at the doctor's office. Here she was. Taking the future by the balls. Or, well, at least being willing to own up to it, whatever it might hold. Other than a brief freak-out in the car—Mel let her borrow her little Camry whenever she needed to come into town— she was even managing to keep her shit together.

She fidgeted with her balled fists. Mostly anyway.

"Are you sure?" Dr. Nunez was a middle-aged woman whose hair was only going a little gray at the temple.

Calla nodded. "My employer gives us good insurance so the test would be covered."

Dr. Nunez's eyes gentled. "You know it's not paying for it that concerns me. I've referred you to a genetic counselor before. Did you ever go see them?"

Calla shook her head. "Didn't seem much point if I couldn't pay for it." If she was honest, Calla would admit she'd just taken that as an out not to learn if she was positive or negative for HD. If she had the mutated gene that would determine the course of the rest of her life. "Anyway, I'm ready now." She straightened her back. "I won't be changing my mind. It's time to know."

Dr. Nunez was quiet another moment before finally nodding. "I'll refer you to the genetic testing facility in Casper."

Calla swallowed and nodded. "Good." Then, eager to change the subject, she asked, "So how's Savannah doing with her mustang? Savannah's what, fifteen, sixteen?" There was a junior's category in the makeover and Calla knew Dr. Nunez's daughter was competing.

Dr. Nunez smiled. "She's sixteen. And the summer has been so exciting for her to get hands on experience training a horse. It's given her something else to do than just watch TV and chase boys."

Calla smiled and Dr. Nunez put her hand on Calla's shoulder. "All right, while I work on the referral I'll have the nurse come in and take some blood. You haven't been in a few years and I'd like to do a complete physical."

Calla heard what she wasn't saying. She wanted to know if she was already exhibiting any symptoms of HD. Calla already told her about her leg spasm. It hadn't happened since and Dr. Nunez seemed confident it was just a normal spasm due to the physicality of Calla's job and training schedule. The doctor also suggested she pick up some magnesium supplements. At the same time, when she'd pressed, Dr. Nunez hadn't been willing to rule out the possibility of it being an indication of early symptomactivity completely.

"Okay." She breathed out.

"And you already gave a urine sample, right?"

"Yeah."

"Great." Dr. Nunez patted her shoulder. "We'll get everything squared away."

Then she left Calla alone in the small exam room.

She was just flipping through a Horse and Rider magazine when the door opened again. Calla looked up, expecting to see the nurse.

Instead it was Dr. Nunez again. And there was something off about her expression. Calla sat up straighter.

"What? What is it?" Did she see some symptom of HD that Calla hadn't recognized? Oh God, she knew it. She just knew she had the gene—

Her eyebrows were scrunched together. "Did you know that you're pregnant?"

"What?" Calla shouted, almost falling off the exam table.

24

CALLA

CALLA FELT WOBBLY on her feet as she walked up the stairs to her dad's nursing home. She'd been living with the reality that she was pregnant for almost an entire week now. She'd been dodging Mack and Liam for most of that time.

And she had no more clue now than when she first heard what the hell she should do about it.

"How is he?" Calla asked one of her dad's nurses once she got inside. *Rita*, by her nametag.

Rita's mouth curved down as her eyebrows lowered in sympathy. "Not so good. Eating's been getting harder for him. Since he was losing so much weight, we had to put him on a feeding tube.

A feeding—? Calla blinked. "Was that really necessary?" She knew he'd been getting skinnier than usual, but still...

Rita put a hand on Calla's arm, eyes full of compassion. "You'll see."

Calla wanted to yank her arm away but managed to stop herself at the last second. She swallowed and tried not to sound like she was gritting her teeth. "Can I go in to see him?"

"Sure, honey. You know the way?"

Calla nodded and then hurried down the hallway not wanting the woman to see her face. A *feeding tube*. The whole reason she was paying this place so much goddamned money was so that they could assist her dad in things like eating when he wasn't able to do it himself. For God's sake, she knew firsthand how frustrating it could be feeding him spoonful by spoonful, especially when he wasn't in the most cheerful mood about it all. But that's what she was paying them for!

She was still steamed when she reached her dad's room. She knocked and went in. If they couldn't show they could give her father the best care possible, well then she'd take her money somewhere els—

"Daddy?" Her voice cracked when she saw her dad.

He was lying in bed, cheeks sunken and eyes staring listlessly at the television. His head and legs bobbed constantly back and forth with the shakes.

"Hi Daddy."

He looked her direction, didn't say anything, then moved his head back to face the screen.

"Whatcha watching?"

Calla looked toward the TV. "Wheel of Fortune, huh," she finally answered for him after a long silence.

"Buy a vowel," he growled at the screen.

Calla looked at the puzzle on the screen. "Daddy they've already got all the vowels up there."

He continued ignoring her as one of the contestants solved the puzzle.

"Buy a vowel," her dad repeated.

Calla's stomach sank. What if the nurse's actions hadn't been extreme. Maybe he was at the point where he needed a feeding tube. He was declining more rapidly. Every time she visited, he was worse, and she came once a week. Was her dad still in there at all?

"New job's working out real good," she tried as the show went to commercial. "Xavier's a fair boss and I'm training a mustang for the Extreme Horse Makeover. You know I always wanted to do that. I'm getting my shot at it this year. Got a great mare named Painter."

Her dad didn't say anything, just kept staring at the screen while a commercial for dishwasher soap played.

"But that's not what I really wanted to talk about today." She took a deep breath. "Daddy, I'm pregnant."

She waited a beat.

And then another.

Still nothing from her father.

She gave him another moment. Sometimes it took him longer to process things than the average person.

But Wheel of Fortune came back from commercial and still he hadn't said anything to her.

"But I don't know what to do, Daddy," she whispered, swallowing back against the tears that threatened. God, she didn't even know whose baby it was. Her cheeks burned with shame. She'd gone bare-back with Liam that time in the shower, but there'd been a couple times when Mack had pulled out early and from what she'd read online, it was rarer but still possible to get pregnant from pre-cum.

Doctors had told her for years she'd have difficulty getting pregnant if she ever tried because of her irregular cycles. For her to have ovulated at the perfect moment on any of those few specific incidents with the guys seemed so unlikely as to be, well... *miraculous*.

If only it wasn't simultaneously the worst news Calla had ever gotten in her life.

"What if the baby has it?" Calla took a step toward her dad, swiping at her eyes as she went. "I got the blood taken for the test earlier today. It'll take three weeks to find out if I test positive or not. But even if I'm negative, there's still a twenty-five percent chance the baby could still have it."

"Buy a vowel," Dad said again, eyes glued to the TV.

"Daddy." Calla swallowed hard against the tears. "Please. I don't know what to do. The father isn't planning to be in the picture." The

Horse Makeover Competition was only weeks away. Mack hadn't said anything about his plans changing. He was leaving, and it was only a matter of time before Liam moved on too.

"If it turns out I'm positive, then maybe I should think about..." Calla balled her fists and looked to the floor. God, she hated even thinking it. But what kind of life could she really give a child if she was going to get sick in a few years? At least she and Dad had had the ranch, for as long as it lasted. But her child wouldn't have anything. It would be cruel to bring them into the world knowing what was in store for—

"Did you hear me, Daddy?" she said louder. "I'm pregnant."

Another commercial came on, and still he didn't look her way.

"Dammit, Daddy, can you hear me?"

She moved to his bed and grabbed the remote from his nightstand. She pushed the power button so the TV snapped off behind her.

That definitely got his attention. He roared and reached for the remote, his movements jerky and uncoordinated. The sudden movement rolled him over in the bed. The only reason he didn't fall off was because of the side rails.

"TV," he screamed. "TV!"

Calla backed up, her thumb fumbling on the remote until she finally hit the button to turn the television back on.

"TV!"

"It's on. I turned it back on!"

Her dad kept shouting, unintelligible words occasionally interspersed with *TV*. A nurse came through the door and Calla looked at her helplessly. "I'm sorry."

"Howard," the nurse said, reaching for her dad's shaking shoulders. "Howard, look over here." She physically directed him so that he faced the television. "That's right. That's right, Howard," she soothed like he was a small child.

That was Calla's breaking point.

Not just because she knew now she'd truly lost her Dad and there might never be time to make it right between them.

But because she saw herself in that bed. Fifteen, twenty years from now. Being held down by a nurse while she spewed demented ramblings. Having lost control of her own body.

She turned around and fled like a coward.

25

LIAM

Liam pushed his extra-large cart with the pallet of feed toward the front of the supply store, looking for Jeremiah as he went. They'd headed in different directions after coming in. Jer was headed to get some wood for fence repair and Liam wondered if he'd—

"Oh hi!" came a chirpy voice. "I thought that was your truck I saw parked out front."

Liam looked down to see the fake-tanned blonde who'd insulted Calla at the Trail Trial the other day. He frowned and tried to move his heavy cart around her but she just stepped in his path again.

"It takes a lot of man to handle that much truck." She smiled flirtatiously. "I thought about getting that model but Daddy talked me into the Ford F450 Crew Cab." She rolled her eyes and shrugged. "*Yes*, it was more expensive, but I always say, never scrimp on the important things." She beamed at Liam.

"You're in me way," was all he said, gesturing to his cart.

"You're not still upset about what you overheard the other day, are you?" Her eyes went big and she put a hand to her chest. No doubt to emphasize the cleavage spilling out of the tight red top she was wearing. "I've been *so* embarrassed about that ever since. My Mama would've washed my mouth out with soap if she'd overheard me." She waved a hand. "It was just a harmless joke but I totally understand if poor Cal took it wrong. I'll apologize to her again the next time I see her. I just think of her as one of the guys but it was wrong of me not to be more considerate of her feelings."

"Anyway," she sidled closer to Liam's side, ignoring the way he jerked back when her arm brushed his. "Liam, like I said, I've felt so bad about the misunderstandings we've had the last couple times we've talked. I wanted to invite you out to my place where we could spend some alone time and really get to know each other. I've got a big stretch of land and a jacuzzi out back that will help relax these muscles."

She moved and put her hands on his shoulders.

What the— He jerked away from her touch again. Could she not get a fucking clue?

"Oh! See? You've got so much tension back there. The jacuzzi will loosen you right up." She leaned in. "I know there aren't a lot of places around here to enjoy the finer things in life, but I've got a bottle of Chateau Margaux that I have just been *dying* to split with someone who would appreciate it."

"I guess I didn't make meself clear enough last time. This is biscuits to a bear." At her confused expression, he clarified. "A waste of *time*. I will never, not ever, want to spend any time with you."

"But you wanted me," she sputtered. "That night at Bubba's. We had a connection. I know if you would just give me a—"

"Are you feckin' delusional?" he asked incredulously. Jaysus. "You were a cow to me girl, Calla. To be honest, breathing the same air as you is makin' me a bit nauseated." He scrunched his nose up to give further effect. "I wouldn't get with you if you were the last woman on earth and sleepin' with you meant the survival of the human race. I'd still find you too disgustin' to lay me hands on. Me cock would shrivel up and fall off first."

The woman's mouth dropped open and then her face went

quickly red with rage. Liam waited for the slap. Perhaps he'd taken it a tad too far there, but he wanted to get it through the poxy bitch's head once and for all.

"Did I miss something?"

The woman's head swung over to Jeremiah as he pushed his cart closer and looked between her and Liam with raised eyebrows.

"I— He—" The woman sputtered several more times before making an infuriated high-pitched noise, turning on her high-heeled boots and stalking off toward the front of the store.

Liam just shrugged his shoulders when Jeremiah leveled his gaze on him. "What?" he said. "The ladies love me. Sometimes I've got to beat them off with the proverbial stick."

"Remind me never to make you my wing man."

"Yeah, yeah," Liam rolled his eyes. "Come on, let's get going." Calla spent the day in Casper visiting her dad and Liam wanted to be there when she got back.

GETTING the rest of their supplies took longer than Liam would've liked and they didn't get home for another hour and a half. It was nine o'clock but Calla still wasn't home yet.

Liam jogged up the stairs and headed for Mack's room. Calla hadn't texted him anything, but maybe Mack had heard from her.

Liam had just pushed Mack's door open the slightest bit when he heard Mack's voice. Liam frowned, pausing. Mack never had anyone in his room. Liam leaned his ear to the door and realized it was just a one-sided conversation.

"—don't have any more info about what he's been up to since he got out?"

Silence.

"Laying low? What the fuck does that mean?"

It must be a phone conversation, because there was another brief pause before Mack's voice sounded again.

"Do you have a location or not?"

Pause.

"Okay." There was scuffling like Mack was reaching for a pen and paper. "But you don't know if he's still at Franco's or if he— Well Jesus, Sammy, what the fuck am I sending you three g's a month for?"

A sigh from Mack. "Yeah, yeah. I know. I'm sorry. This shit's just got me on edge. You know I appreciate you, Sam. Look after Brenda and Sammy Jr. I'll be in touch."

Footsteps sounded and Liam pulled back from the door. But it didn't open. Just more footsteps. Mack was pacing. He did that when he got antsy. Liam could just see the way he was probably stretching his jaw and shoulders.

He'd definitely be coming to Liam's room tonight. He always did on days he got tense like that—well, as long as Calla came first. Mack never came without Calla.

Just another one of the many mysteries that was Mack.

Along with—who was Mack on the phone with? Someone he was sending three grand a month for information. About who? Why? And where the hell did he get that kind of cash?

Liam's eyes cut back to the door and he knocked on it.

"What?" came Mack's growling reply.

Liam smirked and pushed the door open.

Mack glared his direction. "What do you want?"

Liam *tsked*. "How was your day, Liam? Oh, really? How interesting. Tell me more."

"Cut the shit." Mack narrowed his eyes.

Liam laughed out loud. "And to think," he said, closing the door behind him as he stepped into Mack's room, "it's taken me this long to learn to appreciate your bracing honesty. It's okay, big guy." He smacked Mack on the shoulder. "This is an open sharing space. Tell me how you really feel. I won't judge."

He walked past Mack further into the room when he didn't say anything. He lifted the lid of Mack's laptop. "Any good porn on here?"

Mack slammed it shut. "What. Do. You. Want?"

"Jaysus, it must be exhaustin' being so damn serious all the time."

"It's called being a grown up. You should try it sometime."

Liam gasped. "Touché." Then he dropped the act. "Have you heard from Calla? She's not back yet."

Mack's eyebrows went up, finally exhibiting another emotion than annoyance at Liam's presence.

"I've tried calling her but she's not picking up."

Mack shrugged. "You know how spotty service is around here. Even if she did have a signal, she's smart enough not to pick up while she drives. Unlike *some* people, she doesn't treat traffic laws like suggestions."

"Ha. Ha. I'm serious. She's never this late."

"What time is it?" Mack asked.

"Nine."

"I don't like it." Liam felt the hairs on the back of his neck prickle at finally admitting it out loud. He walked over to the window and put his hands around his eyes to peer out into the darkness. "Anything could happen out there on the road. The deer are fecking suicidal around here. I had two jump in front of me car just last week."

"Yeah, well," Mack said, grabbing his laptop and sitting down with it on his bed, "she's driven these roads all her life. Pretty sure she knows what she's doing."

Liam glared at Mack. "Do you have an emotional bone in your feckin' body? Our girl is out there, God knows where, and you're just gonna sit there and what?" Liam reached for the laptop again. "Check your Instagram feed?"

Mack jerked the laptop away at the last second and closed the lid again. "Why are you here again? I don't buy any of this concerned Prince Charming bullshit." He gestured Liam up and down.

"Why do ya always have to be such a poxy bastard about everything? Jaysus. Did your mother drop you on your head as a small child or somethin'?"

"That's it," Mack growled. He tossed his laptop to the side and got to his feet.

"Ooo," Liam said, putting a hand over his mouth. "The big scary man is comin' for me. Run for me life!"

Liam grinned when Mack's glare went a shade darker. At least pissin' with him would help distract Liam from worrying about Calla.

Besides, he only had a few more weeks of this. Fuckin' with Mackenzie Knight whenever he pleased. After that, Mack would move on, and it would just be him and Calla.

Which was good. It was what he'd wanted in the first place. To get the girl.

So why did the thought of never seeing the big angry bastard in front of him feel like a kick to his gut?

The thought had the smile falling from Liam's face. Did he actually *care* about—

Jaysus. *No.*

He wasn't that much of a fecking idiot. Or a masochist.

Right as Mack grabbed for Liam's shirt, Liam jumped back and heard the sound of the front door slamming below.

"Calla," he and Mack said at the same time, their gazes locking. Good. Time to put this back on familiar fecking territory. With Calla firmly between them.

They both went for the door at the same time. Mack got there first, the wanker. He met Calla halfway down the stairs.

"You okay, honey? You're late. We were worried."

Liam rolled his eyes. What a crock of shite.

He ignored Mack and joined them.

"Did you have any trouble on the road? Are you hungry? We kept a plate of food for you in the fridge."

"For Christ's sake, she just walked in the door." Mack shoved Liam to the side so he could pass by with Calla on his arm. "Let her breathe before firing twenty fucking questions."

Liam would have tried to batter the bastard, but Calla was leaning on him like she was glad for the support.

Shite. Something *was* wrong. Liam knew it. She hadn't been acting herself all week. Something was off.

"I ate on the road." Calla's voice was little more than a whisper and it sounded scratchy. Like she'd been crying. Liam's head jerked up to Mack and he nodded. He heard it too. "I'm just tired."

Why wasn't she confiding in them?

Mack didn't lead Calla to her room. Instead, he took her straight to Liam's. The rest of the guys were downstairs watching a game and at this point, Liam didn't care if anyone saw them. Calla needed them and it wasn't like the twins or Nicholas were gossips.

Liam suspected Xavier knew something of what was going on, but if he did, he wasn't saying anything about it either.

Mack led her to Liam's bed and sat her down while Liam shut the door behind them. He hurried over to Calla and sat beside her on the bed, grabbing her hand in his. It was ice cold. He rubbed it between his palms.

"Baby, what's going on? Talk to us."

"Nothing," she answered, too quickly.

"You're a bad liar," Mack said gently, pushing a lock of hair behind her ear. She wore it down more and more often.

Calla's hazel eyes flashed up to them before dropping back down to her lap. She bit her bottom lip and her throat moved as she swallowed hard. "It's my dad... he's... really sick." She covered her face with her hands and her back started shaking. "I don't think he even recognized me."

"Shh, come here." Mack pulled her into his chest. Liam moved up close against her back. Jaysus, she felt so fragile between them. Her body shook like a leaf as she sobbed.

Liam shared another worried glance with Mack and then wrapped his arms around her so that she was enclosed all the way around by them.

Finally she pulled back from Mack's chest, tear tracks fresh on her cheeks. She looked first at Mack, then at Liam.

"I just want to forget. Please. Can you help me forget for tonight?"

"Baby," Liam said, rubbing a comforting hand down her spine. "are you sure you don't want to—"

Calla turned in their arms and cut Liam off with a kiss. She wasn't shy about it either. The more nights they all spent together, the bolder she'd grown. More and more she told them exactly where and how she wanted to be touched. What made her feel good. Watching her come to life sexually had been one of the most fecking amazing things Liam had ever witnessed.

So Liam trusted her to know what she needed right now and he kissed her back. Her hands immediately started scrabbling at the bottom of his shirt. He obliged by pulling it off over his head. Her hands roamed up his chest. And then down, her deft little fingers tugging at his button.

"Jaysus, woman," Liam groaned into her hot little mouth.

Mack nestled his nose into her neck from behind. "Christ you smell good," he murmured. "Like some kind of flower."

Calla laughed a little, hiccupping as tears still fell and she turned around to kiss Mack. Liam followed and kissed the salty tears from her cheeks.

"Beautiful Calla," he whispered. "Goddess Calla."

"Come here," Mack murmured, taking her hand and tugging her in the direction of the bed. She followed, arms around his neck. She kept kissing him while they moved. Liam stayed with her too, nuzzling his nose into the back of her neck.

Mack tugged her t-shirt off over her head and Liam undid the bra clasp at her back, sliding it down her shoulders. Next Mack worked on the button of her jeans before tugging them down, too. Between them, they had her undressed in under a minute.

Mack was gentle as he pushed her back on the bed. She arched up so she could keep kissing him. It was like she couldn't bear to lose contact for even a second. She reached out for Liam the next moment, moving from Mack's lips to his.

He frowned but kissed her deep. She seemed frantic. Was it just her dad she was upset over? How long had she been crying? She'd been gone all day. He hated to think of her crying while she'd been driving the dark roads between here and Casper.

"Baby," he started but she just shook her head like she was anticipating any of the many questions he had.

"I want you tonight." She looked from Liam to Mack. "I'm ready. I want you both at the same time."

Mack's eyes shot to Liam. Did she mean—

"I've been stretching myself," she continued, eyes cast down like she was embarrassed. "Every night. I wanted it to be a surprise." Her gaze flicked between Liam and Mack. "But I can't wait anymore. I want to feel you both at once. I need it."

Shite. She *did* mean—

Mack's eyebrows furrowed. "I don't want to hurt you—"

"You won't," Calla hurried to say. "I told you. I've been stretching."

"With what?" Liam asked. Did she really know what she was asking? Did she think just stretching herself with a finger was anywhere near—

She licked her lips and looked down again. "Just a small toy. I've had it for a while."

Liam could only stare at her.

"Holy shit, that's the hottest fucking thing I've ever heard," Mack growled, grabbing Calla and kissing her roughly. Liam had to agree. Even the idea of her playing with her arse like that each night to get herself ready for them—Jaysus, his cock throbbed at the image.

Mack pulled her until they were both laying down. But then he rolled Calla so that she was facing Liam.

"Eat her out," Mack ordered Liam. "I want her cunt sopping, you hear me?"

Liam bristled at being ordered around. He mock saluted. "Yes, sir."

Mack leveled him with a glare but Liam ignored him, kissing down Calla's body. "Open up, baby," he said when he came to the apex of her thighs. He coaxed her to lift one leg and Jaysus—her scent hit him along with a wave of lust.

He licked down her cleft and buried his tongue inside her cunt.

Her body shuddered and she reached down to bury a hand in his hair. Christ, he loved how responsive she was. It wasn't just a show she was putting on for him, either. Every reaction he and Mack wrung from Calla's body was the genuine article.

He moved up to lick around her clit when her fingernails dug into his scalp. He pulled back the slightest bit and saw Mack behind her. He was doing something to her that was driving her crazy.

Shite, was that how she reacted when someone played with her arse?

Liam moved his hand around to her back entrance, wanting to feel what Mack was doing. His hand collided with Mack's. Mack didn't push him away. Liam felt down Mack's arm covered in wiry hair all the way to his hand. Then to his fingers.

Jaysus, he had two buried in Calla's arse. He'd lubed them up because they were slick. He had them shoved in past the second knuckle. He worked them in and out, in and out.

Liam sucked more furiously at her clit.

"Come for us honey," Mack growled. "Give us your first one just like this."

Calla threw her own hand over her mouth to stifle her cries as she climaxed, thrusting her cunt into Liam's face over and over.

He lapped up every drop of her, loving how crazy they could drive her. He kept sucking on her clit until her body had gone lax with only little aftershocks occasionally making her legs jerk.

He pulled back and looked to Mack.

"All right, honey," Mack said. "I'm gonna lower you on me. You need to slow down or stop, you just say so. You got me?"

Calla looked over her shoulder at Mack and nodded, biting her bottom lip.

"You nervous, baby?" Liam asked, cupping her face and drawing her back around to look at him while Mack stacked up all the pillows at the head of the bed and sat back against them.

She shook her head. "I know you'll take care of me."

Her hazel eyes were full of such trust, it about knocked Liam on his arse. Who was this girl to put so much trust in him? He was a poncy little shite who'd never appreciated all the privileges he'd been given his whole life.

Mack lifted her by her waist so she was straddling him in reverse cowgirl position. Calla crouched and Liam held her hands to help her balance. His breath quickened as he looked around her and saw Mack smear lube up and down his long cock. Then he took it and positioned himself at Calla's arse.

"Here we go, baby." Liam kissed Calla as Mack fed his cock into her arse. Liam felt the second Mack penetrated—Calla gasped and her hands squeezed Liam's.

"That's right. You're doing so good, honey," Mack said from below them. His hands were on Calla's waist, lowering her down onto himself.

"I'm going in another inch. Fuck you feel good. So fuckin' tight." Mack's voice was strained in a way Liam had never heard before.

Liam pulled back from kissing Calla to look over her shoulder at Mack. His face was red, veins standing at attention on both his neck and his forehead, it was taking so much for him to hold back.

"Look what you're doing to him," Liam whispered to Calla, kissing down her neck to her breast. "You're driving both of us insane." He rubbed his cock into her stomach. He wanted her hands on him but he didn't want to take her attention off the feel of Mack taking her virgin arse.

"Christ," Mack bit out through clenched teeth. "Calla. *Fuck*." He took a huge heaving breath as he settled Calla even deeper. Her eyes popped open wide and she gasped again, swallowing hard.

"You alright?" Liam asked.

She nodded frantically. "It's just— I've never felt anything—" She huffed out a short laugh. "It's like nothing I've ever felt before." A concentrated look came over her face.

"Christ honey, you clench on me like that again and I'm gonna fucking lose it."

Calla looked entirely pleased with herself. She was so feckin' adorable. Liam went back up on his knees so he could kiss her deep.

She wrapped her arms around him and pulled him up and into her. His cock bobbed against where she was slick and he groaned low.

"Now you," Mack said. "Take her pussy. Let her feel both of us at once."

Liam pulled away from Calla to reach over to open the nightstand drawer. He was surprised when Calla put her hand on his arm. Her

eyes were hesitant, then shadowed. "You don't have to. Wear one. I'm
— It won't—"

Liam put his hand under her chin. "Never be shy with me, baby.
You telling me it's safe because your monthly's off?"

She nodded, eyes still down.

"Baby that's the best news I've heard all week." The thought of
having her bare made his cock stiffen so much it was almost painful.

"Get inside her," Mack growled. "I need to move."

Liam smiled lazily at Mack. "Can't rush seduction." He took his
cock in hand and brushed it up and down against Calla's pussy lips.

"Jaysus, she's so wet," he whispered.

"Then get the fuck inside her. I want her stuffed full. She's ours
and she needs to know what that feels like."

Calla made a little needy whine at that and her hazel eyes were
full of need when Liam looked at her.

Feckin' hell, he couldn't stand it another second. He lifted her left
leg up and shoved home.

"*Oh,*" she gasped, her eyes going wide again.

This must be what heaven felt like. Right here, hiding in plain
sight—*heaven.* This feeling. These two people. His cock buried to the
hilt in Calla with Mack up her arse, all their limbs tangled up
together.

Liam pushed Calla's body down until she was laying back against
Mack's chest. He lifted her leg up over his shoulder, pulled back and
then thrust back in. He hissed through his teeth at how good it felt.

Calla turned her head to the side and Mack met her lips greedily.
They were both so hot. When Mack moved his hips, Liam could feel
both Calla *and* Mack— Jaysus, it was—

Calla turned back to Liam and then her lips were on his. He'd
swear he could taste Mack on her.

And it was like she read his mind. Because she pulled back from
him and cupped his cheeks. Her eyes closed and her mouth dropped
open, head tipping back as he and Mack continued fucking her. She
sucked in a quick breath and then her eyes opened. And, still holding
his cheeks, she pulled him forward.

But not to her own lips.

She put her hand on the back of his neck and pulled him until he was bent over her shoulder. Face to face with Mackenzie.

"Kiss him," Calla whispered, her chest heaving between them. "This is all of us. Feel it. Oh *God*. I want you to feel it *all*."

Liam looked to Mack, alarmed. No. He and Mack weren't like that. Sure he'd let Mack fuck him that time, and *maybe* he'd sucked Mack's dick a few *more* times—but that was just animal. Bodies fucking. That was all they were to each other.

But when Mack took over for Calla gripping the back of Liam's neck and his lips crashed against Liam's, everything he thought he knew flew out the window.

Mack's jaw was rough with five-o-clock shadow and his lips were hard and thin. Nothing like Calla's giving softness. But Mack kissed him like... Like he wanted to fucking own him.

Liam's eyes had dropped closed but they flew open again and he pulled back from Mack.

Wrong move.

Because that meant he was looking Mack straight in the eye. And what he saw there— Jaysus. Did Mack really— Want *him*? Want him like *that*? Liam blinked, confused even as he thrust even more forcefully into Calla, matching Mack's hips.

Christ. So good. Like nothing he'd ever—

"You're both mine," Mack snarled, reaching around Calla to grasp Liam's waist.

"Yours," Calla gasped, rolling and grinding her hips against Liam. "*Oh*, it's coming." Her body was slick with sweat between them.

"Give it to us," Mack said, withdrawing and then jerking his hips back up beneath her. She jolted every time and all the lines of her face went taut as she chased her pleasure.

"Not yet," Liam said, thrusting even more furiously. He looked back and forth from Calla's face to Mack's. He couldn't decide who he wanted to watch as climax came closer and closer. What he really wanted was to hold it off forever. To stay right here in this moment of before, all of them connected, right on that edge of fucking bliss with both of them.

He stilled inside Calla for a moment, focusing only on the slight friction provided when Mack's cock thrust up her arse and knocked against the wall where Liam's cock was buried. It was too much for him. He had to start thrusting after that.

"Baby." Liam had said it to Calla, but Mack's eyes met his again.

"I know," she said, lifting one hand behind her and hooking it around Mack's neck. She drew Liam close with the other.

Their heads all came together, sweat and breaths mingling. Liam's chest went tight. He didn't know what he— This all felt too—

"*Now*," Mack said.

Calla was the first to lose it. The way her pussy squeezed around Liam's cock, he couldn't help but to lunge forward as deep as he could in response. He dropped his head over Calla's shoulder. Mack met him there, kissing him, and when the very tips of their tongues touched—

Liam roared into Mack's mouth with the rush of his climax. Mack swallowed it all and drew even more out of him.

Liam pulled out and pushed in again, and then again. No. He wasn't ready to let it go. Just a little longer. A little bit more—

Calla clenched around him and he broke away from Mack so he could kiss her. After the roughness of Mack's mouth, her soft lips felt even more sensuous. He could spend a lifetime comparing and contrasting the different ways their mouths felt and tasted.

He brushed his thumb over Calla's breasts and her body gave another shudder. Liam moved his hand beneath her and traced down from Mack's collar bone to his nipple. So much smaller and tighter. He plucked at it and got a slap to the arse for it.

Liam yelped and glared at Mack. Calla laughed at them and rolled with Liam to the side. Mack was spooned behind her and she snuggled her head on his bicep. She wrapped her arm around Liam's waist and pulled him close.

Liam felt the moment Mack went to pull away. To leave like he always did. Liam's stomach swooped with disappointment.

But then, instead of pulling away from Calla, he shifted to wrap his arm more firmly around her waist.

"Roll over," he ordered gruffly.

Liam was confused for a second. Then he realized Mack was talking to him. He blinked a couple times and rolled over.

Calla scooted up against his back, notching her knees behind his. And then Liam felt the weight of Mack's arm settling over both their waists.

Liam's breath caught.

What did all this mean? And why had tonight felt less like fucking and more like making lo—

He shut down the thought before he could finish it and squeezed his eyes shut. Why the hell was he suddenly looking for meaning in shite? A shag was a shag. That was all there was to it.

But when he finally fell asleep, it was to a restless dream of charging into a burning castle to rescue a princess. Only to get trapped by the flames himself.

Until a certain brawny, tattooed fireman came in and rescued them both.

26

CALLA

"A TOAST to our three soon-to-be champions!" Mel stood up from the table and clanged the side of her glass with her spoon. It was the night before the Extreme Horse Makeover competition and they'd all come out to a nearby bar and grill on the outskirts of Denver for dinner and drinks. It was no Bubba's, but it would do in a pinch.

Almost everyone from the ranch sat around the two tables that had been pushed together. They'd all done their normal chores before coming down today and Nicholas was holding down the fort until they got home tomorrow. Mel and Xavier had even brought the kids. Reece was occupying them at the furthest end of the table, the baby in his lap.

Calla leaned into Liam's side, smiling at Mel.

"Tomorrow Mackenzie, Liam, and Calla will take their mustangs to the Extreme Horse Makeover competition."

Mel grinned at each one of them in turn. "No matter how much each one sells for at auction, you're already winners. By training these horses, you've made it so they can find forever homes instead of spending another winter starving out there or locked up in the BLM holding facilities. A round of applause to our trainers!"

The table erupted with clapping.

"And a round for the bar, on Mel's Horse Ranch!" she yelled even louder. A roar of approval came from the crowd around them, along with clapping and a few wolf whistles.

"Alright now," Xavier said, pulling Mel down into his lap. "Don't anybody be getting any ideas. This here's my woman."

"Oh I am, am I?" Mel arched an eyebrow at Xavier.

"You bet your ass, babe."

She grinned and kissed him. Long enough that the table started making a racket and Mel pulled away with an embarrassed blush.

Xavier just laughed and smacked her ass before letting her go.

Calla watched it all with a smile on her face but an ache in her chest. The last few weeks had been nothing short of perfect. Things with Liam and Mackenzie couldn't be better. Painter was a dream. She'd never been happier in her whole life.

Which was the problem, wasn't it?

Because for every second of happiness, she heard a ticking clock in the background. Ticking down to the competition. Mack hadn't said anything about changing his mind about leaving afterwards. There were things he kept from her and Liam, she was sure of it. Important things.

Ha. She was one to talk. Every week that passed, she felt her body changing more and more. The nausea had been mild, thank God for that. But there was a little being growing inside her. One that was part her and part Liam or Mack. Twelve weeks. It was the size of a lime. That was what the website said.

Calla cursed herself for ever looking it up. Now she had to imagine the little lime in there opening and closing their fingers and curling their toes. That was what happened at this stage in development.

How the hell was she supposed to do what she might need to do, knowing that?

The appointment to get the results of her Huntington's test was next week. Four days and she'd know. Four days and she might have to make the hardest decision of her life.

Under the table, her hand went to her lower stomach. It had just started stretching and protruding slightly. She'd been begging off going to Liam's room the past week, saying she needed to rest up for the competition. Mel had let her pick through her closet for tonight's shindig and she'd chosen a dark plum colored *peasant top*. At least that was what Mel had called it. It had a plunging neckline but was loose everywhere else.

From the way Liam kept not so subtly checking out her cleavage, she'd say it was a good choice all around.

The smile died on her lips, though.

She was lying to him. To both of them. They'd never forgive her if they found out. And if she had to—

"You okay?"

"Huh?" Calla looked up to find Mack scrutinizing her.

"Is everything okay?" His eyebrows were furrowed.

"Fine," she said, aiming for breezy. She wasn't sure she succeeded from the way Mack glanced over her head. No doubt sharing a look with Liam. She both loved and sometimes hated it when they did that. Watching the barriers come down between them in the bedroom was beautiful to watch. But she couldn't say she relished having two times the observational power turned her way, especially lately.

"If we're talking about things to celebrate," Hunter said, standing up, "Isobel and I have some news."

Calla looked up, glad to be distracted from her own thoughts. Hunter volunteered each year at the Makeover as an extra on-site veterinarian. Calla had known him forever since they'd both grown up around here, though he was a few years ahead of her in school. She only gotten to know him on a more personal level when he took over for Dr. Roberts at the only large animal veterinarian clinic in two counties. She'd gotten to know his wife Isobel a little over the past year too. She was good for him, had brought the life back into him after everything that happened with his first wife.

"We're pregnant," Isobel said, beaming as she stood up and hugged Hunter's side.

Calla's smile went brittle.

Pregnant. And they were obviously so happy about it. Of course they were. Everyone around the table congratulated them. Because pregnancies were usually something to celebrate.

"How far along are you?" Mel asked, hand going to her own extended stomach.

"Six months now," Isobel said. "We find out if it's a boy or girl at our next appointment in a few weeks."

Mel clapped. "Our babies are going to be twinsies. Ours is due in five and a half."

Calla took a drink of her sparkling soda to swallow down her jealousy.

Mel's face went sour. "We tried to find out if they were a boy or a girl but they wouldn't give the nurse a clear shot during the ultrasound. I swear," she glared at Xavier, "if you give me another boy—"

Xavier just grinned and held a forkful of potato salad toward his wife's lips.

Mel shoved the fork out of her face. "Which do you want?"

"I want a daughter but Hunter wants a boy."

"Just think about when they're a teenager," Hunter broke in. "If you have a boy you only have to worry about one dick. With a girl you have to worry about *all* the dicks."

Calla almost spit out her soda at that. Isobel smacked Hunter on the arm as everybody laughed.

Calla smiled. Good. She could be happy for Isobel and Hunter. It would be okay. She could keep her emotions in check.

"You're a smart man." Liam fist-bumped Hunter. Then he shook his head, "Jaysus, you're both braver than me. I never want kids."

Calla's chest clenched and she clutched her glass of soda. He *never* wanted kids?

"Never?" Mel echoed her thoughts, one eyebrow arched.

"It would cut into his time staring at himself in the mirror," Mack muttered.

Liam smirked at Mack. "Oh let me guess, you think you'll be father of the year whenever you have kids? All your tattoos on display when you pick them up from preschool?"

Mack held up his hands. "No kids for me either."

Oh don't hold back now. Anyone else want to shove a knife in her guts while they were at it?

Calla's lips pursed and she took another long sip of soda.

"Well I'm having a passel of them," Reece said from the end of the table, leaning in so they could hear him over the noisy restaurant.

"Oh yeah?" Jeremiah looked at his twin. "And how exactly are you going to support them?"

Reece rolled his eyes. "Don't go getting all high and mighty on me just because you're Mr. College now. The rest of us get by just fine. I've got a fool-proof plan, if you must know."

"And that is?" Jeremiah asked.

Reece bounced the baby on his knee and grinned. "I'm gonna marry a rich woman, obviously. Well," he bobbed his head, "that's Plan B anyway. Just in case I don't win the lottery."

Jeremiah's eyebrows lifted. "What concerns me is I can't tell if you're serious or not."

"What?" Reece sounded offended. "I'm a catch."

Jeremiah snorted but Reece ignored him and went on, "I'll be the perfect stay-at-home dad while wify goes off and earns the bacon. And twins run in the family. So we'll have a few pairs of them. And Liam," Reece turned toward him, "Don't think I buy it for one second."

"What?" Liam popped a handful of beer nuts in his mouth.

"You say you don't want kids now," Reece shook his head. "But you'll feel it one day. Just look at this adorable little guy." He grinned down at the baby while he spooned some sort of mushy orange goop in his mouth. The baby shook his head back and forth and the spoonful went all down his front.

Then he started wailing while Reece dipped the spoon back into the small jar on the table and made *choo choo* noises as he lifted it back to the baby's mouth. "Train's coming. Yummy train is coming!"

Liam just stared on, shaking his head. "Sorry, don't see meself suddenly deciding I need me eardrums shattered on a regular basis. Or that I really *hate* getting a good night's sleep every night."

Isobel smacked Liam on the back of his head.

"Thank you," Mel smiled at her. "I couldn't have reached him from all the way over here."

But Liam just held up his hands. "Hey, I just know me own limitations, that's all."

Calla tipped her glass up and drank more. About now she was really wishing there was some actual vodka in her vodka soda, instead of just soda. Soon the cup was empty but she kept it tipped up, not ready to deal with the conversation or anyone at the table yet.

She stood up abruptly. "I'm gonna go get a refill."

She didn't wait to hear anyone's response. She made a beeline for the restroom. She had to get her shit together before she could face anyone or she was gonna freakin' lose it.

She went straight for the sinks, turned on the tap, and splashed cold water on her cheeks. Then she looked at herself in the mirror.

She barely recognized herself. Mel had helped her put on some mascara and lipstick before they came out, and to style her hair in loose waves. She backed up from the mirror and ran her hands down her body, breasts to hips. In the purple top and sleek black skirt she'd borrowed from Mel, the illusion was almost complete.

She looked nothing like the Calla who'd walked into Liam leaving Bethany from a bathroom very much like this one.

In a few more months, no one would be mistaking her for a man, that was for sure. She let out a humorless laugh and then leaned her hands on the sink and dropped her head. What the hell was she *doing*? Better yet, what was she *going* to do?

She turned away from the mirror in disgust and slammed out of the bathroom door.

And right into Liam's arms.

"Hey beautiful," he laughed, catching her when she stumbled in surprise.

"Way to scare the shit out of her, asshole," Mack said from where he stood behind Liam.

"No, I'm fine," Calla said. She slipped her arms around Liam and pressed her head against his chest. God, he felt so good. Forget about burying her head in the sand. She wanted to bury herself in him and Mack.

"Hey, what's all this about?" Liam asked, putting his arms around her and hugging her back. "Are you okay, love?"

Love. If only he meant that the way she wanted him to. No, that was stupid. What was she thinking? She squeezed her eyes shut and then pulled away from him, forcing a smile. "I'm fine."

"You sure?" Mack asked, eyebrows furrowed like he could smell her bullshit from a mile away.

"God," Calla rolled her eyes, putting on a façade of bravado. "I just had to use the bathroom. No crisis here. Chill out."

Liam smirked. "What? Chicks aren't angelic creatures who never piss or shit? Your blowin' me mind here, baby."

"Ha," Calla said. She made to leave the back hallway but Liam put a hand on her elbow to stop her.

"Wait, there's something I been wanting to give you."

Calla stopped, surprised. "Give me?"

Liam just grinned and pulled a small oblong box out of his jacket pocket. What—?

He lifted off the lid and there was a silver necklace inside with a small oval pendant on it. Calla reached and ran the tip of her index finger down the thin chain to the delicate filigree tree engraved on the outside of the pendant.

"It's beautiful," Calla said, her voice high and tight. God, she felt like she was about to start crying. Fucking *hormones*.

"Let me put it on you." Liam smiled, obviously pleased with her reaction.

Mack watched on from beside them, arms crossed over his chest, a slight frown on his face. Was he feeling left out?

"Would you mind if Mack put it on?" Calla searched Liam's eyes.

Liam looked over at Mack in surprise. "Not at all. Go ahead." He waved Mack close.

Mack looked uncertain for a second. "It's his gift. I don't want to—"

"We share everything, don't we?" Calla asked.

At least for now.

Chills ran down her body when Mack's calloused hands brushed her neck as he draped the necklace around her. She lifted her hair off her neck as he fumbled with the clasp.

"This is the most beautiful thing I've ever worn," she whispered to Liam. No need for him to know it was the only jewelry she'd worn in a long time—since her mother had left anyway. She used to play at trying on her mother's things but had thrown away the few pieces her mom left behind and never looked back.

Mack finally managed the clasp and stepped back. Calla lowered her hair and Liam came forward, centering the pendent right over the dip of her cleavage.

"You're so beautiful," Liam said.

"Perfect," Mack whispered.

Calla's cheeks burned and she was glad that she'd nixed the blush when Mel offered it earlier. She was pretty sure her cheeks were plenty pink all on their own.

"Wanna dance?" Liam held out his arm to her. There was a small dance floor off to the left of the main seating area and it was filled with people.

Calla smiled and it was genuine this time. God, it was always like this when she was with them. All her worries and fears disappeared. Even when it was *them* and the future she was worried about.

She grabbed Mack's hand with the arm Liam wasn't holding and dragged him along behind them.

The atmosphere and energy of the small crowd on the dance floor was hard not to get caught up in. Mack pulled Calla into his arms as that Florida-Georgia line song, *HOLY*, came on over the speakers. Liam stepped up right behind her.

Just like the first night they'd all danced together.

Liam moved her hair behind her ear and whisper sung the lyrics in her ear, "You're holy, holy, holy, holy, I'm high on loving you."

Loving? Did he just—

She swung her head around to look at Liam but he'd dipped his face into her hair. She blinked in the dim light of the dance floor, heart and mind racing a mile a minute as she swayed back and forth in their arms.

It was just a song lyric. It didn't mean anything.

Did it? What if it did?

No. *God*. If he loved her, why would he say it for the first time off-handed in a song like that. She was a neurotic mess. *Fucking hormones!!*

She squeezed her eyes shut. *Turn off brain. Please, just for tonight.* She clutched Mack with one arm and then lifted the other behind her to hold the back of Liam's neck.

Which reminded her of that night she'd held them close as they'd both taken her. Her panties went damp.

And for the first time all night, all her worries quieted. It was just them. Mack and Liam's bodies warm on either side of her. The music surrounding them. Perfection.

The next song was a little faster but neither Mack or Liam moved. Calla moved her hips back and forth, grinning when she felt Liam's hard on against her ass. When she slid forward and ground against the front of Mack's jeans, she smiled even wider feeling he was hard too. It was such a rush to be able to drive both of them so crazy.

She went up on tiptoe so she could whisper in Mack's ear. "I'm so wet."

He growled and pulled her even more roughly against him.

Toby Keith's *I Love This Bar* came on and a roar of approval came up from the crowd. People shouted along to the familiar lyrics.

"I'll go close out our bar tab," Liam said. Mack nodded at him as he continued holding Calla close even though what they were doing could only loosely be called dancing. She loved every second of it.

By the time Liam came back, they were on to a slow dance and Mack had pulled her so close her body was absolutely cemented against his. Liam pulled her back from Mack and enfolded her in his arms, his hips swaying as he two-stepped with her in a small circle.

"That was my dance you just stole," Mack growled from behind Liam.

Liam looked over his shoulder and smirked Mack's direction. "Guess you'll have to put me in me place once we get back to the hotel."

Mack's eyes went dark and Liam licked his lips.

"Oh, I'll make it a night you won't forget," Mack promised.

Calla grinned at both of them, grabbed their arms, and dragged them toward the door.

They could barely keep their hands off each other but Calla forced Mack to sit up front and Liam in back just to torture them. Calla drove since she hadn't had anything to drink.

What she didn't foresee was Mack torturing her right back. His hand inched up her leg the entire fifteen-minute ride back to the hotel, along with him whispering the dirty, dirty things he wanted to do to her and Liam.

She was so turned on by the time she pulled into a parking spot that opened up right in front of the hotel, she was about to jump one or the other of them. Or both. Yes, both sounded like a good idea.

But your stomach.

Screw it. She'd just keep her shirt on. She dragged Liam's face down and kissed him hard as they walked through the front door, Mack's hands on her waist from behind.

But then Liam jerked away from her. "What the *fuck*?"

Calla blinked, taken aback by Liam's loud voice.

"What's up his ass?" Mack asked.

Calla frowned and shook her head as Liam strode right up to a middle-aged man in a suit who was sitting in one of the lobby chairs.

"What the fuck are you doing here."

"Well there ya are. Finally. I was beginning to think that blonde slag who kept callin' saying you'd be here was lying and wasting me time."

Liam just stared at the man, frozen.

"Well come on now." The man glared at Liam. "Give your da a hello at least."

His da—? Calla had barely taken Liam's father in before a gorgeous, statuesque redhead came running over from the reception desk.

"Baby! I've missed you so much!" She threw her arms around Liam and planted a kiss right on his lips.

27

LIAM

LIAM WAS STUNNED FROZEN for a moment. And then his brain started processing again.

Brigid was kissing him. While Calla and Mack watched.

He wrenched back from Brigid to glare at her and his da. Only to find Calla skirting them and running toward the elevators while Mack looked at him murderously.

"*Shite*. Calla!" Liam went to chase after her but Mack stopped him with an iron grip on his elbow. Calla opened the door to the stairs and disappeared. Dammit. He had to go make it right.

"Let go of me," Liam spoke to Mack through gritted teeth. "This isn't what it looks like."

Mack's jaw worked. "It better not be. If you hurt her, I swear I'll—"

"Yeah, yeah," Liam muttered, jerking out of Mack's grasp and running up the stairs after Calla. Mack was right on his heels. Jaysus, talk about déjà vu.

"Liam!" Brigid called after him right before the door to the stairs shut. "Wait. I just want to talk. Please!"

What a clusterfuck. Liam ignored Brigid and caught up to Calla right before she shut the door to her room on the second floor.

"Calla," he breathed out, stopping her door from closing. She stepped back and allowed him to push his way in.

"That down there, it's not what you think. She doesn't mean anything to me anymore."

Calla's head came up, hazel eyes vulnerable and full of uncertainty. "But she did? Once?" Then she shook her head. "I'm sorry. I don't know why I'm acting like this." She turned away from him. "It's not like we have— We're just—" She waved a hand. "I know we agreed it's not a relationship or anything—"

Liam went to her and spun her around to look at him. "That's shite and you know it. This summer's been—" Now it was him who didn't know the right words to say or how to put it. One thing he did know. "It's sure as fuck a relationship."

He took her shoulders and dropped his mouth to hers but she pulled away at the last second. Her eyes were still full of hurt. "She kissed you."

Liam squeezed his eyes shut and breathed out. "I'm sorry, baby. She's me past. We were together for about six months a couple years ago. That's all."

Calla nodded but her mouth was tight like she was barely holding back her emotions.

"She's nothing to me. What you, Mack and me have, it's everything. Do you understand? Now, I have to go down there to talk to me Da and Brigid. It might take a bit, but I need you to trust me. Can you do that?"

Calla nodded rapidly, swallowing hard as she met his eyes. His brave girl. "I promise I'll explain as soon as I can."

She nodded again and he pressed a quick, hard kiss to her forehead.

When he turned to go back downstairs, he found Mack standing in the doorway, arms crossed over his chest. He watched Liam like he was sure Liam was about to fuck them over.

"Take care of her until I get back," Liam said to Mack, meeting him glare for glare.

"I'm okay, don't worry about me," Calla said, joining them at the door and running a hand down Liam's back comfortingly. "You talk to your dad. We'll be here when you get back."

Liam swallowed, then ran back downstairs where Da and Brigid were waiting for him.

"What was that?" Brigid asked, eyes narrowed as she looked past him up the stairs.

Liam could only stare at her incredulously. "As if you have any right to ask me that. Tell me, how's Sean these days? What, did he lose all his money in another get-rich-quick scheme? That why you're here? Your personal ATM run out again?"

Brigid winced and pursed her lips. "That's not fair. Liam, please, we just need to talk. Your da and I have things we need to—"

Liam scoffed cynically. "I think we all said everything there was to say two years ago when I left. Right, *Da*? Oh wait," he paused dramatically, "I might not have the right to call you that. So, Ciarán, you disinherit me yet? That why you're here? So I can sign the papers freeing you of me legally?"

Learning Ciarán O'Neill might not actually be his father had been one of the great blows of his life. At the same time, it explained so many things.

It was two years ago. His mom had been sick. Dying of liver failure. They hadn't spoken in years but he remembered the ma she'd once been. How they used to spend summers together in the country. Riding horses and painting. How loving and happy she'd once been before the drinking and drugs.

He was in the first stable relationship of his life with Brigid and he thought, maybe, just maybe, he could reconcile with his ma and find some real sort of happiness. Wasn't that what you were supposed to do when you were an adult?

Ma had looked terrible when he visited her in the hospital. Her skin was yellowish and papery, with her veins standing out in her thin, emaciated body. She was short of breath and seemed easily confused. It was right near the end.

"Ma," he'd leaned over her hospital bed, taking her hand. "It's me. It's Liam."

Her eyes had slowly drifted up to his face.

"You," she rasped.

"Yes, Ma, it's me." He'd swiped at the stupid tears in his eyes. She'd been so beautiful once, *so* kind and loving. His earliest memories were of her holding him close and singing to him before bedtime. She was still in there somewhere, beneath the husk of woman destroyed by drugs and drinking, he had to believe that.

Her eyes slowly tracked up to his face and she met his gaze. "You ruined me life."

Liam yanked away from her like she'd struck him. Maybe he'd heard her wrong. "Ma, I don't know what you—"

She fell into a coughing fit that shook her entire body. He sat there helplessly, not knowing what to do.

He reached out for her arm but she batted him away. "You and your da ruined me." Then she laughed and it was a dry, brittle sound. "Course he might not be your da at all. I hope you are the stablemaster's bastard."

"What are you talking about?" Liam asked, so loud she winced away from him. Shite. He ran a hand through his hair. But what she'd just— No, she was just confused. The nurses warned him this might happen. This wasn't his ma at all. She didn't m—

"Not that your da ever had the balls—" another long coughing fit "—to find out for sure if you were his or not. Didn't trust himself not to disinherit ya and kick ya to the streets. And what a scandal that woulda been. His pride couldn't have borne it."

But when he'd run out of there and gone to his da's office to get him to contradict Ma and tell him she didn't know what she was talking about, his dad didn't deny it.

They got in a huge row that ended with his da yelling, "As useless as ya are with your life and considering your whore of a mother, of course I wondered every day if you were even me son."

Liam had always felt deep down his da didn't love him. At least now he knew why.

"Congratulations," Liam had said, yanking open the door to his da's office, "You got your wish. I'm not your son anymore." Then he'd slammed the door behind him.

They hadn't spoken or had any contact since. His ma died a week and a half later, and Liam pulled up a map of the United States on his laptop, closed his eyes, and blindly put his finger on the screen. Couldn't say he'd ever heard of *Wyoming* before, but he looked up jobs that would let him have a low profile and was on a plane the next day. Working on a horse ranch had a certain irony. After all, there was apparently just as much chance his real da was a nobody stable-master as a billionaire media mogul.

"If you'd let me get a word in edgewise," Ciarán said, red faced. "I could tell ya why I'm here." He looked around the lobby where people were staring at them. They were making a scene. Something he knew Ciarán hated.

Liam smiled. "No, you know what? I think I prefer how we've communicated the past two years. Not at all."

Liam knew he was being immature. But everything had been going so good. Calla and Mack, it was all—

"It's time to end this charade and come back home where you belong." Ciarán stood up straighter, speaking with that superior tone that always put Liam's teeth on edge.

But he wasn't a child anymore. Ciarán might have held him at an arm's length his whole life, but it was Liam's choice to do the leaving for once. He left Ciarán. Ireland. Everything.

And if Ciarán thought he had the right to just march right back in, he had another thing coming.

"You should go now." Liam walked back toward the front sliding doors of the hotel. "You aren't welcome here." He looked past Ciarán to Brigid. "Either of you."

Ciarán stared at him a long moment. Then he waved a hand. "It's late and you're pissed." He strode not toward the door, but over to the elevator. "We'll talk tomorrow, somewhere *private*, when you haven't spent the evening swimming in Guinness. We're staying in the penthouse."

Liam bit his tongue. He wasn't drunk. He'd only had a beer and a half earlier, over several hours. Unlike back in Dublin, he didn't have to drink himself into a stupor each night so he could be numb to just how miserable his existence was.

"I'll be just a minute," Brigid called after Ciarán. Then she turned to Liam. He could still feel eyes on them from all sides. If he was *really* lucky, this little throw down would show up on TMZ tomorrow. As much as he hated that shite, he refused to go anywhere with either Ciarán or Brigid.

"Well, for a getaway, you certainly chose a place that's," she looked around, eyes lingering on a chandelier made out of antlers, "*eclectic.*"

"You can follow Ciarán back to your rooms and then out the damn door tomorrow. I don't have a thing to say to you."

Her eyes flashed hurt and she took a step toward him before stopping again, folding her arms across her stomach and looking down. "You don't know how sorry I am for the things I said that day." She looked up, eyebrows furrowed like she was stricken. "I wished I could take it back a hundred times. But I couldn't find you to apologize and beg you—" Her voice broke and she took another step toward him.

Liam's jaw clenched as she came even closer and ran her hand down his chest. "—Beg you to give me another chance. We were good together." She bit her lip, eyelashes batting. "Best I ever had."

Liam jerked back from her and glared, head shaking. "You must think I'm an awful fuckin' eejit to fall for your shite again. You tossed Sean over for me because he was bust and I was bank. Then when it looked like I might go bust too, you were just as ready to drop me and go looking for another lad."

"That's not true," Brigid said, coming up to him again. He grabbed her wrists before she could land them on him. "I just got scared.

Haven't you ever been scared? Liam, I loved you." Her voice was impassioned as she searched his eyes. "I still do."

He shook his head in disgust. When he'd gone to her after the fight with his da, all she could focus on was the money. Saying he needed to get DNA tested to prove who his da was since only Ciarán's 'natural born son' would be given a ten percent share in the company he'd built. That was the language Ciarán had the lawyers put in the legal paperwork—just one of the little details that had come out in the row earlier. Just in case Liam wasn't his son. He'd been hedging his bets where Liam was concerned his whole life. Never willing to *quite* invest all his money, or his time, or his love—

And then there Brigid had been doing the same.

Liam grabbed her hands and begged her to come.

To run away with him.

No money, no prospects.

Just him.

And she'd backed away from him like he'd been diagnosed with leprosy.

"You lost your chance with me," Liam said, affecting a hard grin. "But seems like you've been spending some quality time with Ciarán. You're the type he usually goes for these days. Young. Pretty. Willing to play the slut for—"

She slapped him.

The sound of her hand against his cheek echoed around the empty room. Gasps came from the small crowd that was gathering in the lobby to watch the show.

"Shite," Brigid swore. "Liam, I'm sorry. I didn't mean—" She reached for him again but he pulled back.

"No, don't take it back." He stretched his jaw. She packed quite a wallop. "I think that's the fitting end to us." He shook his head. "If you knew me at all, you woulda known all I ever wanted was someone who wanted me for *me*. Starting the way we did, I don't know why I ever thought that person would be you."

"Liam, I *can* be that pers— Wait, where are you going?" She followed him as she went out the front door and headed for his truck. He needed to take a drive. Clear his head.

"Wait. Liam. Please!" she pleaded.

He slammed his truck door in her face, then peeled out. Then he sped out of there, leaving his da and the woman he once thought he loved in his dust.

28

MACK

CALLA FELL asleep in Mack's arms about an hour after Liam left them. He'd texted Liam several times to ask what was going on but got nothing back.

Calla said he was probably just catching up with his dad. Mack didn't tell her he saw Liam storming out of the hotel when he'd followed him back downstairs earlier. Or that that woman, Brigid, had gone right after him.

Calla always believed the best in people. So Mack had just nodded along, not believing it for a minute. People like Liam always stuck to their own kind in the end. The fact that he himself had started allowing Liam just the little bit *in* made Mack furious with himself.

But if he was honest, Liam *had* wormed his way under Mack's skin. Calla too.

Mack would find his thoughts straying to the softness of Calla's hair at the most random moments. Whenever he made a break-through with Torpedo, she was the first one he wanted to tell. And whenever he had a setback, he immediately wanted to take out his frustrations on Liam's ass.

Though really, there'd even been more tender moments between him and the bloody Irishman lately. Who would have thought? Just this morning, early as fuck, he'd woken up hard as a rock and gone in to grab Liam so they could go give Calla a wake-up call she wouldn't forget.

And he'd stood there for a good five minutes just watching Liam sleep.

What the fuck was *that* about?

Thank Christ for the rude awakening of Liam's past coming back to remind both of them exactly who Liam Delaney O'Neill was.

Because the clock had wound down. Time was up. Mack was supposed to split town as soon as Torpedo was auctioned tomorrow. But he hadn't yet made any plans. Or packed any of his things.

He sifted his hands through Calla's soft hair as she slept against his chest. His gut clenched and he felt fucking nauseated at the thought of leaving them.

What if he didn—

Shit. No. He couldn't think like that...

Could he?

He jerked forward. Calla stirred in his arms and he froze. When she settled, he moved her gently so that she was laying on the bed.

Then he got up and paced back toward the window.

The thought returned—*what if?*

What if he didn't go back for Bone? What if he forgot that part of his life had ever happened? What if the happiness he'd found here *could* actually last?

He sat for hours watching Calla sleep. Waiting for Liam to come home. The others got back from the bar a little after Liam left but they were quiet and didn't wake Calla.

By three a.m. he'd memorized every contour of Calla's face but he wasn't any closer to deciding what he should do. He climbed into bed beside Calla. Her body was so warm and when he slept with her and Liam, the nightmares didn't come.

He was so tired. So, so tired.

Ever since Ben had died, Mack spent every spare moment thinking about taking his revenge on Bone. Fuck the consequences.

He was born shit and he'd die shit, right?

There was nothing but darkness for him. No future. No joy. Just doing what needed doing and then either spending the rest of his days rotting in a cell for it, or, more likely, getting cut down by another of the Devil's Spawn.

But... maybe, just maybe, choosing his future was as simple as that—a choice. Shit could be fertilizer, right? If there was the right person nurturing whatever was growing.

His eyes fell on Calla again. Someone bright and full of life like her.

Christ, he was tired. Fucking delirious if he was having such flowery fuckin' thoughts.

He let his head drop back against the pillows. Calla was so warm in his arms. She even smelled like sunshine.

He fell asleep, that old song playing in his head, *you are my sunshine, my only sunshine.*

"Do you think he's okay?" Calla asked for what felt like the hundredth time as she and Mack parked the trailer in the designated area. They were towing Calla's horse and Xavier and Mel were bringing Tornado over from the stables where they'd boarded them for the night.

One look at Calla's anxious face made Mack want to punch Liam in the fucking face. Especially on a day that was this important to her. She'd only brought it up once, but Mack knew she had hopes of winning one of the cash prizes today. She had a real shot at it. What she'd accomplished with Painter in three months was fucking phenomenal.

But she needed every ounce of focus she had. Which Liam fucking knew.

"You saw the text," Mack said, trying to make his voice reassuring even though he felt anything but. "He's fine. He'll be here soon." The text had been three lines long. *See you this morning at arena. Went for drive last night. Didn't want to wake you when I got back.*

Calla put a hand on his arm, stopping him from getting out of the car. "It's okay if last night upset you. I know you two can be..." she looked to the roof of the car before meeting his gaze again, "volatile. But I know how much you care about him."

Mack paused, frowning. Shit, was she right? Was he so mad at the bastard because he was worried about him?

He pushed the car door open. "Wouldn't have killed him to have fucking called," he mumbled under his breath.

Calla came around the front of the truck cab and threw her arms around his waist. "Everything's going to be okay." She looked up at him, eyes searching. "Right?"

His chest went tight at seeing her uncertainty. "You bet your ass. Everything's gonna be great." He gave her a squeeze, and then a quick smack on the ass. "Now let's go get your prizewinner ready."

She smiled and nodded. He was about to follow her to the back of the trailer rig when his phone buzzed in his pocket.

He pulled it out and glanced at the screen.

Sammy was Facetiming him.

Mack frowned. Sammy knew the competition was today. He wouldn't be calling if he didn't have something important.

"I'm gonna go check on Torpedo, okay, hon?" Mack called out to Calla.

"See you in there."

Mack was already striding away. The phone stopped ringing but started right back up again. Mack finally answered when he got to an empty part of the huge parking lot where no one would overhear him.

"What's up, Sammy?"

But it wasn't Sammy's face he saw on the other end. It was some fucking meathead.

"Who the fuck are y—"

"Bone's got a message for you," the meathead said.

Mack's blood went cold. The screen shifted like the guy was moving the phone around. It settled on a computer screen that was obviously some kind of camera feed.

And what Mack saw almost made him lose his breakfast.

There was just enough light to see Sammy, naked, bloody, and strung up on a hook like he was a slab of meat at the butchers. He was screaming in agony.

"Please! Please, don't—"

Mack almost dropped the phone. "Sam!" he shouted.

And then came that evil fucking laugh that haunted Mack's dreams.

Bone's face filled the computer screen a second later. He grinned, showing off his stained, yellow teeth. "Baby boy, I heard you been asking around about me. You wanted to arrange a reunion all you had to do was ask me direct."

Bile rose up Mack's throat

"Instead, I learn you got one of our own playing snitch for you."

Bone moved out of the way and Sammy's body took up the frame again. Some of the blood and grime on his chest was dark, but some was bright red like Bone had slashed him right before placing the call. Mack's stomach bottomed out at seeing his friend like this.

"Gotta say I didn't mind having the excuse to get me a little plaything," Bone's voice came over the video of Sammy. "It's so goddamned boring on the outside. I miss having my pick of the fresh meat."

Bone circled one of Sammy's nipples with a sharp hunting knife. "Remember the first day you walked the block, baby boy?"

"*Fuck!*" Mack yelled when Bone sliced Sammy's nipple off. Sammy screamed and writhed on the hook. Mack dropped to his knees, staring at the phone.

"Foreplay just gets me so excited," came Bone's voice again. "Maybe you *have* missed me all these years and that's why you sent this fucking idiot to try to learn about me. So I'd know just where to come and find you. Because Sammy here? He sang like a songbird as soon as I pulled off the first fingernail. Wyoming, huh? I didn't make you out for a city boy."

Mack sat paralyzed, eyes glued to the screen.

"Feel free to stay and watch the show. I'll be seeing you soon, baby boy."

Sammy whimpered something Mack couldn't make out. There was another five minutes to the video and Mack wanted to throw the goddamned thing across the fucking parking lot. But maybe there was some deal he could make with Bone. Maybe he could offer to exchange himself for—

Sammy's scream filled the phone speakers and Mack could only sit helplessly by for the rest of the video while Bone raped his friend and then slit his throat.

Bone's demonic laugh was the last thing Mack heard before the phone call was ended.

29

LIAM

LIAM FELT like shite as he pulled in to the arena parking lot.

"Fuck," he swore as he swerved to miss an oncoming car in the lot. The loud honk only had him swearing more as he grabbed his head and stomped on the break.

Driving around last night hadn't done shite for his head and neither had coming back to the hotel and emptying the minibar.

He should have gone to Calla or Mack. But seeing Da and then all that bullshit with Brigid—it had him feeling exactly like nothing had changed in the last two years. That he was the exact same spoiled little cunt that had run away from his daddy issues with his tail between his legs—

Wait, was that Mack?

Out in the far parking lot. A man stood out in the middle of nowhere with his hands on his head. He looked a hell of a lot like Mack.

Liam squinted and leaned over the steering wheel. Liam knew the way Mack carried himself. The way he walked. Knew everything about the lad if he were honest with himself.

Which is why you shoulda gone to talk things over with him and Calla last night instead of drinking yourself stupid.

Because dammit, he *wasn't* the same. He had changed. And Calla and Mack had helped him change.

He looked around and checked his mirrors before putting the truck in drive again and heading out to where Mack was standing. He slowed down and brought the truck and trailer to a stop. Mack didn't even look up. He was just standing there in the middle of nowhere with hunched shoulders, staring at the ground.

Liam honked his horn but Mack only looked his way briefly. Then he just kept walking.

Shite. Liam shoulda known the lanky bastard wouldn't let last night go so easy. He slammed the truck in park and then jumped down from the cab.

"Mack," he called. "Mackenzie!"

He jogged up beside Mack but when he tried to put a hand on his arm, Mack jerked away so roughly it made Liam stumble.

"What the fuck?" Liam said. Then he breathed out. Mack just kept walking and Liam gritted his teeth and then jogged after him again.

"Look, I'm sorry for how shite went down last night. I should have come right back to you and Calla like I said I would. But things are bad with me da. He might not even be me real da. I might be the son of the fecking stableman. And then Brigid, the woman, she was there to complicate shite and— Jaysus, would you just stop for a second and listen to me? I'm trying to apologize here."

Mack stopped and whirled on him. Liam took a step back at the look of mottled rage on his face. What the—

"You think I care about your bullshit rich boy daddy issues? Wake the fuck up!" Mack yelled, throwing out his arms. "Some people have real fucking problems."

"Why do you always have to be such a shite about everything?"

Liam fired back. "I'm sorry if me problems are too white-collar for ya."

Mack got right up in his face. "Admit it. You're gonna make up with your dad and then drop Calla because that's what rich, self-entitled users like you do. The help is good for a fuck but that's it, right? Isn't that what you told me?"

Liam pulled back, sneering in disgust and shaking his head. "I can't believe I felt bad for walking out on you last night. You're a piece of shite who can't see something good when it's right in your face. You're so busy being sure everyone in the world is out to get you. Calla deserves so much."

A shadow crossed Mack's face but then he threw his hands up again. "I don't have time for this bullshit." He turned and resumed walking away.

"Excuse me, are you Liam O'Neill?" Liam's attention was jerked away from Mackenzie's disappearing form by a woman sticking a microphone in his face. "Son of media mogul Sean O'Neill and Irish Film and Television Award winning actress Ailis O'Neill?"

Shite. How had the fucking paparazzi found out he was here?

"Is it true you've been having an affair with Isobel Snow? Last year's Missing Heiress?"

"What?" Liam asked, then shook his head, trying to edge around the woman. She just moved in front of him again.

"There are reports of you and Isobel in a cozy cuddle last night at the Mile High Bar and Grill. Can you confirm or deny these rumors?"

Isobel? What the fuck were they on about? Jaysus, these fucking vultures would make up anything for a story.

Which was nothing to what would happen if they sniffed out the actual truth.

Shite. He headed toward a side entrance to the arena.

He had to find Calla. *Now*.

30

CALLA

"MACK! I've been looking for you everywhere," Calla said, hurrying up to him as he yanked the safety chains off the trailer and then disconnected the wiring cable.

He jerked upright and for a second, Calla had the strangest feeling Mack was about to get in the truck and slam the door right in her face. But then he paused and leaned back over, lifting the coupler off the ball hitch. He kept his face averted. Why couldn't he look at her?

"What?" Calla asked in alarm. "What's happened? Is Liam okay?"

"That snob will always be just fine." Mack's voice was full of acrimony as he dropped the trailer hitch.

"Did you two have another fight?" She followed on his heels as he walked around to the driver's side and got up in the cab. She wedged herself in the open door. He would *not* be going anywhere until she got some answers.

Mack just shook his head. "Look, it doesn't matter." He looked forward through the windshield, jaw working. "It's time for me to move on, that's all."

Move on? Like...

"You're leaving?" She could barely get the words past her suddenly dry throat.

Mack looked down and then away. "I always said I would." He tossed the wrench he'd been using on the hitch into the passenger side floorboards. "It was time I was hitting the road."

Calla could only stare on in confusion. "But Torpedo. You have to show him today. This doesn't make any sense. Where are you even—"

"Back East. Got some things I got to take care of. They can't wait." He still didn't look toward her.

"And then what?" she asked incredulously. "Will you come back?"

He shook his head. "Told you. I'm movin' on."

This time Calla took several steps back. How could he...? She felt like she'd just been slammed in the chest by a semi.

"I don't understand."

"What don't you understand?" Mack turned her way angrily. "This was always my plan. I gave it to you straight from the beginning. You said you were okay with it."

Calla's jaw set. "Things changed. You know they did. What we've shared," she glared at him. "I didn't imagine that."

Mack just shook his head stubbornly. "It doesn't matter. None of it matters. I got a path I'm meant to walk. And it ain't with you."

"I'm pregnant." The words fell out of her mouth without her thinking them through. Mack's head jerked in her direction.

And it just kept spewing out. "I don't know if you or Liam is the father. With the timeframe the doctor gave me, it could be either of yours. I didn't think I could— I've always been irregular and—" She stopped and looked down. "Anyway, I'm not sure if I should keep it. What my dad has, it's genetic. I could have it too, and so could the baby. I don't know what to do."

Finally letting it go felt like having a hundred pounds lifted off her shoulders. But God, what now? Would he be furious at her for keeping it a secret all this time?

But when Mack climbed down out of the cab, he took her face gently in her hands. "You'll be a wonderful mother." His voice was so soft it was barely a whisper. His eyebrows drew together. "But believe me, you don't want me. You and Liam will raise that baby and be able to give them everything. The life they deserve."

He was breaking her heart. Couldn't he see that? "But—"

His eyebrows suddenly furrowed. "Should you still be doing the mustang competition?"

Oh so he cared about the baby in the abstract, as long as he didn't have to ever see it?

She pulled away from him. "I changed my routine. I'm only doing one galloping pass and the rest is low impact stuff. A lot of experienced, professional women riders keep riding when they're pregnant."

She didn't know why she was bothering to defend her choices to him. He didn't want her. She wasn't worth staying for.

"I'm sorry, Calla," he repeated. "This just isn't my path."

She turned around and ran back toward the arena before his words could pierce her any deeper.

She heard a roar go up from the crowd beyond.

The opening ceremony was starting.

Somehow she had to put her heartbreak aside because she had a competition to win.

31

CALLA

"ALL RIGHT GIRL," Calla patted Painter as she munched on hay from the hay net Calla had set up in the temporary stall. "It's almost time."

If she kept talking to Painter and focused on the competition, there wasn't enough space left over to think about Mack. Right?

So why did her chest feel like a melon carver had been used to scoop out her insides?

"Calla! Thank Jaysus."

"Liam!" Calla felt tears welling up in her eyes as Liam hurried toward her in the narrow path between makeshift stalls.

She climbed over the fence gate that made up Painter's stall and flung herself into Liam's arms.

"I need to talk to you," he said urgently, grabbing her hands and looking nervously behind him again.

"What's going on? Did Mack talk to you?"

She knew she should have told them both about the baby sooner. Her heart galloped as she waited for his answer, but he didn't say a word. Instead he pulled her behind him down the path between the stalls. Other contestants watched them as they went.

"Liam, what are you—"

"Just a second. I want to get us somewhere private."

"Okay, but Painter and I are on soon. The junior competition will be over in half an hour, so I can't be gone too long—"

Liam just kept pulling her along until they were underneath the stands of the arena.

"Liam," Calla said, tugging on the hand he was firmly gripping. "Talk to me."

It was dim underneath the stands, but she could still see the tension on his face.

"I have something to tell you." Liam finally said. "I want you to hear it from me first." He looked around anxiously.

Um. Wasn't that supposed to be her line?

"You're scaring me." She grabbed both of Liam's hands. "What's wrong? Are you sick?" Her eyes widened in fear. Oh God, what if he'd been diagnosed with something—

"No, no," Liam shook his head rapidly and Calla felt almost light-headed with relief. "Nothing like that." He took a deep breath. "The thing is, I have a lot of money. Like, a *lot*."

Calla blinked. What was he going on about? "So?"

Liam stared at her like he was waiting for some big reaction. "I'm a billionaire. Back in Ireland, me da owns Prism Media group. They're the conglomerate that bought out half the European and Australian news companies and even one of the bigger American news corporations."

Calla gave a tiny shake of her head. Where was he going with all this? "I know," she said. "So?"

Liam frowned and pulled back a little. "What do you mean, you *know*?"

"Uh," she shook her head, "yeah. You're Liam O'Neill. Son of actress Ailis Duncan. Well, she became Ailis O'Neill, after she married your dad. But yeah. I know who you are."

Liam jerked to his feet, staring down at Calla like she'd suddenly sprouted horns.

"What?" she asked, standing up and reaching for him, but he jerked his hand back.

"*How* do you know?"

She threw her hands in the air and shrugged. "I don't know. They showed that movie, *Irish Spring*, the one that won all those awards, in the world cinema class I took in college. It was my favorite elective."

Liam took another step back from her and raked a hand through his hair.

Calla didn't know why he was so freaked out, but she kept going. "When I saw you at the bar last year, I thought you looked familiar. The more I thought about it, I finally realized who you reminded me of. Your mom. You look so much like her. When I googled her, I saw a picture of you two. You must have been a teenager when it was taken." She smiled and lifted a hand toward him. "You had the most adorable floppy hair—"

"Stop!" he yelled. Calla flinched and her eyes flew open as he wrenched away. "What? I—"

"You fucking knew who I was? This whole time?" He looked at her and it was like his eyes were pleading for her to say no. But she wasn't going to lie about something so silly.

"Yeah. I've known the whole time." She shook her head. "I didn't realize—" She felt completely bewildered. "Is it some big secret?"

"Yes," he shouted, throwing his hands up in the air. "You've known," he whispered, more like he was talking to himself than to her. "You've known all along."

"That first time we had sex in the shower, you *knew*." His eyes flashed and he shoved an accusatory finger in her face. "You lied," he said. "You couldn't believe what had just happened because, and I quote, *you're you*. I asked you what you meant and you made up some bullshit about liking me laugh."

Calla's mouth dropped open. "It wasn't your laugh. I said I like how you made other people laugh."

"Bull*shit*," he accused. "You saw me and thought, here's me chance to cash in. Or at least get your fifteen minutes. Did you call the paparazzi in today?"

"I— Wha—" Each word cut off sharply and she finally threw her hands out in frustration. "I saw you and looked you up and thought: *Huh, a celebrity. In Hawthorne. How cool.* That was it. My entire thought process at the time."

Liam shook his head. "You're such a fucking liar."

She sputtered but he continued, "You just *happened* to come work for Xavier when you went broke? Remembered how that billionaire you'd been stalking worked there and thought, *huh, here's me meal ticket!*"

"How can you even—" She sputtered. "You were the one who approached *me*. I'd never even—"

"You know," he cut her off, his face cruel, "let's just fast-forward this little scene to the end. I'm sure as a fan of cinema, you'll appreciate that. Come Sunday, I'm outta here."

"Well good riddance!" Calla yelled back, her cheeks hot. "To you and Mack both." It took everything she had not to put her hands to her stomach. God, she couldn't imagine the things he'd accuse her of if she told him about the baby. She backed up out from underneath the stands.

"Anyone who doesn't know me after sleeping with me for three months isn't someone I could ever really care for."

Liam scoffed. "As if you care for anything other than me bank balance."

"You..." Calla reached down and grabbed a clod of dirt from the ground and hurled it his direction. He barely dodged it, but then he started clapping.

"Bravo. This really is the performance of the decade. Ma would be so proud. Too bad you'll never get to rifle through her things. Or get anywhere near me billions."

Calla's entire body shook with rage. But then her shoulders slumped. She turned to walk away, not wanting Liam to see the power he had to hurt her. But no. Screw that. He thought he could just go around and carelessly shit on the people who lo—

She cut the thought off even as it formed. God, was it true? Did she love this selfish bastard?

The pain was almost enough to crack her in two.

"I let you in." She hit her chest with her palm. "You and Mack. I let you both in. Like I never had anyone before. And then you both broke my h—" She stopped when she realized Liam wasn't looking at her but had his face stubbornly set to the side.

"Goddamn you, Liam O'Neill."

With that, she spun on her heel and strode back toward Painter. More determined than ever to win the prize money and be able to have control over her own future without ever depending on anyone else ever again.

32

BETHANY

BETHANY THOUGHT the little bitch would never leave her damn horse alone for a single minute. But then Liam came by and of course Cal chased off after him like a dog in heat.

Bethany shook her head.

It was time to show that little whore where she belonged once and for all. The Carters were trash and always would be.

Bethany had always hated Cal. There was just something *about* her. She was nothing but poor white trash but she acted like a *snob*, never hanging around with anyone else or making friends. Like she thought she was so much better than all of them.

But it wasn't until Bethany had walked in on her Daddy with Calla's whore of a mother in his study one day that she knew what hatred really was. Bethany had only been twelve at the time but she knew what it meant when a woman was sitting on a man's lap with her arms around him.

Daddy had sworn he'd get rid of her. And he did. He even got her to leave town.

But there was still her spawn left.

Calla. The uppity little bitch who wouldn't disappear no matter how Bethany tried to ignore her. Always trying to pretend she was equal to her betters.

Every time Bethany came in second place to Cal and her ugly mongrel horse, it was a thorn that dug deeper and deeper under her skin.

But then, finally, *finally*, natural order was restoring itself to the world.

Daddy bought out the Carter ranch, leaving Cal with almost nothing. She had to work as a ranch hand for God's sake.

And Bethany's plans to capture Liam O'Neill's attention and secure her place as billionaire royalty had been *this* close to falling into place.

Until Cal fucking Carter had put her whore fucking nose where it didn't belong and fucked everything up.

Bethany wasn't runner up to Miss Natrona County Jr. two years in a row so she could lose the biggest prize of her life to the town fucking *tomboy*.

And Bethany *knew* if Cal hadn't been distracting Liam with her little   I'm-poor-and-helpless-and-oh-yeah-also-a-whore-who'll-let-you-stick-it-anywhere act, he would have been able to see Bethany for the treasure she was.

Daddy always said no man would ever be good enough for his little princess and it was true. None of the grimy Wyoming farmers were. But Liam was a prince if she'd ever met one and they were *meant* to be together. She'd known it ever since she took a picture of him in the bar, googled his face, and found out he was worth approximately three-point-seven billion.

But then to be so roundly *humiliated* in front of him and all because of that tomboy he-she *freak*! Ugh! Bethany's whole body went hot when she remembered Liam's words to her at the feed store. No one talked to her like that. Ever.

And all because, like, Cal had poisoned him against her.

Well Bethany was putting things right. There was an order to the world. And she was restoring it.

No Carter would ever get in her way again.

Bethany approached Cal's horse. It neighed and shifted back and forth on its hooves, tail lifting.

"It's all right," Bethany said, voice gentle. She needed this stupid horse to stand still for what she was planning. When she stepped forward and grabbed the bridle, the mare's eyes went wide. Bethany clicked her teeth and ordered her to stay, and the horse went still.

Which was, in itself, a little annoying, because *fine*, it was well trained. So what? Bethany's mustang would have been superior, hands down. But she couldn't compete, could she? Because they'd given her a lame horse.

The stupid thing had week joints and went lame right after the trail trials. She'd only been training it in basic reining and cutting skills. And sure, she was pushing a little—but none of her purebred horses would have batted an eye at the exercises.

She gave it two whole weeks off training to rest its strained joints. But after just an hour of getting back out in the training paddock, it was limping again.

So now here she was at a horse competition with no horse. Daddy had even called the BLM and tried to make a generous donation if only they'd give her another horse but they said it was too far into the competition for that.

That was the final straw. Like, you could only push a woman so far.

So she'd called and called for weeks until she finally got through all the stupid secretaries and whatever until she could finally talk to Liam's dad and tell him where his son was. There wasn't a reward or anything, but she figured there was the smallest chance Liam would be so grateful for reuniting him with his father, he'd give her another chance. And if not, well, at least that bitch Cal wouldn't get him.

She wasn't about to let her win this competition either.

She ran her hand down the flank of Cal's horse's.

"Just stand still, stupid horse," she whispered in a soothing voice. She glanced around, didn't see anyone, and pulled the small buzzer out of her pocket. It was about the size of a cigarette lighter and it easily slipped underneath the back of the saddle against the horse's flank. The horse turned and looked toward her, ears flicking back and forth.

"Oh you'll be fine," Bethany muttered, taping the small device in place. "People use these things on race horses all the time." Sure it was illegal but God, if those stupid animal rights activists had their way, everyone would be, like, eating tofu and kale for every meal.

Bethany pulled the remote out of her pocket to test the buzzer. Before she could, though, she heard voices coming her way.

"Shit." She slipped through the bars of the stall and down the hall before anyone could see her.

She smiled as she took the long way around to the arena seating. She couldn't wait to watch the show.

33

CALLA

CALLA WAS JOGGING BACK toward where she'd left Painter stalled and almost ran into the back end of a horse.

"Oh!" she said, pulling up short as the horse and two people leading it turned to look at her.

"Dr. Nunez?"

A young woman stood beside her. The doctor's daughter, Calla bet.

"Calla." Dr. Nunez's eyes lit up at seeing her but then she averted her gaze like she'd just remembered something.

Like that Calla was her patient and they had an appointment next week to reveal Calla's test results.

"Did the results come back already?"

Dr. Nunez head jerked up to Calla and then she quickly looked away again. "It's good to see you, Calla. Good luck today. Come on, Savannah." She pulled on the horse's reins like that's how she meant to leave it.

Holy shit. Calla grabbed her elbow. "If you know, you have to tell me. Please," she begged. "Think about if it was your daughter. I have to know." Maybe a low blow, but God, the knowledge about Calla's entire future could be standing right in front of her.

Dr. Nunez's eyes flicked toward her daughter. "'Vannah, why don't you take Mariposa back down to her stall. I'll be right there."

Savannah nodded and led the horse further down the tunnel back toward the temporary stalls.

Calla squeezed Dr. Nunez's arm. "Please."

Dr. Nunez sighed, then looked around them. Behind them, cheers and applause came from the arena.

"This is completely unprofessional. And you're about to compete. The last thing I should be—"

"So I have it?" Calla pressed. "I tested positive? Is that what you're saying?" She knew it. She'd been stupid to think for even a second that—

"No," Dr. Nunez exclaimed. Then she pressed her eyes shut a moment before opening them again and pulling Calla off to the side of the tunnel hallway. Her eyes gentled. "Your test came back negative for Huntingtons."

Negative?

Calla collapsed back against the wall, blinking in shock.

"Not only that," Dr. Nunez smiled gently, "but your CAG repeats were so low, there's no chance any of your offspring will have it either."

Calla choked and then bent over, hands on her stomach.

She couldn't believe her ears. Did she—

She shot up straight. "You're sure? There's *no* chance—?"

"None," Dr. Nunez assured her.

"Thank you," Calla said. "I don't know how I can ever— Just, *thank you.*"

Calla felt like crying. And dancing. And whooping in elation at the top of her lungs. She hugged Dr. Nunez and thanked her again.

Then she ran the rest of the way back to Painter's stall.

"What's up with you?" she asked when Painter neighed anxiously after she stepped in the stall. She laughed and rubbed down her nose. "Today is our lucky day."

She frowned as she said it. Because it wasn't half an hour ago that both Mack and Liam had broken her heart.

But her son or daughter wouldn't get Huntingtons. And she'd be able to raise them without ever having to worry about abandoning them by getting sick herself.

It meant everything.

"Come on, girl," she said to Painter, opening the gate and leading her out. "Don't want to be late to the party."

As Calla led her around to where competitors had lined up by the chute that led into the arena, her mind raced. For the first time, she could really start planning her future. And even if it didn't have either of the men of her dreams in it, she would make it a damn good one.

"You and me, little lime," she whispered, patting her stomach. "You and me."

34

MACK

MACK WAS *this* close to leaving them all behind without another look back. He shifted from park into first gear. But then he froze.

Pregnant. She was pregnant.

It could be yours.

No. Christ. How could he even feel a stab of hope or joy at the thought? He was *so* fucked up. He was born shit and any baby he made would be—

His mind rejected the thought before he could finish it.

The baby was half Calla. And something that came from her couldn't be anything less than perfect.

He squeezed his eyes shut and as soon as he did, he saw Sammy's bloody, broken body.

Christ. That had happened because of Mack. He needed to get as far away from Calla and Liam before Bone ever knew a thing about them.

Mack slammed the steering wheel. He heard the roar of the

cheering crowd. There were speakers on the outside of the arena that broadcast everything happening inside.

And then Mack heard, "Next up, Cal Carter, representing Mel's Horse Rescue with her mustang, Painter!"

He'd leave. He would. But after one last glimpse of her.

He slammed the door to his truck and ran into the arena. He had to push his way through a group of reporters bottlenecked at the entrance of the arena where a harried looking security guard was holding them back.

"Mackenzie. Mackenzie Knight?"

"It's Mackenzie!"

Mack looked up sharply at all the eyes quickly turning his way. How the fuck did any of these people know his name?

"This picture of you and billionaire playboy Liam O'Neill was snapped last night." One of the reporters held up a tablet showing some internet site with a clear picture of him, Calla, and Liam dancing. Close. Closer than close.

Shit.

"Tell us, is Liam cheating on Isobel Snow, last year's Missing Heiress?"

"What's your relationship to Liam O'Neill?"

"Can you comment on rumors that Liam suffers from amnesia and hasn't known where he's been the past year and a half?"

"Get the fuck outta my way," Mack growled, finally managing to push through the reporters and to a curtained off area. There were two entrances to the arena and Mack made his way around to the one furthest from the reporters.

He slid through the competitors and horses lined up there until he was right up against the gate so he could see into the arena without going up into the stands. Calla was already taking Painter through her paces.

"Looks like you had the right idea about getting out of town."

Mack jerked his head around and there was Liam, back propped up against the opposite wall.

"I met your adoring public," Mack muttered, eyes going back to Calla.

Liam went on like Mack hadn't said anything. "I'm out of here as soon as I can pack me things up at the ranch." Liam pulled his wide-brimmed hat low.

Mack glanced his way. "Oh yeah? What's Calla got to say about that?"

"She doesn't get a say." Liam's jaw tensed. "She was playing me this whole time."

Mack turned his head at that. "What the fuck are you talking about?"

"She knew exactly who I was. And how much I'm worth."

"Huh," Mack said. "So?"

Liam scoffed. "What do you mean, *so*? The rest is self-explanatory."

Goddammit no one got on his nerves like this fucker. He wanted to order him to grab his knees so he could tan his ass.

But shit. He was done with all that. Still, Liam needed to get his head out of his ass. Mack wouldn't be here to watch out for Calla so Liam better step the fuck up. "And what she'd have to say about it?" With effort he kept his voice mostly level. "Did she try to ask for money for the baby or something?"

Liam's face went red. "*Baby?* What fucking *baby?*"

"She didn't even tell you she was pregnant? Jesus," Mack shook his head, "you really fucked things up, didn't you?"

"Me? You're telling me she's fucking pregnant! It's even more proof she's trying to trap me and get at me mon—"

Mack grabbed Liam by the front of his shirt and slammed him up against the side of the chute. The horse who was first in line at the gate snorted and stamped its feet, while the owner started bitching at Mack.

Mack ignored him. "You better not finish that fucking sentence." He shoved Liam against the wall again, then let him go. He shook his head at Liam. "Christ, you're what I'm leaving her to?"

"I'm going to have to ask you two to move away from the—"

"Shut the fuck up," Mack growled at the arena volunteer and turned his back on Liam so he could watch Calla.

Liam was a fucking idiot thinking she was after him for his money. Woman like Calla, she didn't want anything she hadn't earned. She was as proud as she was stubborn. And too good for either of them.

She rode Painter out into the middle of the arena like she was born to sit on a horse. They moved together as one, like they'd been working together for years instead of just months. And the way Painter responded to Calla's tiniest nudge or click, there was no way you could tell the mare had been a wild mustang not three months ago. Fuck Liam and all his digs about mustangs being inferior to other horses. Fuck Liam in general.

Calla had already made it through several obstacles no problem. She next directed Painter to do several turnaround spins in place, first clockwise, then, after a slight pause, in the other direction.

Then she had the horse back up several steps before taking off at a trot, then a canter, then an all-out gallop across the arena. She brought the horse to a sliding stop, pulled out a pop gun and let out several loud *pop pop pops* as she backed the horse up again. Painter continued through the steps without flinching at the noise.

Mack let out a low whistle. Damn, Calla was impressive. Mack had been proud when he'd been able to get his gelding to stand still for a whole five seconds. Meanwhile Calla's horse was running circles around them all. She really had a chance at the prize money.

He found himself holding his breath as she approached the last set of obstacles. They were set up on his side of the arena and he could make out the concentration and calm determination on Calla's face. First she led Painter through a veil of hanging streamers. Then she urged Painter up, hoof by hoof, onto a wobbly wooden platform that pivoted on a fulcrum.

Painter set her first two hooves on it, no problem. But when she moved her back hooves up, something went wrong. Painter's neck suddenly jerked and her eyes went wild.

And then she bolted.

She leapt off the wooden platform, jarring Calla to the side and almost off the saddle.

"Calla!" Mack jumped up on the gate.

Calla righted herself on her saddle and was clearly pulling on the reins to try to get Painter to stop. But her eyes were wide with some kind of hellfire and she just kept going. Calla had enough control to get her to turn slightly left around the curve of the arena oval, but she was still galloping hell for leather. They flew past Mack and on down the arena.

Mack was about to jump the fence but one of the chute workers held him back.

"Please sir, get down! You're not allowed in the arena during another contestant's ride."

"She's in trouble," Mack snarled, yanking away from the man as he tried to see what was going on with Calla and Painter.

They were reaching the opposite end of the arena. It looked like Calla was trying to get Painter to turn again since she wasn't slowing down.

It didn't work this time.

Calla's body flew off the back end of the horse as Painter kept galloping off without her. Calla flipped once in the air before landing on the arena floor in a puff of dirt.

"Calla!" Mack shouted.

"Let go of me, you bastard! She's hurt!" It was Liam's voice from behind him. All Mack knew was that no one was holding him back anymore.

He jumped the gate and started running for Calla. Goddammit, why was the arena so fucking big? He was only halfway there when paramedics came out with a stretcher. They slipped a neck brace around her neck.

Fuck. Was she unconscious? Had she broken her arm? A leg? A fucking spinal injury?

What about the baby?

He pumped his legs even harder.

The paramedics lifted Calla and were moving her out of the far exit of the arena. Shit. He was glad they were so efficient but he just needed to know if she was okay.

They disappeared into a wall of people who had gathered at the arena tunnel. Mack was there fifteen seconds later.

"Out of my way," he growled, trying to push through the crowd and see where they'd taken Calla.

"Liam! Liam O'Neill!" called a man in a suit holding a microphone, eyes focused behind Mack. "What is your relationship to Calla Carter? How are you feeling right now as she's being taken away with unspecified injuries?"

"Are you in a relationship with Isobel Snow?" asked someone else.

"Are you cheating on Isobel with Calla?"

"Liam, why did you run away to America? Is it because the rumors about your father being your family's long-time gardener are true and Ciarán disinherited you?"

"Get out of my fucking way!" Mack roared as the vultures came at them from all fucking sides. He glanced over his shoulder and saw Liam having an even worse time of it. Camera flashes popped off every other second.

Mack growled and grabbed Liam's upper arm, hauling him forward with him.

"No fucking comment," Mack shouted, putting his shoulder forward and using it like a battering ram to shove through the wall of people.

"Hey!"

"You can't just—"

One bastard with a camera was knocked to the floor. He immediately started sputtering about suing but Mack kept plowing on. These fuckers had the gall to be thinking about their goddamned story when he didn't even know if Calla was okay.

When he and Liam made it past the first ring of reporters, Mack shouted to anyone who would listen, "Where'd they take the injured woman?"

A pimply-faced teenager with a Horse Makeover lanyard around his neck looked at him with wide eyes. "Uh, the ambulance is parked around back. This way," he jerked a thumb over his shoulder.

Mack let go of Liam and grabbed the boy's upper arm. "Show us."

The teenager swallowed.

"Faster," Mack growled. That got the kid moving, even if he did look terrified. Mack didn't care. He just needed to know what the fuck was going on with Calla.

The kid led them out of the arena and to the left. "The ambulance was parked right here—" the kid started but then he jumped back. "Holy shit!"

He bent over and threw up.

"What the hell?" Liam asked.

But as Mack looked down on the two bloody bodies in EMT uniforms with *D*'s carved into their foreheads—the calling card of the Devil's Spawn—a horrible fucking certainty settled on him.

"Bone's got her."

35

LIAM

"WHAT THE FUCK DOES THAT MEAN?" Liam spun on him, shoving his shoulders. "Who's Bone?"

Mack grabbed his head with his hands. "Shit. I don't know." His eyes came back to Liam and whatever it was, it wasn't good.

"Well tell me what you do fucking know," Liam shouted at him.

Mack took one more look at the two men on the ground, each with a pool of blood underneath them from their slashed necks. Jaysus. Liam turned away before he got sick just like the lad.

"First, we get out of here," Mack said, voice tight. "Call the police," Mack said to the white-faced teenager. "Tell them Calla Carter's been kidnapped by Daniel Jones in these EMT's ambulance."

Then he grabbed Liam's upper arm and started dragging him toward the parking lot.

"Let me the go." Liam jerked his arm out of Mack's grasp. "You don't get to order me around. You're the one who's dragged Calla into whatever the fuck this is."

Mack flinched at that. Not that it gave Liam much gratification.

For once, he didn't care about getting in hits with Mack. But he probably did need the big bastard's help getting Calla back. It looked like he had the same thought as Liam as they both were jogging in the direction of the trucks they'd driven in.

"So tell me what I need to know about whoever took Calla," Liam said as he reached his truck. They worked quickly to unhitch the trailer from the back. Then Liam went and yanked open the driver's side door.

Mack tried to pull him out of the way. "I'm driving."

"Fuck you are," Liam said. "She's me truck. And—" he shoved Mack back with a hand on his chest— "I drive because I know where the fuck she is."

Mack blinked at that. "How—"

"You're wasting me time," Liam said. "Are you going to get in or we gonna waste more time in this pissing contest?"

"Fine," Mack said. "But let me get something from my truck." He backed up and ran toward the other truck.

Liam huffed out a frustrated breath and pulled his phone out of his pocket. Mack was back in a couple minutes, up in the cab and slamming the passenger door behind him.

Mack looked at him incredulously. "You really think it's time to be checking your goddamned messages?"

Liam didn't even bother with a comeback. "I'm tracking Calla. I got worried because she takes those trips up to Casper each week and is always driving home in the dark. So that necklace I gave her last night? It has a GPS tracker in it."

Mack just stared at him for a second. "I could fucking kiss you right now."

"Yeah, yeah." Liam held out the phone so Mack could see. "Looks like they're taking her on back roads. Avoiding the highway."

Mack nodded, taking the phone. "You drive. I'll tell you what we're walking into."

That was when Liam saw what Mack had in his other hand. A gun. A fucking gun.

36

MACK

LIAM STARED AT THE GUN, then shook his head as he put the truck in gear. "Talk. Why the fuck did those two dead guys back there have D's carved in their heads? And what the hell do they want with Calla?"

Liam peeled out of the parking lot as Mack gave Liam the abridged version of what had happened with Bone and Ben.

"It was personal between Bone and me, let's just say that," Mack said. A fucking understatement, but Liam didn't need to know the gritty details.

Bone liked keeping his pets around until they broke. When Mack stopped fighting back, Bone thought he'd done just that. But he saw he'd made a mistake when Mack thrived after getting away from him. Mack stealing Ben away made it all the worse. It didn't matter that Bone killed Ben. To Bone, they'd never be square. Sending Sammy to spy on Bone had just made everything worse. He was such a fucking idiot.

He gritted his teeth as he continued, "Things were okay between me and Pres when I got out. The Devil's Spawn are mainly just a prison gang. There were members outside, but usually just to support the inside members and keep the supply chain strong. It didn't operate like a normal MC."

"So you don't think this President sent his thugs after you?"

Mack shook his head, his jaw hardening. "No. Timing of it? No. This is Bone. Plain and simple." Mack watched the GPS as Liam turned off onto a side road. Then he looked at the blinking dot on the map on Liam's phone. *Smart.* Bone had taken the long way around but Liam was circumventing the route by taking a diagonal road that would put them right behind the ambulance.

"He knew where I was gonna be and then he was either watching and saw us all together last night or this morning. Or he saw that damn picture online."

And Bone had always liked to hurt him by taking what he held dear.

What the fuck had he done to Calla's horse? That seemed way too elaborate a plan just to snatch her. Didn't seem like Bone's style. He'd been more of a fist to the throat kind of a guy. Not too bright but brutal as all fuck. Maybe Bone hadn't done anything and he'd just taken advantage of the circumstance. Bad luck for the fucking EMTs.

And Calla.

Mack's hands fisted as Liam floored it. Mack's eyes flipped back and forth between the GPS and the blinking dot on Liam's phone.

Please let Calla be okay. Mack wasn't a praying man but he swore he'd go to church every Sunday if only Calla was okay.

If Bone was just going to kill her right off, he would have left her with the paramedics.

No, Bone would want Mack to know she'd suffered Bone's particular brand of violence before killing her.

They slowed down as they came up behind a small Toyota going the speed limit and Mack's knee jiggled impatiently. The red dot passed the juncture of where their road met up with the ambulance's. They were only maybe a minute behind.

"Faster or we won't be able to catch up with them."

"I'm working on it," Liam said. He laid on the horn as he passed the Toyota and slid back into the right lane just as an oncoming car barreled by, honking their own horn.

"Fuck," Mack swore, grabbing onto the handle on the ceiling as Liam's truck swerved, readjusting. "You're gonna get the goddamned cops on our ass."

"Sounds good to me. The more the merrier."

Mack didn't know about that. He'd prefer to dole out his own form of justice before the cops got involved. He kept the Glock in his truck in case he ran into any dangerous wildlife. Mountain lion sightings were rare, but they still happened. Now, though, he recognized that Bone was the monster he'd really bought the gun for.

They finally reached the T junction where they turned right onto the road the ambulance was on. Mack checked the red dot. He didn't know the scale of the little map, but it didn't look like they were far ahead. Even at top speed, the ambulance couldn't be booking it *that* fast. Especially not compared to Liam's lead foot.

There were fewer and fewer signs of the city the further out they went. The road they turned onto was a narrow, scenic two-lane highway. Trees lined either side. Liam honked and passed a couple cars and then—

"There they are!" Liam shouted as the ambulance came in to view. It didn't have lights or sirens on and it swerved back and forth on the road.

"Jaysus, is the fucker drunk?"

"Get in front of 'em," Mack said, straining against his buckle and rolling down his window to get a better look. He pulled out his Glock and loaded the chamber.

"What the fuck are you going to do?" Liam shouted, glancing back and forth between the gun and the road.

"Pay attention to the goddamned road," Mack said, eyes locked on the ambulance.

"You're mad as a box of feckin' frogs," Liam muttered through gritted teeth. They sped up until they were passing the ambulance.

"Bone's driving," Mack called. At the same moment Bone looked down and saw Mack hanging out the window. And the bastard grinned. Fucking *grinned*.

"Get in front of him," Mack said, still watching Bone. "Force him to stop."

Liam had obviously been of the same mind because even as Mack said it, they passed and were about to pull in front of the ambulance. At least until Bone jerked on his wheel and rammed into them.

"Shite!" Liam yelled, just managing to right the truck before they fishtailed off the road. In the distance, another truck was heading their way in the oncoming lane. To their left was a large lake.

"Pass them," Mack yelled.

"I'm trying!" Liam slammed his foot on the gas and the truck lurched forward. Mack was thrown back against the seat. His fingers went white-knuckled on the grab handle overhead and he sent another prayer up as the truck heading toward them started honking.

Liam had just about passed the ambulance when it jerked in their direction again, this time clipping them on the back taillight.

Shit!

They almost spun right into the ambulance's way. What the fuck was Bone thinking? Mack barely had a second to think before the truck's wheels burnt rubber Liam yet again managed to steady them. They cut in front of the ambulance right in time to avoid the oncoming truck.

"Holy shite," Liam shouted as it whizzed by, the horn blaring in one constant honk. Mack swung around to look out the back window at the ambulance.

Mack could just barely make out Bone's ugly mug behind the wheel, features mottled with rage. And shit, even after all this time, Mack felt a kick of terror in his guts. Bone still had that power over him.

He swung around. "Let's end this," he said and Liam nodded. He punched the gas even more, furthering the distance between them and the ambulance.

Then, the road clear of on-coming traffic, he spun the truck sideways, blocking both lanes of the road. There were trees on one side of the road and the lake on the other.

Nowhere for Bone to go. He had no choice but to stop.

Liam pushed open his door and jumped down. "Just in case the crazy fecker tries to go through."

Mack nodded. But he could already see that the ambulance was slowing down. They had the bastard cornered and he knew it.

His fingers closed around his Glock as he tucked it in the back of his pants and walked around the truck to stand by Liam.

The ambulance slowed even more.

And then Bone turned it at the last moment and drove through the flimsy metal barrier into the fucking lake.

37

MACK

"CALLA!" Liam shouted, running to the lake's edge after the ambulance.

Mack followed right on his heels, his heartbeat a pounding drum in his ears. Liam jumped in the water, swimming to where the ambulance was nose down and slowly sinking.

But then Mack caught sight of movement on the road.

It was Bone, crawling and then stumbling to his feet.

Motherfucker must have bailed right before sending the rig over into the lake. Mack yanked the gun out of the back of his pants and walked toward Bone.

"Mack, help! I can't get the doors open!"

Mack looked back at Liam, in the water and yanking at the back door of the ambulance. It wasn't giving even though Liam looked like he was yanking with all his might.

Then he looked back at Bone, who was obviously winded but was still grinning at Mack. "Yes Mackenzie, go try to rescue your girlfriend. If it's not too late, that is."

"You son of a—"

"Mack!" Liam screamed.

"What a dilemma," Bone mocked, putting his fist under his chin. "Do you deal with me and let your girlfriend die? Or let me go so you can go try to save her?" He laughed. "This is why you were always so fun to play with. You cared so damn much." He threw his hands up in the air. "What's it gonna be, baby boy? Me or her?"

"Who says I have to choose?" Mack said coldly.

He whipped his gun around, aimed, and shot Bone's dick off.

Then he turned and ran for Liam and Calla.

38

LIAM

LIAM only barely registered the gun shot behind him. He looked back, saw Mack still standing, then went back to what he was doing. The back door was locked, so he'd given up on that and swum around to the front of the ambulance. It was totally submerged. Jaysus the whole thing was sinking so damn fast. It had only been thirty or forty seconds and already the front was full of water.

"Calla!" he heard Mack shouting and banging on the back door. At least the bastard had finally got his priorities straight and was in the damn water.

Liam yanked on the front door. It didn't give at first but after bracing his feet and yanking some more, it finally opened.

Liam took a giant breath of air and ducked underneath the water. He swam into the front seat. It was dark inside, a little bit of light filtering through the submerged windshield. Enough to see that it was the kind of ambulance that opened to the back compartment, thank Jaysus.

It was awkward to maneuver his lanky body through the narrow opening to get to the back. He got the top of himself through but his bottom half became tangled, his foot stuck on the steering wheel. Shite!

He was getting short on air and the back of the ambulance was completely dark. He couldn't see a thing. Including where Calla was. Or where the surface was so he knew how close he was to catching a breath.

He finally kicked and kicked until he got his legs untangled so he could slip all the way through the opening to the back of the ambulance. He swam up and broke the surface. He took a huge breath and then immediately started searching.

"Calla?" He moved his hands around in the wet darkness.

That's when he heard the most beautiful sound in the world. Muffled cries came from his left and, following the noise, his hands closed on Calla's drenched frame, sitting on a gurney.

Jaysus the water was up to her chest. He felt along her body until he came to her face. Some sort of rag was stuffed in her mouth. He yanked it out and she started crying, "Thank you. Thank God. Oh God. Thank you. Thank you."

"Gotta say, this is the first time I've been called God outside the bedroom."

"Oh my God, if I could smack you right now, I would," she laughed and cried at the same time. "Get me out of here. I'm hand-cuffed to this damn thing."

Shite. Liam felt down her arms to her wrists. On both sides she was cuffed to the handles of the huge gurney. There was no way they were going out the way he came in. And they were running out of time.

"I'm gonna see if I can get the doors open from the inside. I'm only letting you go for a second, okay."

"Okay," she said, but her voice shook so much Liam could tell she was terrified in spite of the fact she'd just been making jokes.

Right then there was an ear-splitting *bang*. And then another one.

Then the ambulance was flooded with light as Mack yanked open the back door. For a second, Liam could only stare. The bastard had shot the lock off the door.

"You could have killed us, you fucking maniac." Then he shook his head. "Help me get her out of here. She's handcuffed to this damn thing."

Mack nodded and waded into the ambulance. He pulled on the handcuffs and obviously saw what Liam had. They weren't getting her out of there apart from the gurney. Liam was already trying to tug at the gurney and get it free from the sinking ambulance. It wasn't budging.

"Mack, help me move this damn thing." He jerked at it some more but while it rattled a bit and sloshed the water, it didn't move.

"I don't want to panic anyone," Calla said, "but *get me the fuck out of here!*"

Liam looked up and saw the water was at her neck. He would not sit here and watch Calla die.

Mack dove down, probably trying to find whatever held the gurney to the ambulance. Good idea. Liam did the same. He felt all along the floor on the right side of the gurney. But there were just the wheels and the floor and nothing holding the two together. What the fuck was it?!

He ran out of air and surfaced. Only to find Calla's head tipped back as she strained to keep her nose above water.

"Goddammit!"

Liam looked around... There! He yanked a bit of clear plastic tubing off the wall. It had a mask on one end and some sort of medical something on the other. He ripped both of them off and put the tube in Calla's mouth just as the water closed over her face.

He held the other end of the tube clear of the water so she could keep breathing through it. But holding it up meant he couldn't help Mack in the search to free the gurney. And they only had so much time before the whole goddamned ambulance filled and sank. Liam had no idea how deep the water was, but it had been an especially snowy winter and all the reservoirs and lakes were full.

Mack came up gasping for air. He took one look at Liam holding the tube out of the water and Calla submerged. His eyes widened and then he took another huge breath and dived back down.

"Come on, Mack," Liam whispered. "I'll take back every time I ever called you a stupid bastard, if you can just figure this out."

The water continued rising. The tubing Liam had found wasn't very long and soon, the water had risen almost to the end of it. Shite, shite, *shite*. He couldn't— They weren't going to be able to— *FUCK!*

He looked around frantically for anything else that might do. Some other tubing that might be longer? But everything was in disarray, half the shit must have fallen off the walls and out of the cabinets when the ambulance crashed into the lake.

He was useless. Calla was going to die. For all his money and power, he was a useless piece of shit who would watch her die right in front of his goddamned eyes—

The gurney suddenly shifted.

Mack did it.

The bastard actually *did it*.

Liam wanted to whoop with joy but instead he shook himself and made sure to hold the tubing clear of the water.

Mack came up to the surface, wading wildly with one arm and tugging at the gurney with the other. Jaysus, he was a terrible swimmer.

"Take the tube so she can breathe," Liam said.

And for once in his life, Mack didn't argue. He reached over the gurney and took the tube carefully while Liam braced his legs against the side of the ambulance and pushed the gurney out the back.

Calla sputtered for breath as her head finally came clear of the surface and Mack tossed the tubing aside, one hand coming to her face. She spit and blinked. Jaysus, Liam couldn't imagine how traumatizing everything she'd just been through was.

Even now. She was still locked to a heavy hunk of metal and they were in a lake.

"We'll get you out of here, baby. Everything's all right now."

She just shivered, apparently out of quick-witted responses. Liam couldn't fucking blame her. He pushed the gurney all the way free of the ambulance, using the doors for the last little bit of leverage before swimming on his own.

Calla's feet immediately began to sink. She yanked her knees up, twisting and floating but being dragged down by her wrists attached to the gurney.

"Mack, can you get her feet?" Liam asked, trying to keep his voice calm. He wasn't sure how good a job he was doing by the way Calla whimpered. He stayed at her head, pumping his legs furiously under the water to keep her afloat.

"We've got you, baby. It's just a little way to shore."

Thank God it wasn't a lie. While the reservoir dropped steeply off from the road, there was enough silt built up by the roadway. When Mack swam around to the foot of the gurney, they were able to wedge the wheels onto solid land.

Behind them, the ambulance kept sinking until only the top corner of the doors was visible. Medical paraphernalia floated all around.

Even wedged on the soil, the water was still deep enough that Calla's waist and legs were submerged. When Mack moved around closer, she threw herself into his arms. Well, as much as she could with her hands still cuffed to the damn gurney. Liam tread water, lifting Calla's cuffed wrist to get a better look at it. There had to be some way to get it off.

Then he heard sirens in the distance. Thank Christ. He'd gotten into his share of scrapes throughout his years where Garda had gotten involved to be wary of the bastards—but he'd never been happier to hear the police were coming. They'd be able to get Calla free.

"Help's coming, baby." Liam pushed some wet hair out of Calla's face and dropped his forehead against hers. Mack kissed her, all three of their heads close together. Just like they should always be.

Which was when he remembered his last words to Calla about her only being with him for his money.

"I'm sorry I was such a fecking idiot and didn't trust you," Liam said, words tumbling out one after the other. "Everyone I ever loved before has let me down. Just wanted me for what I could give them." Even his da. He was only worth something to Ciarán if he could prove himself worthy of the O'Neill name and legacy—a standard which his da always set impossibly high. Maybe because he never really believed Liam was his son.

"But you aren't everyone else. You're Calla." He grabbed her face between his hands. "You're the woman I love." Jaysus. It was so obvious now. "I was a coward not telling you before." He hadn't even been willing to admit it to himself. Not before that horrible moment when the ambulance went over the road into the lake and his heart stopped beating.

Calla was worth taking a chance on. She was worth everything. And Mack. He had Liam's heart too, the big bastard. Calla was the glue, but the three of them were the perfect fit. When he was with them, it felt more right than anything had in his life. Two people who wanted him just for... well, *himself*. Who found him worthy all on his own.

Liam grasped Mack's bicep and pulled him close as they both embraced Calla. For her part she cried and laughed and hugged them back.

Until a loud growling shout came from above.

"You'll never be anything but my *bitch*."

Mack jerked back from Calla and Liam right as the figure above them, blood streaming from his—*crotch?!*—leapt down from the road, knife raised over his head.

39

MACK

MACK DIDN'T EVEN HAVE time for a full thought before—

SLAM. Bone's weight hit him full force and knocked him back into the water. *The knife. Block the arm holding the knife.*

Shit! Burning pain lit up Mack's left forearm. Fucker had sliced him. Still. Better his arm than his throat. Mack wrestled to get hold of Bone's wrist, both of them sinking deeper into the water as they struggled for control of the knife.

There. He finally grabbed Bone's wrist. He tried to elbow Bone's throat but upside down in the disorienting dark water, Mack could barely tell his ass from his ankles. He struck out several times, once even making contact with... something.

But then a thick arm came around his throat. Fuck. Bone had gotten behind him somehow. Mack held on tighter than ever to the wrist holding the knife.

He was short on air, though. Seriously short. It wasn't like he'd gotten much advance notice of Bone's attack. If he didn't get a breath soon, he'd pass out. And be easy fucking pickings.

Then Bone would go for Liam and Calla. Liam might be able to hold his own in a fight, but Bone had a knife. And Calla was still handcuffed to that damn gurney.

No. He would not let anything happen to them because of his fucked up past.

With a roar into the water, Mack jerked Bone's hand holding the knife up and stabbed it into Bone's other arm around his throat.

Bone's grip immediately loosened and he ripped the knife out of his own flesh. Mack took the chance to swim to the surface and grab a huge breath. But Bone was only more enraged. He came at Mack, knife swinging.

Mack yanked the gun out of the back of his pants and he pulled the trigger right in Bone's face.

Bone stopped, wincing. But then he laughed when nothing happened. Shit. The waterlogged gun hadn't fired.

Mack felt his eyes widen as he swam frantically backwards.

"Think fast."

Then a soaking medical duffel bag hit Bone in the head from behind, throwing off his attack on Mack. Bone swung around, tossing off the blue duffel but getting tangled in the straps. Mack wasn't about to lose the opportunity.

He grabbed Bone's knife arm from behind, wrenching it back with enough force to— *Crack*. Like the sound of a wooden baseball bat smacking a ball. There went Bone's bone.

He screamed and dropped the knife.

He still struggled when Mack grabbed and shoved his face under water but he was weak. After the blood loss and then his arm being broken, for once, he was weak and Mack was strong.

"Who's my best little bitch whore? Bone's breath on Mack's ear while he raped him. "You love being my little baby boy, don't you?"

"Go fuck yourself in hell," Mack spat.

Bone fucked him even more mercilessly. "You're clenching on my cock like you love it. You're my favorite, you know that? Out of all the bitches I've ever had, you're my favorite. My special little baby boy.

Mack shoved him even further beneath the water's surface.

He'd never hurt Mack again. He'd never hurt *anyone* again.

"Mack. Mack!"

Mack ignored Liam shouting his name. Until Liam rammed into him from the side, forcing him to let Bone up for air.

Bone gasped as soon as his head hit the surface.

"What the fuck are you thinking?" Mack shouted, grabbing Bone and shoving him underneath again.

But Liam just shook his head, mouth agape. "You can't just kill him like this. Listen," he gestured at the road. "The cops are almost here."

"We'll say it's self-defense."

"You're going to make Calla lie for you?" Liam demanded. "After everything she's been through today. All because of you?"

Mack kept shaking his head. "You don't know what he did." He spoke through his teeth.

Liam's face softened. Compassion. It took Mack aback. As did Liam's next words. "From where you shot him, I can guess." Liam moved closer. "He'll never hurt anyone like that again."

Mack looked over and saw Calla watching them, sitting up, obviously tense as she waited to see what Mack would do. Beautiful, innocent Calla, who deserved so much better than to witness anything as ugly as this.

"Do this and you might go back to jail," Liam went on, voice pleading. "Don't do it. Choose Calla. Choose *me*."

Mack looked at Liam. His handsome, boyish features were strained with earnestness.

"Fuck," Mack shouted, lifting a gasping and sputtering Bone back out of the water and hauling him over toward the incline where the reservoir met the road, far away from Calla. If Bone tried anything else, Mack would still be happy to bash his head in with some of the smooth stones near the base of the road.

The sirens were louder than ever, right over head. Liam swam back over to Calla and started to climb up the muddy, rocky embankment.

"Down here!" Liam yelled. "We're down here. We need help. And bolt cutters!"

40

CALLA

CALLA's own heartbeat was galloping a million miles an hour as the doctor moved the ultrasound wand over her stomach in order to see if her baby was okay.

Wown, wown, wown, wown, wown.

A smile split the doctor's face. "You hear that?" He held the wand steady and watched the screen. He was a tall man with more white than gray in his hair. "One hundred forty beats per minute is well within the healthy range. We can run a couple more tests to double check, but you haven't had any spotting and I see no reason to think there's anything wrong with your pregnancy."

"But I passed out when I fell off Painter. My horse," Calla clarified.

"You said you felt like you had the wind knocked out of you when you came to in the ambulance, right?"

Calla nodded.

"Did you have much to eat this morning?"

Calla shook her head and looked down at her lap. "No. I mean, I had half a bagel, but that was it." More like a fourth of a bagel if she was being honest. Mack had urged her to eat more but she'd felt nauseous. Morning sickness still hit some days. She claimed it was nerves because of the competition. God, that seemed like it was a million years ago now.

After the police had gotten her free of the cuffs attaching her to that horrible coffin of a gurney, another ambulance brought her to the hospital. She'd about hyperventilated when they put her in the back of it. Liam and Mack hadn't been able to come either because the police were still questioning them.

"Well," the doctor said, running his pen-light over her pupils again, "barring the results of your blood test, I'd venture to say that it was just a combination of low blood sugar and the shock of the fall that had you briefly passing out. And after the stress of everything that happened to you today," he patted her shoulder, "I suggest focusing on rest and nutrition for the next few days. But like I said, I don't see any reason you shouldn't continue with a healthy pregnancy."

Calla blinked but couldn't hold back any more. She put her hands to her face and started crying.

"Oh. There, there, Ms. Carter."

"Calla!"

Calla looked up at Liam's worried voice. "Are you all right? I'm sorry we took so long. The cops kept asking a million questions."

Liam jogged past the doctor to her side. Mack was behind him but he stopped in the doorway.

"Are you okay?" Liam asked again, slipping an arm under her head and pulling her to his chest. She didn't realize how tense she'd been until all her muscles relaxed at his touch. She went limp against him, reaching her other hand out for Mack.

He stared at her for a long moment before coming forward and clasping it. Finally. *Finally* she could breathe out.

"Everything's fine," she said, laughing and crying at the same time. "The baby's fine."

The next moment, though, her head was filling with images of what happened earlier.

God, when she'd come to in the ambulance only to find an attendant strapping her waist to the gurney. And then—she shuddered remembering how that man, that *monster*, ripped the second ambulance attendant backwards and how the blood sprayed when he slit his throat—

She shuddered.

"What is it?" Liam said. "Baby, you're killing us here."

She could tell he meant it, too. He sounded anguished. He didn't deserve it. She knew both he and Mackenzie had been through the ringer today too.

"Just..." She looked from Liam to Mack. "Thank you. If you hadn't gotten there when you did..." She shuddered again and pressed the hands they were holding to her stomach.

Mack jerked his hand away and she looked up at him startled.

He ran his hand through his hair. "I need to go."

He stood up abruptly.

"Wha—" Calla said at the same time Liam said, "You're not going fecking anywhere."

Mack swallowed, looking from one to the other. He shook his head and looked down. "I almost got you killed. The bab—" His voice broke and he looked toward the window, jaw flexing with emotion.

"You saved me." Calla reached for his hand again but again, he pulled it away.

"Stop it," he bit out, eyes flashing at her. "I know what I am. I'm ugly and fucked up inside. Why do you think I got these tattoos?" He yanked up his shirt sleeve to expose one of the bug-eyed devils inked on his skin. "It's what he made me. I'm damaged fucking goods and you deserve better than me. You deserve a man like him." Mack's eyes went to Liam.

"Mackenzie," Calla cried. How could he think that of himself? He'd been used and abused so horribly, but didn't he see? That was over now. "Don't you see? I felt ugly and alone my whole life until you two. We belong together. We're each other's family. And now we're about to add one more."

Mack's face went pained as he glanced at her hand on her stomach.

Don't pull away. Please. Don't pull away again, she begged silently.

"For Christ's sake, there you are," boomed a voice from the doorway. Calla's head swung that direction just in time to see Liam's father striding into the room.

41

LIAM

"I HAD to find out from the fecking paparazzi where me own son was. They're flocked outside like buzzards over a kill." Ciarán looked Liam up and down. "Well, you look a bit waterlogged but not too much worse for wear. Now let's end this nonsense and come home with me on the private jet."

Liam could only stare at him in disbelief. Did he not see the woman in the hospital bed whose hand he was holding?

He stood up straighter. Enough. "Da, this is me girl, Calla. And that there," he pointed to the ultrasound picture that had been printed off, "may or not be me biological son or daughter. Either way, I'm going to love them as if they were."

His father's back stiffened. "You have to find out. You can do a test before its born. If I would have had that chance, it would have changed everything." Emotion choked his father's voice.

Liam could only blink in disbelief at the man he'd spent his whole life either worshiping or hating. "So you coulda kicked me and ma to the curb if you found out I was the stablemaster's bastard before I was even born? Is that what you're sayin' straight to me face?"

Ciarán shook his head. "If you would have let me get two words in the other day, you would've heard me when I told you I did a DNA test. With some hairs from your comb you left behind. You'd only been gone a month at the time, but I realized it was time to know. To put this behind us once and for all." Liam couldn't be sure, but it looked like there might be a sheen to Ciarán's eye. "You're mine after all. You're me son. But then I didn't know where you were. Not until that woman got in touch with us. You have to believe me, lad, if I'd known all along, it would have been different."

He shook his head. "But learning about the affair when you were still a boy and knowing there was a chance you weren't mine—"

"So Ma was right," Liam huffed out a short mirthless laugh. "I didn't believe her at first when she told me the reason you'd never tested me DNA against yours was 'cause you didn't trust yourself not to throw me out like last week's garbage if you found out I wasn't yours."

"But you *are* mine—"

"It shouldn't have mattered!" Liam shouted, hands going to the sides of his head. "Jaysus, I've spent the last two years ever since ma told me the truth trying to prove to meself that I *was* your son. People only ever wanted me for what I could give them. If you disinherited me and I lost it all, where'd that leave me?"

"Son, I—"

"Don't," Liam bit out, running a hand roughly down the back of his neck and staring at the floor. There was silence for a second before Liam looked back up. "It wasn't ever about the money to me." He stared Da down. "All I ever wanted was you. I didn't even realize it, either. Not 'til the last few months."

He looked at Calla and then Mack. "I didn't know what it meant to love someone who loved you back. Not because of what you could do for them. But just for you. Just because you made each other happy."

He focused on Mack. "I'm sorry for how I've been to you. But you gotta know everything you just said was complete shite. Here I was trying to prove I was better than you, like it meant I was his son somehow."

He shook his head, pain tightening his gut as Mack frowned. "But every step of the way, you've proved you're a better man than me. You're the best man I've ever met." Mack took a step back at that, but Liam followed him, getting right up in front of him. "Seems the only place I could admit that was the bedroom. But you took me as I am. It's just one of the reasons I love you."

Then he kissed Mack in front of God, his dad, and anyone who happened to be passing by.

His father made a disgusted noise and turned around. "When you're done with these juvenile stunts, call me office." He headed for the door.

"This is all I've got to say to ya." Liam gave his dad the middle finger, never taking his eyes off Mackenzie. Then he intertwined his fingers with Mack's and pulled him back toward Calla on the bed.

Calla had tears in her eyes.

Liam's neck heated but he didn't let go of Mack's hand. "So. If you didn't hear, I'm not interested in ever findin' out which one of us donated to make the little sprout."

Calla laughed and this time when she reached for their hands and put them to her belly, Mack didn't pull away. The look on his face was priceless, Liam wished he had a camera to capture it. It was full of shock and awe while he also looked a little like he was about to pass out.

"Family," Mack finally whispered, echoing Calla's earlier sentiment. He squeezed both their hands and bowed his head to Calla's stomach.

EPILOGUE

MACK

"Is the blindfold really necessary?" Calla asked, tilting her head toward Mack. He was driving and he frowned her way. Liam reached up from the back seat and waved his hand right in front of her face, but she didn't react. Mack smiled.

"You bet your arse it's necessary. What's the point of a grand gesture if it isn't grand?"

Mack pulled onto the long gravel driveway and Calla grabbed for the door to steady herself when the truck started bouncing up and down.

"Whoa," she said. "So we're officially somewhere off the beaten path."

Mack glanced in the rearview mirror and saw Liam looking smug as fuck. Shit, he'd never hear the end of how this was Liam's great idea. Rest of his life, the Irish wanker would brag about how he knew just how to make all Calla's dreams come true.

But then Mack smiled. After all, it was his name going on the paperwork.

Mack slowed the truck down as they came up to the house.

"Wait's almost over," Mack said. He parked in front of the house and then Liam got out of the truck and opened Mel's door for her.

"Can I take the blindfold off now?"

"Not yet," Liam said.

Mack came around the front of the truck to their side and took Calla's other hand.

"Now," he and Liam said together.

Calla reached up and pulled the blindfold off. She blinked a few times in the bright noon sunlight. Then her brow scrunched.

She looked from Liam to Mack. "I don't understand. Why are we at my family's old ranch?"

Liam's grin was so wide it was gonna break his damn face. "Gotta have a place to bring our baby home to, yeah?"

Calla blinked some more. "What do you—"

"We bought the place," Mack said.

Calla's mouth dropped open and her eyes went wide. "But how—"

"Turns out there was a reason Mack got a full ride to Harvard. He's a right smart bastard."

Calla looked to Mack. He put a hand on the back of his neck. "I just happened to see there was a future in cryptocurrencies. So I made a small investment."

Calla started smiling but Mack could see she was still confused. Apparently, Liam could see it too.

"Fecking Bitcoin," Liam said, shaking his head. "Mack bought five-hundred dollars of it in 2011, and now it's worth fifteen million. Can you fecking believe that?"

"Holy shit," Calla breathed out. She grabbed Mack's arm. Her eyes ping-ponged back and forth between them before settling on Mack's. "Is he serious?"

Mack nodded. He'd worked his ass off at the mechanics shop in town all through high school and had a few grand saved up by the time he went to college... and then prison.

Pres occasionally got a cell phone smuggled in and Mack had used the fifteen minutes of internet Pres granted him to try to do something with the little money he had. Otherwise he knew he'd be fucked when he got out. He'd first heard about cryptocurrencies at Harvard and had read up on it, so that's where he put five hundred bucks. He'd tried a couple other investments but that was the only one that took off so fucking insanely.

"Can you believe it?" Liam asked. "Now I'm broke but this lanky bastard is our sugar daddy."

Mack looked at Liam. "Never. Call. Me. That. Again."

Liam laughed and clapped him on the back. Mack did have to say, though, Liam was taking the whole not-having-a-penny-to-his-name thing surprisingly well. His dad was 'cutting him off until he came to his senses.' Liam had responded to that text with a selfie of himself kissing Mack while simultaneously squeezing Calla's ass. Really, it was quite impressive he'd fit them all in a single camera frame.

"So you bought back my old house?"

"And the ranch," Liam said. "And an additional five hundred acres on either side of it."

Calla stumbled a little and Mack grabbed her arm to steady her. "Holy shit," she whispered again.

"Know you dreamed about setting up a horse training and boarding place, so there's money in the budget for that."

Calla just shook her head. "But how? That's Ned Cunningham's land and he'd nev—"

Mack felt his blood rise at even hearing the name. "Turns out he's so ashamed of having a lying, cheating, whore of a daughter, he's selling out and moving to California."

"I heard that after the sheriff arrested B— Betty? Bailey? Whatever her name is. Anyway, after she got arrested and everyone learned what she did, some folks who Cunningham was in debt to called in their markers. So he had no choice but to sell."

"Six months in jail and a four-thousand-dollar fine is a fucking injustice," Mack muttered. Stunt like that—using a buzzer on a recent broke mustang— Mack's teeth ground together. The bitch had meant for Calla to get thrown. And plenty of the best horsewomen and men got seriously injured every year. Just last year Mack had seen a guy on a spooked horse get thrown and then dragged a quarter of a mile when his foot got tied up in the stirrup. Even thinking of how easily Calla could have lost the baby made sweat break out on Mack's forehead.

But apparently, Daddy Cunningham still had enough money for a slick lawyer. He'd gotten his daughter's charge pled down to *assault causing bodily harm.*

Then again, Mack himself had finally enjoyed the benefit of a good lawyer for once. Of course it had helped that Liam claimed he'd been the one to shoot Bone. Said the gun was his too.

Mack had never in his life had someone go to the mat like that for him. Seemed like the bastard meant it when he said he loved him. Wonders would never fucking cease.

"I don't care about Bethany," Calla waved a hand. "Can we get back to the part where you bought my family's ranch?" She bounced up and down on her toes, looking around.

A neigh sounded in the distance and Calla froze. Again, her mouth dropped open. "You didn't," she whispered.

"We did." Another grin lit Liam's face.

Calla took off sprinting around the side of the house toward the barn and horse paddock. Her shrill scream of excitement carried clear across the yard. "Prissy!"

She was over the gate and hugging her horse's neck by the time Mack and Liam got there. When she looked back at them, tears shone in her eyes. "I can never repay you."

She ran over, climbed the wooden fence of the paddock, and dragged both Liam and Mack close.

Christ but it was the best feeling in the world. Their two bodies, warm and alive against them. Family. It was Calla who first said it and every day Mack woke up with Calla and Liam in bed beside him, he could still barely believe it.

He ran his hand down her side to her stomach. A month after the Horse Makeover competition and their little one was growing strong.

"No repayment necessary," Mack said, clearing his throat when the words came out rough. "That's the point of family, right?"

Calla beamed up at him and she went up on her tiptoes to kiss first him, then Liam.

While she was kissing Liam, Liam gestured behind her back at Mack.

Oh. Right. The other thing.

He dropped on one knee and as soon as Calla broke away from Liam, he did the same.

"What are you—?" If Mack thought Calla's eyes were wide before, it was nothing to the saucers they became now.

Liam pulled the ring box out of his pocket. "Calla Carter, will you marry us?"

Calla's hand went to her mouth and more tears glistened in her eyes.

"Mack won the coin toss," Liam went on, "so it'll be his name that goes on the official papers, but it's between all of us."

Calla just kept standing there, staring down at them.

"Shit," Mack said, starting to get up. This was too soon. She hadn't even got used to the—

"Yes!" Calla shouted, dropping down and hugging them both close. "Yes. A million times yes!"

She sounded happy but she was crying. Her back heaved up and down she was crying so hard.

"Darlin," Mack held her closer, "don't cry."

Calla pulled back. "They're happy tears."

"How about just the happy, and no tears?" Mack kissed her deep.

She kissed him back and finally her shaking slowed and then stopped. Mack pulled back but only long enough to turn her toward Liam.

Liam put the engagement ring on her finger, then cupped her face and kissed her. It was gentle at first, but it quickly got frantic.

Fuck, it was so hot when they went after each other like that.

"Let's take this inside," Mack said, standing up and hauling Calla with him. He smirked at the look of denied lust on Liam's face.

Mack took Calla's hand and led her inside. "We haven't had much time to set up house yet but," he led her back to the master bedroom that had a single piece of furniture.

The bed.

"We ordered it special," Liam said, pulling his shirt off over his head and then kissing Calla again. "It's an ultra king-sized bed."

"No more having your mattress hogging ass pushing me off in the middle of the night," Mack said, coming up behind Liam and massaging his shoulders.

Liam shuddered at the touch and Mack's cock stiffened even more than it already was.

Calla broke off from Liam's kiss and then moved behind Mack. She tugged at the bottom of his shirt and he paused to pull it off over his head. Then she started massaging him the way he was doing to Liam. Christ he loved having her hands on him.

"Liam and I were talking," Calla said, her voice husky.

Mack turned his head to look back at her and he raised an eyebrow. "Oh?"

Calla bit her lip in a way that had Mack's cock poking into Liam's ass. Liam ground back against him.

"What about?"

Liam turned in Mack's arms and cupped his face like he had Calla's earlier. He ran his lips back and forth against Mack's, the stubble on their faces scraping one another. Calla's arms snaked around his waist and her hand dropped to grip his cock.

"About how we want you to know what it feels like to be the one in the middle," Calla whispered. "Receiving all the worship."

Liam jerked Mack toward the bed, pulling him off balance. He stumbled a few steps and Liam took the opportunity to drag him down to the huge bed with him.

Liam landed on top but Mack growled and quickly flipped them so that Liam was underneath. Liam's breathing went stuttered and Calla joined them on the bed. She'd been wearing a soft little cotton dress but it was a puddle of fabric on the ground. She slid her bra and panties off before crawling toward them in a way that made Mack want to fuck her senseless.

He went to grab her so he could do just that when Liam said, "Turn over and up on your knees."

Mack shot Liam a look. It was a look that should have communicated—*we've already settled this. I'm the top.* Always.

But Liam just grinned. "We'll take it easy on you. Promise." Then he winked at Mack.

Mack was about to put the bastard in his place but Calla put a hand on Mack's chest. "Please? Do you trust us?"

Mack stared at her face and the want he so clearly saw there. Did he trust them? Well yeah, but—

"Please," Calla said again.

And shit, how was he supposed to say no when she was flashing those soulful hazel eyes his way. Not to mention she'd grabbed his cock again and he thought he might start begging if he didn't have a hot, wet hole to stick it in soon.

"So how do you want me?" He directed it at Calla. He didn't think he could quite handle the smug look that was undoubtedly on Liam's face.

"On your knees." Calla's eyes sparkled with excitement.

Mack's chest went tight at exposing himself like that. How many nights had Bone shoved him face down into the bunk and then—

Bone can't hurt you anymore. Or anyone else. This is Calla and Liam. You trust them. You love them.

Mack swallowed hard and forced himself to roll over. He couldn't help how tense his entire body went, though.

"Shh," Calla whispered, rubbing a soothing hand down his spine. She must have sensed his tension.

He hated that. He was supposed to be the strong one. He was supposed to—

"Fuck," he shouted as a mouth closed around his cock. He looked down and there was Liam's head between his legs, mouth circling his cock. He was on his back, hand at Mack's shaft, feeding the crown in and out of his lips.

His blue eyes sought Mack out. They were wide. Unsure. Looked like he wasn't the only one who felt vulnerable in this position.

For some reason that made Mack relax. This was Liam and this was Calla.

He even managed to stay mostly still when he felt a probing finger at his anus.

But that was because he was paralyzed.

This is my *ass, baby boy. No one will ever fuck it as good as I do. I fucking own you. Stop that goddamned whimpering. You want to walk tomorrow? Because I'll—*

"Mackenzie?" Calla's voice broke Mack out of the memory that was so fucking vivid, for a second, he'd been back there. Under Bone's stinking body.

"Honey," she asked, "are you okay? Because I can st—"

"Keep going," Mack said through gritted teeth. He refused to let Bone have any more of his life than he'd already stolen. Not that it was that simple. How many times had he told himself not to give that fucker another thought?

He'd hoped the nightmares would end now that Bone was locked up again—and dickless. Mack had the satisfaction of learning that the surgeons hadn't been able to do anything but sew together the little bit of flesh that was left after Mack shot the damn thing to smithereens. Bone was left like a sexless Ken doll, pissing out of a permanently inserted catheter. Nurses were surprisingly chatty when it came to a serial rapist who'd murdered two EMTs in cold blood.

Even knowing all that, Mack had still woken up a couple times in the dead of night, the old nightmares riding him.

Unlike in the past, though, Liam and Calla's warm bodies tucked against his had soothed him enough to be able to go back to sleep more quickly than he used to. So maybe he'd never be cured in a single stroke. But he'd be damned sure to do everything he could to take back what that monster had stolen.

One of Calla's fingers pushed against his asshole. He sucked in a breath. Her finger was slick. She must have lubed it. Christ, how long had she and Liam been planning this?

"Shh," Calla whispered again. "That's right. Let me in. Let us love you."

Liam licked around his crown and then sucked him in again.

"Jesus Christ," he moaned, his head falling down against his forearms. Calla took the opportunity to slip her finger inside. First one, and then another.

Initially Mack squeezed his eyes shut—but it was too easy to imagine Bone was the one behind him. So he opened his eyes and looked down his chest to where Liam was enthusiastically slurping at his cock.

Fuuuuuuuuuuuuuuck. Having both of them work on him at the same time. That was so fucking h—

"*Oh*," he grunted, his whole body jerking as Calla's fingers zeroed in on that spot.

Liam let go of Mack's cock long enough to say, "Gently. Make sure to go gently."

But Mack shook his head as he gave into the sensation. "No. Harder. Jesus. Fuck. Harder."

It was so good. Fuck. It was indescribable. To have something that had been only associated with horror, now to be so fucking good...

His cock hit the back of Liam's throat but Liam didn't pull off him. No, he swallowed him even more. He was clearly unused to the sensation. Calla was usually the one sucking him off. Liam hadn't had much practice. But what he didn't have in technique he made up for in eagerness. His long tongue never stopped moving.

It was fucking sensational. And with Calla's fingers working their goddamned magic. Within minutes Mack was grabbing the sheets and roaring as he had one of the hardest, most intense orgasms of his entire life.

He slid to the side and collapsed, feeling like Liam had just sucked the life out of him. Both Liam and Calla were smiling—Liam with a satisfied grin and Calla with that gentle tilt to her lips.

Goddammit but he loved them. The feeling almost tore his fucking heart apart it was so piercing.

"Make love to her," he said, barely getting the words out he was so out of breath.

Liam crawled up the bed and Calla joined him. She crawled over Mack, kissing him long and lazily.

He closed his eyes and sank into the sensation. The solid bump of her stomach pressed into him. Their child. Growing inside her. It was so fucking insane.

He couldn't believe he was here. Wanted. Loved.

Calla let out a sudden breathy little gasp and Mack lifted his heavy eyes to look over her shoulder. Liam's face was a mask of concentration.

Damn, he was taking her ass.

Mack felt his cock stir back to life. Holy shit. The orgasm he had, he thought he'd be satisfied for a whole week. A goddamned month.

But with Calla's body jerking over his as Liam took her ass, his cock got stiffer and stiffer.

He pulled Calla's head down for a deep kiss even as he reached to line up his cock at her entrance. Jesus she was wet. So wet and wanting. Always wanting.

As Mack slid home inside her, feeling Liam's cock through the thin wall of her body, he thought: *fuck. This is it. This is perfection.*

He'd spent so much of his life filled with hate. Waging his one-man war against evil. Willing to die for it.

Only to discover that there was also a certain kind of beautiful in the world so precious that once you found it, there was nothing to do except *live* for it. Breathe for it. Give every last ounce of your being for it.

It was a lesson he was learning late.

But one he'd happily spend the rest of his life perfecting.

HUNGRY FOR MORE **DARK ROMANCE** BY STASIA BLACK?

Check out *Innocence*, a dark mafia romance...

Find out what happens when Marcus, king of the criminal underworld, finds his new obsession in Cora. He'll give her everything she desires. Except for one thing.
Her freedom.

Want to know how Liam and Mack got to be where they were at the start of *The Virgin Next Door*? Click to grab this sexy short story collection that explores each man's past.

Download at: https://BookHip.com/SPLNWT

ACKNOWLEDGMENTS

Aimee Bowyer, thank you SO much! Your amazing turnaround and feedback on this book before Christmas was so immensely helpful. I never feel like I can breathe about a book until it's had the once over by you. Giganto HUGS!

Melissa Pascoe—you are such a fabulous PA, thank you so much for helping me have time to WRITE! And thank you to for your feedback on this book. Your enthusiasm was awesome to get on this project.

This book would be an ugly mess of miscapitalizations, grammar mistakes, and missing words without the proofreading genius of Maria Pease from The Paisley Editor. She's awesome! Fellow authors, highest recommendations!

And thanks as always to super hubby. Love you forever.

ALSO BY STASIA BLACK

DARK MAFIA ROMANCE

Innocence

Awakening

Queen of the Underworld

Innocence Boxset

LOVE SO DARK SERIES

Cut So Deep

Break So Soft

Hurt So Good

THE MARRIAGE RAFFLE SERIES

Theirs to Protect

Theirs to Pleasure

Theirs to Wed

Theirs to Defy

Theirs to Ransom

STUD RANCH STANDALONE SERIES

The Virgin and the Beast: a Beauty and the Beast Tale

Hunter: a Snow White Romance

The Virgin Next Door: a Ménage Romance

ABOUT THE AUTHOR

STASIA BLACK grew up in Texas, recently spent a freezing five-year stint in Minnesota, and now is happily planted in sunny California, which she will never, ever leave.

She loves writing, reading, listening to podcasts, and has recently taken up biking after a twenty-year sabbatical (and has the bumps and bruises to prove it). She lives with her own personal cheerleader, aka, her handsome husband, and their teenage son. Wow. Typing that makes her feel old. And writing about herself in the third person makes her feel a little like a nutjob, but ahem! Where were we?

Stasia's drawn to romantic stories that don't take the easy way out. She wants to see beneath people's veneer and poke into their dark places, their twisted motives, and their deepest desires. Basically, she wants to create characters that make readers alternately laugh, cry ugly tears, want to toss their kindles across the room, and then declare they have a new FBB (forever book boyfriend).

Join Stasia's Facebook Group for Readers for access to deleted scenes, to chat with me and other fans and also get access to exclusive giveaways:
Stasia's Babes

facebook.com/stasiablackauthor
twitter.com/stasiawritesmut
instagram.com/stasiablackauthor

Printed in Great Britain
by Amazon